"I'm saying, Lieutenant, that tomorrow night I'm going back into the zone and I'm going to do my best to kill Apollonius. If I fail, save who can, but if dawn breaks and I haven't returned – for the good of the country, for the world maybe – to stop this plague of disease and violence from spreading – Manhattan must be destroyed."

PADWOLF PUBLISHING BOOKS BY JOHN L. FRENCH
PAST SINS
THE NIGHTMARE STRIKES
THE GREY MONK: SOULS ON FIRE
RITES OF PASSAGE: a DMA casefile of Agent Karver and Bianca
Jones (with Patrick Thomas)
BAD COP NO DONUT [editor]
MERMAIDS 13 [editor]

OTHER BOOKS BY JOHN L. FRENCH
HERE THERE BE MONSTERS: *a Bianca Jones collection*
BIANCA JONES: BLOOD IS THE LIFE
THE DEVIL OF HARBOR CITY
PARADISE DENIED
TO HELL IN A FAST CAR [editor]
WITH GREAT POWER [editor with Greg Schauer]
BULLETS & BRIMSTONE a Mystic Investigators™ book (with
Patrick Thomas)
FROM THE SHADOWS a Mystic Investigators™ book featuring
the Nightmare
(with Patrick Thomas)
THE ASSASSINS' BALL (with Patrick Thomas)

THE NIGHTMARE STRIKES!

JOHN L. FRENCH

PADWOLF PUBLISHING

PADWOLF PUBLISHING INC.
WWW.PADWOLF.COM

THE NIGHTMARE STRIKES © 2015 John L. French

Cover Art Roy Mauritsen and Patrick Thomas
Cover design Roy Mauritsen

ISBN 13 digit 978-1-890096-60-1

Publication History
The Undead Killer *Zombies in Time and Space*, Wildcat Books 2010
A Plague on the Land *Apocalypse 13,* Padwolf Publishing 2012
After the Fall *Hellfire Lounge 2*, Marietta Publishing 2012
Not Quite in Time excerpted from "Defying the Odds," *From the Shadows,* (by John L. French and Patrick Thomas) Dark Quest Books 2012
Wolf Hunt *Tales from the Pulp Side*, Purloined Pendant 2013
Cursed Luck *LUCKY 13*, Padwolf Publishing 2014
The Fabulous Eggoriginal to this book
The Choice of the Phoenix original to this book
Bathed in Fire original to this book

To Karl Harris
Who fights the darkness and serves the Light.

Table of Contents

A Message from the Nightmare:

I, Michael Shaw, once known as the Nightmare, have reviewed the tales told in this book. I find that, for the most part, they accurately relate certain events in which I was involved.

The author and publisher have my permission to reveal these stories to the public.

THE UNDEAD KILLER

Waiting alone in the dark, Michael Shaw idly wondered just how much oxygen was in the vault and how long he could safely stay inside it. After all, his passing out would mean that all the trouble he went through to crack the combination then relock the heavy door behind him would have been for naught. It would also ruin the big surprise and wouldn't do his health any good either.

Well, Michael, he thought, *you got yourself into this mess, you might as well see it through.* He hoped that when the vault door finally He hoped that when the vault door finally opened he had enough air in his lungs for a really good laugh. With nothing else to do, he thought back to earlier that night.

The mugger waited in the dark alley for his next victim to walk by. A gent with a heavy wallet, some dame with a purse hanging off her arm, a drunk he could snatch and roll. He didn't care, as long as whoever it was looked like an easy mark.

"Hello, Ronnie."

The voice startled the crook. He would have sworn he was alone. He had checked the alley twice and hadn't seen anyone. And there was no other way in or out. That could only mean …

It was one of *them*. One of those crazy crime fighters who dressed in black and killed people – people like him.

Well, he hadn't done anything, not yet anyway, nothing to get killed over. And maybe if he moved real slow he could edge his way toward the street without getting drilled by a blazing .45.

"Going somewhere?" came the voice from the darkness. Ronnie stopped, thought about running, then thought about that blazing .45. He stayed where he was. The figure moved into the dim glow of the alley's only light.

He was a tall man, dressed in the color of the night – pants and shirt, trench coat and hat, all black. Also black was the hood he wore, the hood that showed only his eyes, his merciless, pale blue eyes.

News about this one had reached Ronnie. "You're the new one, ain't ya? The one called the Nightmare?"

"That's right, Ronnie," was the cold, emotionless reply. "I'm the Nightmare from which no one awakes." A gun was drawn.

"No! Wait! I ain't done nothing!"

"Not tonight, Ronnie, not yet. But what about the nights to come? What of them, Ronnie? Will you still be doing nothing then? Better to make sure." The gun was aimed.

"Wait!" Ronnie cried desperately. "I know something!" To save his life Ronnie talked about what he had heard earlier that evening in Blind Tom's, how he was finishing his bottle of cheap rye while the men in the next booth spoke of a bank heist that would go off that evening. The First Farmers Bank of Manhattan. Lots of payroll cash, lots of jewels.

The Nightmare listened and liked what he heard. He nodded once.

"Run away, Ronnie."

The mugger did not have to be told twice. With the sound of mocking laughter following him he fled into the street.

"I'm the Nightmare from which no one awakes." Michael Shaw shook his head in the dark. I've got to come up with better lines. Then he heard tumblers clicking and readied himself.

The job was supposed to be easy. No night watchman on duty. The beat cop lured away by a doll claiming to have been molested. The combination supplied by an assistant manager with a big gambling debt. Damn fool thought this would clear him. He'd soon learn that you never get clear.

Five men were on the job. One to foreman and open the door, three more to carry the loot and a lookout with a Tommy just in case.

"Damn it, Ox, hold that flash steady. I can't read the guy's writing."

"Hurry it up, Archie, that dame ain't gonna hold the cop up too long."

"Shows how much you know. I told her to rip her dress and show her stuff. That cop will keep as long as she lets him stare. Hey, is this a three or an eight?"

After a few false starts, Archie finally got the right combination. The safe was unlocked and the big door swung open. Then from the darkness of the vault came laughter.

"Crap!" cried Fred and struggled to free his piece. "Gunner, get over here. The rest of you …"

Archie' words were lost in the sound of two booming .45's. Four would-be robbers fell before even getting off a round. Gunner, hearing laughter followed by shots, chose to live another day and fled the scene. When stopped by responding police three blocks away he swore that he had just found the Thompson he was still carrying and was bringing it to the police station. No one believed him and he was taken to the station where he was booked on suspicion of everything.

"Somebody talked."

That was the simple pronouncement of gang boss Wolf Hopkins. It was followed by quick denials then sudden silence as each man sought ways of deflecting any forthcoming blame onto someone else. None of the four men standing in front of Hopkins wanted his boss's attention directed solely at him.

Wolf Hopkins was Gotham's newest gang leaders, having taken over and consolidated two of the town's smaller mobs. He did this in a way unique to the city. He convinced the mob bosses to retire and turn their businesses over to him.

His method of persuasion was direct, efficient and cruel. In each case he selected a close but not immediate relative of his target. In Bennie Cohen's case it was his maiden aunt, in Salvatore DiPeitro's it was his second cousin. Neither of these two was involved in any way with their relative's business, only the accident of birth and the whim of a ruthless man marked them for death. Their mutilated bodies were delivered to their kinsmen's front door early one Monday morning. By Monday afternoon both men had received messages from Hopkins, promising that similar violence would fall upon closer family members if his demands were not met. The threats were ignored and the messengers killed.

Tuesday afternoon Cohen's sister was shot down in the street. Tuesday night someone set DiPeitro's dog on fire. By Wednesday evening both men had left town.

Doing nothing to break their silence, Hopkins slowly eyed the four men standing before him. He watched them sweat, he savored the tension, he enjoyed watching them worry about being picked as the traitor. They knew the penalty – death of a loved one followed by their own painful demise.

Hopkins finally spoke.

"This job was planned on the q.t. Except for the five of us, only those four losers in the city morgue knew when it was going to happen."

Polecat Johnny dared to interrupt. "And Gunner," he reminded Hopkins.

"Ah yes, Gunner, who right now may or may not be singing to the police. If so, then our station house source will be sure to give us the lyrics to his song. Either way," Hopkins pointed to Bull Evans, "When we're finished here, call the mouthpiece and get Gunner released and you," the mob chief turned to Charlie Heywood, "Gunner has a niece over in Philly. Get a line on her, just in case.

"And now gentlemen," Hopkins continued, "any idea whose mouth needs to be shut for good?"

A few more minutes of uncomfortable silence followed, each man imagining his family being wiped out one by one. Finally, Jake Green remembered something.

"Me and couple of the guys you sent out, Archie and Ox, were in the Blind Tom's going over final plans. A lowlife mugger, Ronnie something or other, was passed out in the booth next to us, or maybe not. Maybe he heard everything we said and traded in on it, gave it to the cops so's they'd let him go."

Hopkins shook his head. "Not the cops, my source tells me our late friends were killed by shots that came from inside the vault. Only one of those black-garbed busybodies would do something like that."

"That would explain why Gunner ran," Bull said, "He'd have shot it out with the cops, but there's something about those guys coming out of the shadows that spooked him."

"He did run, didn't he?" mused Hopkins. "Gentlemen, do we have any room in our organization for cowards?" And with that question he sealed a man's fate. Two days after being released on bail, Gunner's body was pulled from the harbor.

"As for this … Ronnie, was it? As for Ronnie, he should have known better than to meddle in our affairs. I'll send the Dead Man after him."

Although they were all hardened criminals, the four lieutenants shuddered at the name of a man they had never met. The Dead Man was their boss's special assassin, only Hopkins knew who he was or where to find him. He was rumored to be unrelenting and unstoppable, his very presence said to be announced by the smell of death. And if the reports of the condition in which his victims were found were even half true, he was more monster than man.

Not knowing what fate awaited him, Ronnie had returned to the alleys, again looking for someone smaller and weaker to prey upon. This time, however, he took precautions, carrying an electric torch to light up the dark places and make sure no one in black was lurking there. In case there was, Ronnie had a .38 in his pocket. Maybe it wasn't as big as the .45s the Nightmare and the others carried, but it would do the job if fired first and fired straight.

An old woman walked by. No, there were two men right behind her. A young girl walked past. Much better, he'd take more than her purse. But she waved at someone and crossed the street. Ronnie felt the weight of the gun in his pocket and considered the liquor store down the block. It was almost closing time, he thought, the cashbox must be full to bursting. But the owner might recognize his face. Ronnie wrapped his hand around his gun. Too bad for him then.

About to leave the alley, Ronnie saw someone coming towards him. A man of indeterminate age, wearing what had once been fine clothes but which were now threadbare and shabby. His pace was slow and deliberate and his gaze was fixed on the alley entrance and Ronnie.

At first the Ronnie thought it was one of the countless stumblebums who inhabited the city – alkies, winos and hopheads whose brains were casualties to their cravings. But as the man approached, Ronnie caught his scent. The man reeked, but not with the typical unwashed, urine-flavored odor. No, this was the smell of rotting garbage, of a dog three days dead in the summer sun, of a maggot-ridden body about to burst. This was the smell of decay, the smell of the grave and of death.

He had heard only the vaguest of rumors about someone called the Dead Man, but they were enough to cause Ronnie to flee back into the alley. Too late did he remember that to prevent anyone sneaking up on him from behind, Ronnie had again chosen another dead end.

The symbolism went unappreciated as Ronnie searched in vain for a hiding place, someplace dark where the thing that was after him would not find him. The stench grew stronger as Ronnie's doom approached.

His back against a wall, Ronnie watched as the Dead Man slowly came closer. Ronnie looked into the shadows, as if trying to will one of the night's avengers to emerge and defend him with their deadly automatics. None of them did, but the thought of them reminded Ronnie that he too was armed, that he had a rod in his pocket with six bullets for the man now stalking him.

Ronnie pulled his .38 from his pocket and held it so the Dead Man could see. The creature was not deterred but kept on with his slow, steady pace. Trying not to gag at the foul odor, Ronnie let him get even closer, waiting for him to close to a distance where he would be impossible to miss. Finally, almost overwhelmed, feeling the vomit rise in his throat, Ronnie fired, emptying the revolver's cylinder into the chest and stomach of the thing that was almost upon him.

Ronnie had watched people die, had seen what happened when they were shot repeatedly in vital areas. Some staggered forward before collapsing, some fell backwards and some simply collapsed. What they did not do was extend their arms and wrap their cold hands around the shooter's neck, they did not squeeze until the shooter's eyes bulged and bowels voided, and after life had left the shooter's body, they did not bend over it and feast.

There was a bar in the east end of the city. Nothing fancy, just drinks well poured at a fair price. It was called Moran's, after the owner. He was a short fellow who didn't say much and always looked as if his mind was a world away. The day following the discovery of what remained of Ronnie, Lieutenant Jerome Easton walked in, looked around and settled himself at a booth in the back, joining the man who was already there.

"I thought you idle rich hung about in gentlemen's clubs, like that one the Commissioner belongs to, what's it called? The Baltic Club?"

Michael Shaw smiled. "Something like that, Lieutenant. But that kind of place is too stuffy for me; too many grim faces. I prefer an honest bar, where a man can get a real drink." Shaw held up a glass containing a pale amber liquid. "Can I get you something? By my count you're two behind already."

"Just coffee tonight, Mr. Shaw."

"On duty, then, despite the suit. Speaking of which, you should see my tailor. I can assure you of a generous police discount."

"Thanks but no thanks. People trust a cop in a cheap suit. Makes him look honest, or at least less crooked. And you're right, I am working. There's been another cannibal killing, some lowlife mugger found in an alley. Most of his face and part of his stomach chewed away."

Shaw's eyes widen and he leaned toward the police detective. "Disgusting ... tell me more. You said 'another.' How many does this make?"

"Five, but you know that already, don't you?"

Of course Shaw knew that. He had also heard of one other that the police had not found. Knowledge like that was the reason he hung about in bars of less savory nature than Moran's. One sat in the corner, bought a drink now and again and listened to the gossip. It was the best way to learn many interesting things. Like the latest news that there was a new killer in town, one called the Dead Man.

Good name that, Shaw thought as he did his best to look shocked at Easton's allegation. Much better than the Nightmare.

"Lieutenant, how would I know anything about that?"

Easton shook his head. "Mr. Shaw, you're telling me that it was just a coincidence that shortly after your chauffeur's daughter got caught in the crossfire between two rival gangs that this Nightmare fellow shows up and single-handedly wipes out both mobs?"

"The girl's death was in all the papers. I suppose some misguided person read about it and decided to do something about that senseless tragedy."

"And I suppose this same person, who by all accounts is your size and build, decided to do something about the lunatic blowing up schools and hospitals?"

"That was the Mad Bomber, wasn't it, Lieutenant? And you were a sergeant then, weren't you. It was bringing in the Bomber that got you promoted."

"At least you left that one alive," Easton mumbled under his breath.

"What's that, Lieutenant, I didn't quite catch that?'

Easton spoke up. "I said we didn't recover all his explosives. But you wouldn't know anything about that, either, would you, Mr. Shaw? Just as you don't know anything about how the Nightmare got involved with some of the other cases you and I have discussed?"

"Life is full of coincidences, Lieutenant."

"Somebody's full of something, Mr. Shaw. And wouldn't it be something if after tonight this Dead Man started having nightmares."

"Yes, it would, Lieutenant."

Easton stood up. An honest cop who always paid his own way, he dropped some coins on the table to pay for his coffee. "Wouldn't break my heart, Mr. Shaw."

Shaw watched as the lieutenant left the bar. A good man, he mused. A smart man who lets himself learn just enough. And that just enough is all that's keeping me from being locked up with those I hunt. But then,

Shaw allowed himself a quiet laugh, at least I'd have them all in one place.

Shaw ordered another drink and started planning how he could catch a dead man. Although his plans for when he found him might just break the good lieutenant's heart.

He started with the now late Ronnie. The fact that Ronnie met his fate shortly after providing the Nightmare with information about the bank heist was likely not a coincidence. And the men from the bank, plus the one who was so quickly bailed out of the precinct station, all worked for Gotham's newest crime boss, Wolf Hopkins.

A little research, a few more nights in less than reputable taverns and saloons revealed to Shaw that none of the cannibal's other victims had worked directly for Hopkins. In fact, in some way or the other, they all had run afoul or posed a threat to the gangs now run by the up and coming mob leader.

Alone in his study, Shaw thought about how his fellow dark avengers would handle the situation. Richard would charge in with guns ablazing, taking down his quarry but only after leveling half the city in doing so. Kent would already know where Hopkins's headquarters was. He would stealthily infiltrate it and find the clue that would lead him straight to the Dead Man. He'd go there straightaway, always assuming he didn't have to rescue an agent or two first.

Shaw liked the city and didn't want to see any part of it destroyed. And he didn't have any agents, not yet anyway.

"I really should get me a few," he said aloud to no one in particular, "or at least a faithful servant and a great looking gal willing to put off marriage until I'm done with this mad crusade." Shaw smiled. "Who am I kidding? If I had a girl like Nina or Carol I'd marry her at once and the Nightmare would be just a memory. Sometimes we can be such damn fools."

And with that thought he went back to plotting his campaign against the Dead Man. The key, Shaw realized, was not in figuring out where he was, but who his next target was going to be. Partly eaten corpses were turning up about a week apart, indicating some kind of pattern. Or maybe a need, if what the killer was called was less a nickname and more a description.

So Shaw waited, watched and sat in bars, keeping his head down and his ears open. And he heard of a new gang, lead by one Rusty Hower. It was pulling stick-ups and running a protection racket down by the docks, a little bookmaking and loan-sharking as well. Nothing that anyone would normally worry about, except that the docks were very close to areas claimed by Hopkins, and the next logical place for him to expand. And it was past time for the Dead Man to feed.

The Nightmare haunted the docks for three nights, hiding in the shadows and watching as Rusty Hower's gangs broke into warehouses and storage containers to steal goods meant for the city's merchants. He witnessed bribes and payoffs, police officers and night watchmen being paid to look the other way. He took notice of these men, some he would report to Easton, others he'd deal with personally. He could use eyes and ears on the docks, and the threat of prison and the promise of cash should be enough to recruit at least a few.

Of the Dead Man there was no sign.

In the darkness the Nightmare wondered how long he should wait, how long he should ignore the crimes occurring before him. He told himself that only material things were being taken, objects easily replaced. But he'd had word of others crimes the Hower Gang had committed – shopkeepers terrorized into paying for protection, debtors who could not pay the usurious interest the gang charged being beaten and crippled. There were even rumors that the wives and daughters of these poor men being forced into carnal slavery to pay off some of the debts.

The Nightmare decided that he'd wait two nights more, two nights before the gang met justice, either at his hands or those of one far more terrible.

On the fifth night, just before he was about to act, the Nightmare's vigil was rewarded.

Hower and two of his men were gathered in a watchman's shed on the far end of the docks. The watchman had been sent off on his rounds and told not to come back for at least an hour. The Nightmare was outside a rear window. With no light at his back, he was invisible in the darkness. With the window cracked just enough he could see and hear perfectly.

Hower pulled a wad of bills from his pocket. Peeling off tens and twenties he gave out most of the cash.

"There you go, guys, this week's cut. The rest goes to Louie and Fred when they get back from seeing that accountant with the 'sure thing.'"

"How sure was it, boss?" asked the shorter of the two henchmen a short man with a wide scar down his face.

Hower laughed. "He asked for two large. I said sure. That was as close as he came. And he damn well better say sure when Fred asks him for it back plus the vig."

"I'm kinda hoping he doesn't," said the other mobbie. "I saw his daughter when I dropped off the dough. Nice and sweet and not a day over sixteen. Be nice to take the interest out on her."

"The mother's not so bad either," offered Scarface.

"They're both nice pieces," Hower agreed. "And if the number cruncher don't come through, we'll hold a weekend party at his house. If he's good maybe we'll let him watch."

As dirty laughter echoed round the tiny shed, the Nightmare was sorely tempted to pull his .45s and throw his own sort of party. These were men who did not deserve to live. He'd find the Dead Man another way.

Then a foul odor wafted his way. Close by and growing stronger, it came from the lot where the Hower gang had parked their cars. It was the smell of death telling the Nightmare that his wait was over. The Dead Man had arrived.

Guns drawn in case they were needed, the Nightmare watched as the door to the shed swung open and a walking corpse came inside. Flesh hung in tatters from its face; its outstretched hands were nothing but bone. It said nothing, it did nothing but stare at the three men with lidless eyes.

"Gun the freak!" yelled Hower and three revolvers appeared as the men began firing.

Three times, five times the skeletal form was hit, then a dozen more. When three hammers clicked on empty shells, the Dead Man was still standing.

There was a sucking sound as the creature drew air into what passed for its lungs. "Mmmyyy tuuuurnnn," came an eerie whisper.

It could only end one way, decided the man watching from outside, a way he did not want to witness. He might be the Nightmare, but he didn't need any himself.

As unstoppable as the Dead Man seemed to be, he was not that quick. As the undead thing slowly made its way toward Hower, Scarface and the other mobbie realized this and decided that this was a good time to seek employment elsewhere. As fleshless hands found their boss's throat, the two ran out into the night.

They did not get far. The Nightmare was waiting for them just outside the shack.

No laughter, no mercy, no chance for the two men who were greater monsters than the one from which they had just fled. The Nightmare had his .45s drawn and used them ruthlessly and efficiently. Four shots, two for each man, and Rusty Hower's men were sent to Hell to await their boss.

The Nightmare waited. Waited for Rusty Hower's screams to die along with him. Waited for the Dead Man to finish his grisly business. Finally, the door of the shack slowly opened. The Dead Man paused in the doorway as the Nightmare stepped into the light.

He had changed. Gone was the skeletal face, the fleshless hands. What came out of the shed appeared nearly human. Even the smell of decay had abated somewhat.

The Dead Man looked at the shadowy figure before him.

"You could try," the Dead Man said after pulling air into his lungs, his speech more distinct than it was in the shack, "but not even those cannons could stop me."

"I have no intention of stopping you," the Nightmare replied. "Not tonight, not with these." And to the Dead Man's surprise the man in black put away his guns. "You're a zombie, aren't you?"

The undead killer paused. He knew he should leave. The Nightmare could not stop him, would not even try. But it had been so long since he had talked to anyone. The man called Hopkins saw him as a tool to be used, provided him with a means to sustain what passed for a life. But that was all. Seeing before him a possible kindred spirit, the Dead Man replied, drawing in air as he needed it.

"Yes, but not as you might understand it. I am from another time, another place."

"What brought you to this time, this city?"

"I once had a life, a real life with a family. Then came a great plague that devastated the world and left me as I am. I was one of the few that were not destroyed outright. Instead I was turned over to men of science, men who wanted to explore the past. To them I was Subject 24, sent back in time because my dead flesh could travel backwards while their living bodies could not."

"And your purpose here?"

"To observe, to learn and when the time comes, to find a quiet place that might not be disturbed for hundreds of years and then to rest, wait and report. Until then I survive as best I can." The Dead Man turned and looked at the shack where rested the remains of Rusty Hower. "I kill them first so they do not become like me." The Nightmare would not have thought it possible, but there was sadness in the zombie's voice.

"Are we to be enemies?"

The Nightmare shook his head at the question. "Not for now, not as long as your prey is men like these." He gestured toward the bodies on the ground. "The fewer of this kind of scum the better as far as I'm concerned. But should things change, then I will find a way to kill you."

The Dead Man's lips twisted in what might have been a smile. "I believe you might."

A light in the distance announced the return of the watchman.

"We'd best be gone," the Nightmare said and the two creatures of the night faded into the darkness.

Two weeks later. Another two men dead and devoured. Both were minor criminals that were rumored to have somehow displeased Wolf Hopkins.

After his meeting with the Dead Man Shaw avoided those places where he would be most likely to encounter Easton and instructed his servants that he was not at home to the good lieutenant. And with the discovery of each new body, Shaw worried as to whether or not he'd made the right decision that night on the docks.

"Not that I had any choice," he told himself. "After watching how little effect gunfire had on him, the Nightmare's .45s would not have stopped that walking corpse."

Shaw knew what would. The only question was if he should use it.

The answer came three days after the discovery of yet another partly eaten body.

Shaw was dining in a most exclusive club, one he was sure that would not only refuse to admit Easton, but one which he believed the police detective did not even know existed. He had forgotten that the lieutenant was a trained investigator and once he decided to find someone that man would eventually be located.

"This seat taken?" Easton asked casually as he came up to Shaw's table. He sat down as if he ate every night in a club whose average dinner would have cost him a month's salary.

"Lieutenant, how did you get in?"

"I showed them my membership card," Easton held up his badge, "and said that you were expecting me. You were expecting me, weren't you, Mr. Shaw?"

A wry smile appeared on Shaw's face. "Eventually, Lieutenant."

"So where's the Dead Man?"

Shaw looked puzzled. "I don't know. The cemetery, the morgue, at the bottom of the harbor. A dead man could be so many places."

"You know damn well!" the detective began to shout, then lowered his voice once he realized that everyone in the restaurant was staring at him. "You know damn well," he continued in a near whisper, "what dead man I'm talking about. The one you, or rather, the Nightmare found and let go a few weeks ago." To forestall the inevitable denial, Easton held up his hand. "Yes, I know, you're not the Nightmare. And before you ask, we matched the slugs in Hower's goons to other Nightmare killings. And judging from what we found in that shack, unless The Nightmare likes his meat rarer than that steak you just finished, he found the Dead Man and let him go."

"I'm sure he had his reasons, Lieutenant."

"And I'm sure I know what they are, Mr. Shaw. And I'd be lying if I didn't admit that there's a part of me that agrees with them. But things have changed."

"How so?"

Easton looked around. "Is there somewhere more private?"

"How did you get here?"

"How else, I took the train."

"Then I'll drive you home, we'll talk on the way."

"It's a long drive."

Shaw shrugged. "I'm the idle rich, remember? I've nothing but time."

Once in the car Easton explained the situation.

"A family of four – wife, husband, two kids. Tourists. They got lost and drove someplace they shouldn't have been. Someplace where Hopkins's boys had just finished pulling off a rubout. All four saw the getaway car. The father saw two of the thugs. With his testimony we can nail the shooters. If they talk, maybe we can put Hopkins away for at least a while."

"If he lives until the trial."

"If they live," Hopkins corrected. "The whole family's on the spot. We can try to hide them, but half the department's on the take from some gang or the other. Someone will talk. We could throw a wall of cops around them, but what good would that do against a guy that, from what I've heard, can't be killed? Sooner or later …"

The drive continued in silence as the two men considered all that sooner or later could bring. Finally, Shaw made a decision.

"I have a cabin upstate. It's more of a small house, all the comforts of home – my home, not yours. It's very nice, just the thing for a family of four. Isolated, easy to defend if it came to that."

"You're not suggesting that I hide them there, are you, Mr. Shaw?"

"No, Lieutenant, I'm suggesting that you tell everyone you're hiding them there. Enough people saw you with me tonight. Let's make your asking me to allow the NYPD the use of my cabin as a safe house the reason. As to where you actually take them, I don't care to know. Just tell everyone that they're taking a trip to the country."

"And what's going to happen in the country?"

"Lieutenant, that's something you don't care to know."

Cardboard cutouts moving around on a model train track. Silhouettes throwing shadows through the window. Mannequins standing guard. A convincing enough illusion.

The Nightmare waited in the darkness of the trees.

The word was out. The Nightmare was sure of it. All that remained was to see who showed up with murder in their hearts. If the hearts were still beating, the Nightmare stood ready to deal with common assassins. There were dry wells deep enough that their bodies would never be found. If however, one of those hearts had long ago ceased to beat, the Nightmare was prepared for that as well. He hoped it was the former. He prayed that a lifeless body could still have a soul.

A car was heard in the distance. Voices carried through the night.

"It's up on the hill, through da path," came one voice. "We'll wait here."

"Yeah," another man said, "Go on up and have a snack."

As the Nightmare waited and prepared himself for what must be done, a man sent back in time to satisfy others' craving for knowledge, a man once alive, a man who in another time had a family of his own began a long climb bent on destroying the lives four innocent people. From his hiding place, the Nightmare clearly saw him in the moonlight. He was as the dark clad avenger had first seen him, a skeletal form with decaying flesh sloughing off him. In the open air his stench was not as bad, but still he carried the odor of death with him.

The Dead Man came to the door of the cabin. The Nightmare watched him enter.

He's looking around, the Nightmare thought. He's not seeing what he expected. He's realizing now that it's a trap. He's slowly turning to leave. He's too late.

The Nightmare pushed down on the plunger, setting off the dynamite he'd planted throughout the cabin, dynamite he'd taken from The Mad Bomber several months back. He knew then that he'd have a use for it.

The explosion lit the night. The shockwave almost flattened the Nightmare and did for a time deafen him. Somewhere down the hill a car sped off to report to their boss.

Daylight. Michael Shaw stood looking into the crater of what had been his upstate getaway.

"I may have used too much dynamite," he mused, not at all upset at his sacrifice.

The blast would not have gone unnoticed. With the authorities no doubt on their way, Shaw made a quick search of the remains. Finding what he hoped, he made his way through the woods.

He walked for well over an hour until he came to long abandoned dry well. From the bag he carried he took the head of the now truly dead man. Looking into lifeless eyes he said,

"I'm sorry it had to end this way. You didn't ask to come to this time and this isn't the resting place you expected. But an unmarked grave is all I can offer. Unless you'd rather be an exhibit in the police museum. You don't deserve that, not after what you've done for us. Not killing the bad guys, although that was helpful. I mean your warning about the coming plague. You didn't say when that was going to happen, but I'll try to see that we're ready for it. Rest in peace."

Shaw dropped the head down the well and spent the morning filling the hole with rocks.

"I'd best get back to the city so someone can tell me that my cabin blew up. Now if he can just keep those witnesses hidden, maybe Easton can do something about Wolf Hopkins. If he can't the Nightmare will."

Walking back to his car, Michael Shaw thought about what the Dead Man had told him.

"A plague of zombies, no one's going to believe that. Sounds like the plot of a horror movie."

A Plague on the Land

A story of the Nightmare and Bianca Jones

Everyone needs a place to unwind, to relax after a long night at work, to meet with those who share similar interests and to discuss common problems. After hours, when the lights went out and daylight was not that far away, Moran's became such a place. One by one, without seeming to disturb any doors or windows Moran may have locked, the hunters of the night gathered. Men and women who hid in shadows and clothed themselves with darkness in their crusade against crime. This is where they met before assuming their civilian disguises, to spend some time with others like themselves. This was their brief chance to relax. By common assent, little business was discussed, maybe a warning here or a word there about which criminal was plotting what crime and who was seeking whom.

"When did it start?" Seamus Moran wondered as he watched a pint of his best seemingly disappear from the counter. "When did the Dark Ones choose my place and why?"

Those were two questions Moran could never answer. He could not remember a time when they did not gather, when spectral laughter was not heard every night after hours.

"Maybe it's something like a family curse," was his thought as the flash of a fire opal drew his attention. He poured its owner another large Bushmill's then returned to his musing. "My cousin Paddy has the same kind of crowd, less violent though. This sort would not be permitted in his place."

Thoughts of Paddy and his place uptown caused Moran to think of home. Not his apartment above the bar, but of that ancestral place from whence he and his came.

Moran was of the Gentry, the fair folk of Eire, that mythical land that was the Spirit of Ireland, a land that was currently in sore distress.

Moran had first thought to consult with Paddy, but the more he heard and the worse the news got, he knew that this was not his cousin's fight. If there was any truth to the tale, it was a killing matter, and the taking of life was something the elder Moran would not do.

"Now these in here …" Moran scanned the shadows of his bar, barely able to make out his costumed patrons, "most of them have no qualms about pulling the trigger when it would do the most good." There were exceptions – the green one was a man of peace, the pink one killed when she had to but mostly avoided it. Otherwise these champions of Justice were killers all.

Justice was what was needed – Justice for his people, Justice for his land. Maybe he could find it here.

Which one? Few of his afterhour's patrons would believe that Moran was anything more than a short barkeep who served them drinks. They were men of cold steel and science, accepting only what they saw or could prove. To them ghosts were luminous paint and witches just deluded women. But there were those who knew differently.

"You look lost in thought, Seamus."

Such as the Nightmare, the man who just spoke.

"That I was, until yourself came along." Moran sighed, fully aware of what he was about to do. "Could I ask a favor?"

"If you want to peak under my mask, it'll cost you a drink."

"Maybe the next time, this is … can you stay after the rest have gone? It's … serious business, your kind of business."

"Look around, Seamus, they've already left. There's no one in place except you and me."

"How do they …"

"Trade secret."

Dawn was near. Michael Shaw, aka the Nightmare, sat unmasked in a booth waiting for Moran to bring breakfast. Over eggs, bacon and a cold glass of orange juice with which to welcome the morning, Moran made his plea.

"I hate like the devil to ask this of you, Michael."

"There's no harm in asking, Seamus. I can always say no."

"That you can, and after hearing what I have to say you probably will. If so, no hard feelings. You and your money will be welcome as long as there's a Moran's, however short a time that may be."

"Well, if there's a threat to my favorite watering hole I'm half convinced already. Now what's the problem?"

"Michael, there's trouble back home."

"So I've been reading."

"Not the Rebellion. That's a fight that's been going on for centuries and may go on for more. It's not Ireland I'm speaking of, it's Eire."

"They're not the same, I take it?"

Moran shook his head. "Every country has a physical plane – England, the United States, Ireland – and a spiritual plane – Albion,

America and for Ireland, Eire. It is the soul of the Land, and Ireland's soul is blighted."

Shaw's eyes widened as his mind leaped. He sensed a revelation coming, one that would lead to new adventures and fresh challenges. "And you know this how?" he asked as he tried to repress a smile in what was a serious matter.

"It, Eire, is the land of my birth, the land I left when I came to America and the United States, the land to which I dream of one day returning."

Shaw lost his struggle as his smile broke free. "If you're from Eire, then given your size, that would make you a … leprechaun?"

"Close enough, Michael Shaw. And if it's my pot of gold you'll be asking about next, well, if you do this for me and make it back then you will have earned your chance at it. All I'll ask is a fair head start and if you catch me, it's yours."

"Seamus, I'll never spend the money I have. I don't do this," Shaw held up the mask of the Nightmare, "for the money. None of us do."

"Why do you do it?"

"Because, my friend, it must be done and we few are able and willing to do it. Now tell me, what ails your land and what must be done to save it?"

In another bar, some miles and many years away, two women met in a secluded booth. One was tall and dark and beautiful. The other was small, fair-skinned and while the man she loved thought of her as beautiful, she herself did not.

"I'm surprised he lets us in here," the smaller woman said, indicating the diminutive man behind the bar.

"It's not us Paddy objects to, Detective Jones, it's our methods. He thinks that there's always another way. If everyone believed that …"

"We wouldn't be needed. But tell me, why does the angel of vengeance need the help of a Baltimore cop?"

"You're much more than a Baltimore cop, Detective."

It was true. Despite her small size and slender build, Bianca Jones hunted monsters. Not just the two-legged kind that preyed on the weak and helpless – killers, rapists, drug dealers – but the terrors from dark places that saw humanity as cattle and play things. She was very good at what she did, but this skill was dearly earned and she was always aware of the dreadful cost of failure.

"Granted, but that doesn't answer my question. Why do you need me?"

"You accept who I am, then. Few do."

Bianca smiled. "In Baltimore we do more than wait for monsters to come to us. We research and prepare. We want to be ready to meet a threat when it arises, not try to develop a plan while half the city is being destroyed. So yes, I've heard of you. Nemesis, goddess of retribution."

The woman in black returned the smile. "One of my many names, but it will do for now. As to why I need you …"

Nemesis drew several tattered pulp magazines from her bag and threw them on the table. They had the title FROM THE SHADOWS emblazoned across the top front and each garish cover featured a man dressed in black wielding oversized pistols while fighting some menace or the other. The captions at the bottom read "In this issue, another exciting adventure of the Nightmare."

Bianca picked up one of the books. "The Nightmare, I heard of him. A character like the Spider or the Pink Reaper."

"Would it surprise you to learn that he was real?"

"After what I seen, little surprises me. I assume there's a point to this?"

Nemesis gave little sign of hearing Bianca's question. "He was much like you, Michael was. No special powers, just an ordinary human doing extraordinary things. He too fought monsters and once helped bring down a god."

Bianca knew the look on Nemesis's face. She saw that look whenever her husband glanced her way. She felt it on her own face when she looked at him.

"You were in love with him."

"I still am and always will be. Yet he is in trouble and I cannot go to him."

Bianca looked at the date on one of the pulps. "If he was alive back then, by now he must be …"

The woman in black shook her head. "Where Michael is is beyond time. When he entered it was somehow closed to all those like me. That he could pass through shows that the way was not barred to mortals. Michael went to save a world but without help he will fail."

"All this time, is he still …."

"The realm of Eire is outside time. I have known of Michael's peril since he left this world. Unable to help him myself, I have waited long to find someone who could, a mortal like him who would dare challenge a god. If you are willing, I could send you to him. That, at least, is within my power."

"And so is bringing me back, I trust."

Nemesis nodded. "If you are successful. If not, there's little point."

Bianca sympathized with the woman across from her. To rescue a child she had stormed the gates of Hell. To save her love she had given up Heaven. But she was a practical woman.

"You're asking me to risk my life and leave the city I've sworn to defend unprotected just to save your old boyfriend. Why should I?"

"A fair question, Detective Jones. You just told me that you like to be ready to meet a threat when it develops. If, in the future, there comes a dire, desperate situation, would it not be a good thing to have the goddess of vengeance standing at your side?"

"Favor for favor, then?"

"It is the way of the worlds, Detective."

"Given the circumstances, call me 'Bianca.' And after you order us another round of drinks, you can explain just what I'm about to agree to."

The Nightmare stood alone in a dark, blasted landscape. Where there had once been green fields was nothing but brown earth. Burned stumps stood where trees had grown and houses were nothing but ruin and rubble.

There was no sign of life – human, animal or otherwise.

With a pistol in his right hand, the Nightmare carefully approached what had been a village. As he grew close he was met by the odors of decay, pestilence, of burned bodies and spilled blood. Not wanting to look, he searched what was left of the villagers' homes. He found what he had expected, signs of sickness and slaughter.

Some had died of a wasting illness, their lives slowly drawn from them, their emaciated bodies still lying in their beds. Other had died more quickly, slain by knife and sword. Still others had been set afire, their contorted, blackened bodies telling the Nightmare that they had been alive when fire was set to their flesh.

Seamus, thought the man in black, *what have you gotten me into? At least I can't say you didn't warn me.* His mind took him back to Moran's just after the bartender had asked his help.

"Those of us who have left Eire have always maintained a connection with it. We are of the Land and the Land is of us and there's no escaping that. It was a grand place and it was said the Lord made it so that a bit of heaven might be on Earth."

"If it was so grand, Seamus, why did you and your cousin leave it?"

"Aye, and a damned good question that is. I cannot speak for Paddy, that one has his own reasons for everything, but as for me, why does any boy leave a home where people love him and he has all he needs? For adventure, for the challenge, so that the boy might become a man. But if it's a good home you never really leave, do you. There's always a little piece inside you, to encourage you in the good times and comfort you in the bad."

Seamus tapped his chest. "Eire was always right here. And feeling it, knowing that it was but a door away, was enough for me. But now, Michael, that feeling is gone and there is a deep hole where once it was. Something bad has happened, but I do not know what."

"How can I help?"

"I can't go back, Michael, I've tried, but the door won't open for me nor for any of my kind. But for you, a noble man with a just cause, it might. You are not of the Land, so maybe it will not reject you as it did me. Find what's wrong. Stop it if you can. And if you cannot, if all is lost and the Soul of Ireland is gone then you must act as the avenger you are and kill the thing or things responsible. For if you do not, then once it has finished with my Land it will move on to others and one day find yours."

Shaw thought for a moment, then asked, "Seamus, in Eire, is there a god of sleep?"

"There are several, Angus for one, Epos Olloatir for another. Why?"

Shaw checked his guns, then put on the mask that covered one face and revealed another. "Pray to them if you can. Tell them the Nightmare is coming and he could use their help."

Seamus Moran then led the Nightmare to a back room of the bar where stood a door without a room.

"For two days it's been like this. Two days since I summoned it to try and go home. As I said, it will not open for me."

With a nod to the smaller man, the Nightmare strode to the portal and easily passed through it.

"To find myself here," the Nightmare said, again surveying the absolute destruction of the landscape and all who lived in it. A glow in the distance caught his attention. Dawn maybe? He waited and, when the sun did not rise to banish the seemingly eternal twilight, he walked toward the light, expecting to find the darkness that caused it.

I'm back in Hell, was Bianca's first thought when she saw where she was. Then she corrected herself. Hell, at least that part of Perdition where she had met and cheated the Devil, was not this bleak. Hell was where nothing grew except pain and where Hope did not exist. This land, this "Erie" as Nemesis had called it, had once been alive and what was left of the village in the distance told her that the people who lived there had had hope for the future.

Now, though, all growth had been stunted and all hope crushed.

And I'm supposed to find one man, one dressed in black yet, in this wasteland.

Looking around, Bianca saw a glow in the distance. With nothing else to go on, she shouldered her pack and headed toward it.

As he approached his goal, the Nightmare was met first by some of the odors he had left in the ruined village. The smell of sickness and burning wafted his way. Then came the sounds of battle. No, battle was not the right word, for there was no clash of steel upon steel. It was the noise of slaughter – men crying out, women screaming, babies crying. Above it all was the sick laughter of those causing it as they gleefully went about their demon's work.

"If it's laughter they like," the Nightmare said to himself, "it's laughter they shall have."

Drawing his weapons, the man in black came close enough to pick out targets and unleashed his own brand of Hell.

At first the invaders of the village did not know what was among them. There was only the flash of lightning and the sound of thunder. Each time this occurred another or their comrades fell, a hole in his head or punched through his armor. He'd fall dead to the ground though there was no enemy close enough to strike him and no sign of spear or arrow.

Then they saw it, a figure all in black, the lightning spurting from his hands with thunder following. Whatever it was, it laughed as it killed, and like the banshee's mournful cry, the laughter promised death.

But these men were not the common criminals that the Nightmare was accustomed to fighting. Killers to a man and evil to their souls, they were warriors still. Once the initial shock wore off, they turned their attention away from the murder of innocents and focused on the threat at hand. They gathered then charged, each man trusting to his fate that he would not be the one to die next and praying to the god that sent him to be the one to strike down this specter.

"This didn't work out as planned," thought the Nightmare. Though he fired as fast as he could, though with each shot another of his foes dropped, those remaining came closer and closer. *They'll be close soon,* he thought, *and my guns will be useless except as clubs.* He thought of withdrawing, of fading back into the darkness of the night, but he was too close to the burning village, the light of the flames making that darkness too far away for him to reach before they caught him and hacked him to bits.

Better to die on his feet. Raising his guns he shot the two men closest to him. Then greeted the coming charge with a laugh of defiance.

Approaching the burning village, Bianca heard gunfire and laughter. From what Nemesis had told her, this meant the Nightmare was close by. A few minutes later she found him, in a fight for his life, firing his .45s into a mass of warriors that kept getting closer no matter how many he shot down.

Guess the lady in black was right, Bianca thought as she came up from behind the crowd of men. *He does need my help.*

It was then the enormity of what she had to do struck her. *So many,* she thought. Bianca was no stranger to death. She had killed both men and monsters before but only once on this scale, the zombie war in New Orleans after Katrina. There, however, she had fought the undead. Here, in Eire, her foes were living men. That they had done terrible things made it easier, but not by much.

Placing her pack on the ground, Bianca removed from two small, round objects. Knowing this day would be relived in dreams for years to come, she pulled the pins on the grenades and threw them into the crowd just as it started its charge.

Twin explosions shook the ground and blew the men closest to them into pieces. They also startled the rest to the point where the black ghost that had killed so many of them was for the moment forgotten.

Some turned to see a small, slender woman standing behind them. She was not laughing and the look on her face was unmistakable. Some sorrow and regret but mostly determination. She meant to kill them. Seeing that she held only what looked like a hollow tube, the men rushed her.

None got close enough to pose a threat. Bianca's Mossberg shotgun roared, its flechette loads tearing her attackers into pieces. Again and again she let loose tiny slivers of death and with each shot her foes fell. And when the Nightmare added his withering fire, the spirit of the warriors broke and they ran like cowards into the night, leaving the two crime fighters alone on the field of battle.

Wading through the blood and gore of the dead, the Nightmare greeted Bianca with, "Thanks. Seamus didn't tell me that he was sending reinforcements." He held out his hand. "I'm called …"

"The Nightmare, I know, aka Michael Shaw, one of the masked vigilantes of the thirties. Later … well, I better not say. I'm Bianca Jones, Detective Sergeant with the Baltimore Police Department. And whoever this Seamus is, he didn't send me."

"Miss Jones, or rather, Sergeant Jones. Let's see. You're a woman police sergeant, carrying a kind of shotgun I've never seen. Your clothing is not the kind that women of my era would wear and you seem to know all about me. So if Seamus didn't send you, who did and from how far into the future have you come?"

"The when doesn't matter and as for who, Leda sends her love."

That name. The name by which Michael Shaw knew and loved Nemesis. There had been evenings of bloodshed and vengeance and one marvelous night of passion. She was his first true love and before this night he had had no hope of ever seeing her again.

"Leda sent you. Does that mean that in your time we …"

Bianca shook her head. "What will be, what Fate allows, I can't reveal. But let me ask you this – what the hell were you thinking, taking on a village of crazed men with sharp weapons?"

The Nightmare shrugged. "It seemed like a good idea at the time. Back … where I come from I laugh and start shooting. Some fight back and die, the rest run away." He looked at the bodies on the ground. "These didn't run."

"That because they're not pulp fiction gangsters who are afraid to die. These are warriors to whom death in battle is a glorious thing. Remember that the next time we face them. And please take off that mask when I'm talking to you. It's like talking to a shadow."

Thinking, *He doesn't wear a mask*, the Nightmare tried to remove his, and failed.

"It won't come off."

"Odd." Like the Nightmare had only a short while ago, Bianca looked at the lifeless bodies around them. "You killed a lot of men today. How many times did you reload those cannons?"

It was then that the Nightmare realized that he had not stopped to reload. "I didn't."

"And how many round do those guns carry?"

Again looking at the dead, the Nightmare replied, "Not that many."

"Strange forces are at work here, Michael. Look at the dead."

He did. Not all appeared to have come from the Land. Many races were represented, some of them not native to the Earth they knew.

"God!" the Nightmare exclaimed.

"More than one, Michael. Let's hope some of them are on our side. Now to find out what's going on in this place."

Thanks to the intervention of the two mortal fighters, this time there were survivors. All had hidden in what had been vain hopes that maybe they would be spared, maybe the killers would not find them, that maybe death would pass them by. Bianca wanted to seek them out.

"No," cautioned the Nightmare, "They're frightened and who knows what they might do if two blood-stained killers sought them out. We'll stand here, weapons away, and let them come to us."

They stood and waited, the tall man in black whose very appearance marked him as a creature of the night and the small woman whose duty it was to mete out justice and vengeance. Slowly, as the residents realized that the screaming and crying had ceased and silence once more ruled their village they began to emerge from their hiding holes.

A strange lot they were, the stuff of myth and legends. Leprechauns like Seamus and his cousin, creatures smaller still who flew on paper-thin wings, beasts who could have torn unarmed men apart but who were no match for trained soldiers. Most appeared human, but there was something about them that hinted that they possibly were something more, or maybe something less.

There were twenty in all, twenty survivors in a village where maybe ten times that number once lived. As they emerged from hiding Bianca and the Nightmare saw that despite their size, appearance or nature they were united in one thing, they were all scared.

As they gathered on the main street it was not long before they noticed the pair. Some fled back into hiding. Others, noting that the newcomers had not attacked, waited. A few, seeing blood on the clothing of the two but no wounds on their bodies, counted the dead behind them, breathed a sigh a relief and said a silent prayer of thanks. One of these few approached.

He was a child-sized creature, smaller than Bianca. As he came nearer his age became evident – graying hair, a lined faced and eyes that had seen too much of life.

"You did this?"

The Nightmare nodded as Bianca answered, "Yes."

What would have been a smile under happier circumstances creased the elder's face. "Then the Mother Goddess heard our pleas. We did not think any of the Fair Ones left." He looked around, as if searching for something. "Where is your army?"

"We do not need an army," the Nightmare replied in what he called his "spooky voice."

"All this? The two of you alone did … this?" Fear and awe was in the old man's voice. He dared to ask. "What are you?"

Bianca would have replied that they were just two people from another land sent to help. The Nightmare had a better sense of the dramatic.

"We are Retribution and Justice. We are Vengeance and Nightmare. We were sent to restore this land."

"Angus, Epos, Arian," whispered the elder as he wondered.

Knowing what it might mean to be named in a magical land, Bianca said firmly, "We are none of these. Our names are our own. And not for you to know. If you must, call us Bán and Tromluí."

The man nodded. "And I am Liam. Your names will be remembered as long as this village stands. You saved us. How may we serve you?"

The cop in Bianca took over. "Tell us what happened. When did the trouble start?"

"When has there not been trouble in Eire? Always there has been war and disease. But nothing like this. Plague and destruction have ravaged all the Land. First the pestilence comes. It kills some and weakens the rest. Then a blight steals the crops away. Sick and hungry, we are no match for the killers that come to finish the job."

"You said all the Land. How do you know this?"

Liam held his hand palm out. A small blue shape fluttered into it. "The piskies spread the news that Eire is besieged with warriors destroying all as they march to the sea."

"Thank you, Liam. Excuse us a moment. Tromluí and I must confer." The elder withdrew.

"What's this 'Tromluí and Bán?'"

"Irish for nightmare and white. Seemed a better idea than taking on the names and attributes of local gods, although that may be too late after your 'Retribution and Justice' pronouncement."

"I was just …"

"I know what you were doing, Michael. In our world it's dramatic and effective. But in a realm like this, words are magic."

"With just the two of against an army, I'll take all the help we can get. How soon do you think those marauders will be back?"

"Once they'll regroup, soon enough. They may wait for some sorcerous help."

"Then we'd best get ready for them."

It hurt her to say it. "Michael, we'd best get going before they do."

"What, but when those killers come back …"

"If we fight to save the village, we'll lose the Land. To save the Land …"

"We let the village die."

It was the logical thing to do, the man who was the Nightmare admitted to himself but that was no comfort at all. He would have argued with Bianca but his companion had waved Liam back.

"The heart of Eire," she asked the elder, "where is it?"

He pointed northeast. "Temair, where stands the Stone of Destiny, where lies the entrance to the otherworld. A day's journey, maybe more. You are going there?"

"Yes," Bianca admitted. "We do not know if this evil began or will end there, but that is where it might be stopped."

There was sadness in the old man's eyes and understanding in his voice as he asked, "And what of us?"

Pointing to the field of fallen men Bianca replied, "There are weapons out there. You can use them to fight and die." Then she pointed to the hills and forest behind the village. "Or you can hide and maybe live."

"A poor choice, Lady Bán."

"Your only one, Liam." To the Nightmare, Bianca said, "Let's go."

"Shouldn't we stop to eat and sleep?'

"Are you tired or hungry? I'm not."

"Neither am I, but I should be."

"Spirits at work again," Bianca said in disgust. "Come on, let's kill some gods."

They had been walking north for most of an hour when the Nightmare asked, "Why are we going to this Temair?"

"It's a place to start. If it is the heart of Eire, whoever's behind this either started there, in which case we may find a trail or is heading there, in which case we'll wait for him."

"What if he's still there?"

"Then we sit down with him and calmly discuss why he turned a paradise into a wasteland and ask him politely to make things right again. Either that or just kill him."

"I think we'd best kill him."

Later, after they had trekked more than half a day, "This land is barren," Bianca observed, "withered crops, burned villages, no life at all. Given what we left, I think the raiders came this way."

"I agree." After studying his surroundings the Nightmare added, "Reminds me of the Great War."

"You fought in World War I?" As soon as she spoke, Bianca realized her mistake.

The Nightmare nodded solemnly. "So there's going to be another one? Don't worry; your news isn't a surprise to anyone paying attention. It's always been a question of when, not if. I don't suppose you'd like to tell me?"

Bianca shook her head. "I've said too much already."

"At least tell me if we win."

"The good guys always do, don't they."

"We usually do, at least so far."

Bianca suddenly realized that she had the power to change history. *Should I tell him*, she wondered. *Tell him about Germany and the Final Solution, Stalin and the Iron Curtain, Pearl Harbor and the Atomic Bomb? He's a hero. He could gather the others and together they could kill Hitler and prevent the Third Reich. There might still be war but it might not be as bad. Or it might be worse.* That was the trouble with power. Using it may not always be the best course of action. Bianca decided to leave well enough alone.

That led her to consider her presence in Eire. Was what they were doing there the best course of action? Maybe the Land was supposed to die so that a better one might be reborn. Maybe their intervention ...

Enough, she yelled at herself. *You're thinking too much. Just do the job you came to do and get out of this hell.*

Hell. If the desolation around them reminded Shaw of the war, it reminded Biancxa of the Plains outside Hell. She and her partner had gone there to rescue an innocent. The journey had forced her to face the worst parts of herself. With help she overcame them and left them on the sands of Perdition.

Now Bianca found herself on a similar journey. Walking with a partner through a mythical land. They did not tire, they were not hungry and their guns did not empty. Magic was working. Maybe they should use it.

"Michael."

"Yes?"

"When the time comes to fight, before you act, before you even draw your guns, tell yourself to become Nightmare."

"I am the Nightmare."

"Not *the* Nightmare, just Nightmare, the terror of dreams brought to life."

"This has something to do with what you said before, about words and names having power."

"It has everything to do with it."

"Worth a try. But if I'm to be Tromluí in fact as well as name, what of Bán?"

"She becomes Vengeance."

It could have been the same day, maybe the next. In a sunless world there were no days or hours and time was merely an illusion.

"Are we there yet?"

"Tired, Michael?"

"Bored."

"Well, if that slight glow on what I think might be the horizon mean anything, you won't be bored for long."

"Then we should start making plans for when we ... wait. What was that?"

"I didn't hear anyth…"

"You wouldn't. Back on Earth I worked and fought in the shadows. I was part of the night. Here it's as if the darkness is a part of me. There is something out there."

Bianca began to bring up her gun.

"No, don't. Gunfire will only attract attention. Let me handle this. You just keep talking."

Bianca turned to ask, "About what?" but the Nightmare was gone.

There was not much cover in the wasted land of Eire – broken stone fences, husks of trees, partly collapsed walls, but what there was was sufficient to hide a small band of men. Somehow the Nightmare knew where each of them was.

Miss Jones was right, he thought. *We are close. This must be the first outpost.* He sensed movement in the night then felt one of the lookouts leaving his post, no doubt to spread word about the intruders.

Can't have that. Suddenly he was flowing through the darkness, travelling faster than he ever could in the mortal plane. There was no conscious thought in this, just a desire to catch the running man. When he did, he used a knife he'd taken off one of his foes from the village to silence the man forever.

There were six others. How he knew that he could not say but reaching through the night he found them, flowed to them and used his knife to end their threat. Then he was back with Bianca.

When he again appeared at her side the detective tried not to appear startled. She almost asked how things had gone then saw his cleaning blood off a wicked looking knife.

"There'll be no warning from this direction," said the Nightmare casually, as of the deaths of seven men had not affected him. "Here."

He handed Bianca a pair of matched blades – long knives, short swords – Bianca wasn't sure. "I don't need these."

"Maybe Bianca Jones doesn't, but Bán soon will. In a crowd guns are of little use except as clubs. These are best for close quarter fighting."

"And how do you know they're be close quarter fighting?"

"To quote one of my colleagues, I know."

The pair had not gone much further when distant noises reached them. The Nightmare knew those sounds from the war, they were the sounds of encamped men.

Stealthily they approached, Bianca following the Nightmare, matching him step for step, moving when he did and stopping when he stopped. Finally they reached the camp.

As the Nightmare called on the night to hide them, the pair surveyed the scene.

"Fifty, maybe seventy-five men," the experienced soldier explained to the detective. "Nothing permanent. Those tents are made to be taken down quickly. Look there." The Nightmare indicated one side of the camp. "Men preparing to leave."

"And there," Bianca drew his attention to the other side, "more men coming in. But from where?"

"Up there, maybe?"

The Nightmare pointed past the far side of the camp to where stood a castle. Temair, the Heart of the Land. It was not the fairy tale palace one reads about in stories. Instead it was a stone fortress, one that appeared easy to defend and difficult to breach.

"Liam said that Temair was a gateway to other worlds."

"From which, Miss Jones, whoever or whatever's behind this may be bringing in troops. We have to get in there."

"Any suggestions, other than knocking on the front door and asking to come in."

"I've gotten into more formidable places. But first we have to get past these men."

"Why not just go around them?'

"That would be my first choice, Miss Jones, except ..." The Nightmare pointed at the camp. Men were gathering their weapons and coming towards them. "I think someone knows we're here. We'll have to go through them."

As the Nightmare drew his .45s Bianca readied her shotgun, made sure her .40 caliber pistol was close to hand. "We'll use our guns until they get close," she said.

"And then?"

"Then we let Tromluí and Bán take over. Start us off, Michael."

"Why not?"

The Nightmare laughed and the pair opened fire.

The order came from the castle. There were intruders approaching from the south. They were to be stopped at all costs.

As the men and those who walked like men gathered, they saw two figures at the edge of the woods, a tall one in black and a youth. Neither was armored. Nor did they appear to be carrying any weapons. *This won't be much of a fight,* most of them thought.

Then there was laughter and thunder and death came for no reason and the men knew them for what they were – wizards or gods. No matter, they were warriors and had their orders. And whatever their nature, the pair would die.

The men rushed forward only to be felled by the Nightmare's bullets or ripped to shreds by Bianca's flechette loads. Still they came, grinning in the face of almost certain death. They knew, or thought they knew, that the pair could not stop them all and sooner rather than later they would be within spear's point or sword's edge and that would be the end of them.

Bianca and the Nightmare knew this as well. As their targets came closer they killed more of them but before they got too close, Bianca said, "Now would be the time, Michael."

"Agreed, and let's pray you're right."

And as they surrendered to their other selves the screaming began.

The two at the woods, the ones that were expected to die easy and messy deaths were suddenly not there. Instead each man faced that which frightened him the most, the things that haunted his dreams and caused him to wake screaming from sleep. Some broke and ran, others stood paralyzed with fright. Still others collapsed in fear.

The man who had been the Nightmare and who was now Tromluí felt their fears and fed on them. Growing stronger, he sent his night terrors further outward, engulfing those still in camp, bringing them to their knees to weep like children.

But there are men who do not fear, or if they do have the strength to overcome it. Horrible monsters, terrible beasts, skinless hags with diseased flesh have no power over them for they have caused more suffering than could ever be dreamt and enjoyed doing so. And there were such men among those advancing, men unaffected by what seemed to be a wizard's curse.

It was these men that caused she who was now Bán to draw her blades and go among them. Against her speed and skill these men had no chance and one by one were cut down. And when none stood against her Bán went down into the camp and continued her bloody work.

When it was over, when there was nothing left but the dead and empty tents, Bianca and the Nightmare slowly came back to themselves.

Bianca looked over the slaughter. "What have we done?"

"What we had to do."

"I'm not so sure. There must have been a better way." She looked down at her hands and the blades they held. Both were bloody. She would have thrown the weapons down had she been sure she would not need them again.

"What have we become?" she asked.

"Something more."

"You enjoyed doing this?" With a wave of her red stained hand Bianca indicated the dead and moaning.

"Not exactly, but … look at how I dress, what I do, how I do it. It would be easier to strike fear into the hearts of evildoers if I could, well, actually strike fear."

"At what cost? Your life, your mind, your soul. How much of Michael Shaw would Tromluí allow to remain, and what if he chose not to stop with the hearts of bad guys? Magic has a price, Michael, just look around you to know what it costs."

Again Bianca looked at her hands. This time she did drop her blades.

"Point taken, but if we don't want to pay another installment we better get up to the castle before whoever sends down more men."

"You start for Temair; I'm going to search out this gateway to the otherworld."

"Leaving so soon? The party's not over."

"Not yet, maybe not ever, but as you said, we do what we have to do."

As Bianca walked away, the Nightmare could not help but think of how much she reminded him of someone else, although Leda would not have left her weapons, nor would she have thought about the cost of using them.

The entrance to the otherworlds. That's what Liam had called it back at the village. If it truly was, it might be her way back, possibly her only way back. That's not why Bianca sought it but it was how she was going to find it. Resisting the impulse to click her heels together she began repeating, "There's no place like home, there's no place like home."

She felt a tug, one which led her to the east of Castle Temair. There she found a mound of earth about the size of a hill, a round hole at its base. Through the hole Bianca sensed Baltimore, her husband Joe and the 21st century. No troops were coming from it, but how long would that last? She did what she had to do. Then, saying goodbye to all she knew and loved, she went to join the Nightmare.

The approach to Temair was guarded, but not well. To one whose practice it was to blend with the shadows it was an easy task in this endless twilight for the Nightmare to avoid the guards.

"But why blend with the shadows when you can become them?" asked a voice inside his head, a voice he knew to be Tromluí's. But Tromluí was a part of him, was he not? "Think, Michael, how easy it would be to slide from one shadow to the next, no fear of detection. Where there was darkness and light, there you would be, striking down your enemies, teaching them the true meaning of fear."

At what cost? the Nightmare wondered, thinking back on Bianca's warning. *My life, my soul, myself?*

Somehow the Nightmare knew that it was not a part of himself that answered. "You need not worry, Michael, I want nothing from you, only the fear of others."

"What have we done?" he echoed Bianca. "What have we created?" Whatever it was, it was not something he could take home with him, nor did he want it inside him.

"While I appreciate the offer, I think I'll pass," he drew his guns, checked their loads. "I'll make do with these."

That part of him that was Tromluí would have protested but as its creator, the Nightmare was able to push it away and out of his conscious mind.

He was now at the castle gates. Ahead of him was the courtyard and next the Great Hall. The Nightmare suspected that that was where he'd find the source of the Land's troubles.

"Well, Michael," he said aloud to himself, "it's just you, your guns and a laugh against who knows what. The way it should be, without the hocus-pocus. Time to play."

And with that he marched toward the Great Hall to face who knows what.

The first thing that hit him was a wave of nausea. He fought back the urge to vomit then struggled not to soil his trousers. His skin grew clammy then hot as a fever threatened to take him. An itchy rash began in places he did not want to think about.

Disease, he knew, was the first to plague the villages. But his symptoms were not plague-like, merely annoying and potentially embarrassing. His maladies did however tell him that he was in the right place.

Then he saw her, a diseased-ridden hag with more sores than skin. Lesions on her body oozed pus when they did not leak blood. She smelled of putrescence and decay. On seeing her, the Nightmare was glad that he could kill from a distance, for he had no wish to get any nearer to the creature than he must.

"Madame," he said politely, "I think it's past time that you saw a physician."

What was probably a cackle came out as a death rattle followed by a prolonged cough. "I doubt if any would heal me, young man. I am the reason for their profession and the source of their wealth. I am Cailleach, and I am Sickness Herself."

Leveling a .45 in her direction, the Nightmare said, "And I have a cure for that sickness."

The diseased goddess laughed again, phlegm gurgling in her throat as she did. "You would think to kill a god? Destroy this form and I will find another."

"And in the meantime the Land will have a chance to heal."

Cailleach smiled, if a show of bleeding gums and blackened teeth could be called a smile."So be it," she said and when the Nightmare fired she made no move to avoid her fate.

He shot her twice, in her head and heart. As she collapsed and began to decay, the Nightmare thought he heard her say, "Beware the stranger and your other self."

Before the Nightmare could consider these words he heard,

"He told us you would come. Where is your other?"

Turning, the Nightmare saw a man at the far end of the hall. He was armored. A sheathed sword hung at his side and in his hands were a shield and spear. The man was tall and well muscled, the image of the perfect warrior.

"You must be War."

The man shrugged. "War, Death, Destruction – it's all the same is it not?"

"Who are you and why do you plague this land?"

"I am called Elphane by some and as for plagues, they were Cailleach's doing. I brought war and destruction. As for why …" It seemed to the Nightmare as if the warrior god had tried to speak but could not. He did, however, turn and look at the doorway behind him.

Pistols in hand, the Nightmare advanced, expecting Elphane's attack at any time.

"Were we to fight, dark one," cautioned the god, "you would lose."

"Were I to fire these, you would die."

At this Elphane smiled. "I can throw this spear faster than a man can blink and it always flies true. My shield is such that nothing can pierce it, indeed, whatever force strikes it is returned threefold against my attacker. And when I draw my sword it cuts so clean that you will not feel your head leave your neck. As I said, dark one, were we to fight you would lose."

Bizarre plans ran through the Nightmare's mind. Could he catch the spear? Could he fire and not hit the shield? If his bullets did strike the shield could he then run in front of the god so that they struck him? Rejecting these ideas he simply asked,

"And if we do not fight?"

"Then how could you lose?"

Nodding in understanding, the man in black holstered his .45s. As he approached the far doorway of the Great Hall Elphane stepped aside. To the Nightmare's questioning glance he replied, "I am the god of death and destruction, not a porter. Enter of your own free will. Beware the stranger and your other self."

That phrase again. Who was the stranger? Was it the "he" who had warned Elphane of his coming? And was his other self Tromluí or could it be Miss Jones? What had become of her and would she somehow betray him?

The room which the Nightmare entered was smaller than the Great Hall and was empty of all but a chair and the man sitting in it. If man he was. He was dressed in white and shone with an inner brightness that made the torches on the walls unnecessary. There had been boredom on his face when the Nightmare came in but that disappeared when he saw the man in black.

Immediately sensing that this being was the one responsible for the troubles plaguing the Land, the Nightmare decided not to waste time. Drawing his .45s he fired but as he did so a shadow rose up before the shining man and seemingly swallowed the bullets.

"You didn't think it would be that easy, did you?" the man asked. "Meet your other self."

At the man's words the Nightmare knew the shadow creature for what it was. It was Tromluí, that part of him that he had rejected.

"You came to this Land to stop me and to stop me you took part of the Land into yourself. And when you rejected it you not only gave me the means to stop you but to use that part of you to enter your world when I am done ravaging this one."

From outside the castle there came the sound of thunder and from the doorway the voice of Bianca Jones.

"Your gateway to other worlds just collapsed." To the Nightmare she explained, "Several grenades going off at one will do that to a hole in a hill. We're probably trapped in this world, but then again, so is he."

As Bianca spoke, the Nightmare noticed that she carried a spear in one hand and a sword in the other. "How did you get those?"

"I'll explain later. In the meantime, who's our new best friend?"

"Fools. You are in the presence of Apollonius of Tyana, the true Messiah over that Nazarene pretender. Long have I wandered the many planes of existence, looking for a world such as this, one whose mortal plane is so beset with strife that I can usurp its very gods and cause them to do my bidding. Know this, I needed that gateway only to bring in warriors with which to overwhelm this land. There are other paths which I may trod. Your souls for one."

And the shade of Bán rose up next to that of Tromluí.

"Your own selves will devour you and through them will I gain access to your world."

As the two spirits began to advance Bianca turned to the Nightmare. "Trade you," she suggested and at his hesitation added, "Trust me."

Seeing no other choice, he agreed. Tromluí which was Nightmare itself enveloped Bianca, filling her being with horrors which would have overwhelmed anyone else. But these terrors paled in comparison to those which the detective has faced in real life. She was a Baltimore City cop and had seen it all – men gunned down for no reason, women brutalized beyond belief, children raped and murdered. Bianca had fought monsters and had walked the plains of Hell. Nothing scared her anymore save the possibility that she would one day fail the people and the city she loved. And since she had lived that fear every day for the past few years, experiencing it again had little effect on her. Powerless over her, Tromluí faded away

As the Nightmare faced Bán he remembered what she as part of Bianca had done to the soldiers outside the castle. And in remembering, smiled. Now and then he saw in this spirit of vengeance an aspect of

Nemesis, the goddess and woman whom he loved. Whispering softly the name "Leda" he let that love shine through. And as Bán had been born of Bianca, and Bianca had been sent by Nemesis, the spirit felt the love. With no vengeance to take, Bán faded.

"Is that all you got?" Bianca asked. Saying "catch" she tossed the sword to the Nightmare.

"Fools," Apollonius said again and unleashed his powers against them. Heat seared one, cold froze the other. They would have fallen, should have fallen but their belief in themselves was stronger than any self-named god. Her skin blistering, Bianca drew back her arm. Barely able to feel his limbs, the Nightmare advanced with his sword.

Bianca let loose the spear that always flew true. It pinned the would-be messiah to his chair. The Nightmare moved closer. One swing and Apollonius did not even feel his head leave his neck.

"Did we win?" asked a very frostbitten Nightmare. Feeling in his fingers and toes was gone and it felt as if his arms and legs were next

"If the bad guy's dead I think so," answered Bianca, her every nerve ending screaming in pain, "but right now it doesn't feel like it."

"F-fire and ice," said the Nightmare through shivering lips. "We're in a magical realm. Do you think …"

"Worth a shot. It's that or die."

Crawling over to each other, they just managed to embrace before losing consciousness.

It was hours, or maybe just minutes later, when they awoke. Both were seemingly healed, the Nightmare with some small tingling in his fingers and Bianca with a decent tan for the first and only time in her life.

The headless body of Apollonius was still in its chair but, like their pain, was beginning to fade.

"That's never a good sign," Bianca said.

"Like us, he was a stranger to the Land. Now we have to find our way back. Any ideas?"

Before she could answer, Elphane came into the room. "May I have my weapons back now?"

"That reminds me, Miss Jones, you never did explain how you got them."

"It seems that there are two answers to my riddle. One was not to fight and the other …"

"While he was bragging about his weapons I kicked him in the balls and took what I needed," Bianca explained.

"Of the two, I liked your answer better, dark one." Elphane looked at what remained of the corpse. "Still, you managed to free the Land from the stranger and for that you have my thanks."

"And mine as well, Michael."

At the sound of a familiar voice the Nightmare looked around to see a smaller than average man.

"Seamus, but I thought …"

"With that one gone," Seamus indicated the now almost vanished body of Apollonius, "the way once again opened, my way, at least. I understand it will take some digging to repair this lady's handiwork." He turned to Bianca. "Seamus Moran, my lady, at your service. And may I say it's nice to meet a lady of the proper height for once."

Taking the proffered hand, Bianca said, "I've met your cousin."

"Then you know that good looks run in the family. That is, they run from Paddy and run to me. Ready to go back, Michael?"

"Wait, what of the Land, what of Eire? How will it heal itself?"

"Rest assured, my lady, the one thing we have is plenty of fertility gods and goddesses. The Land will heal amid much pleasure. Michael, it's time I saw you home."

"Past time, I'd say, Seamus, but what of Miss Jones?"

"She'd be more than welcome. She'd fit in well with your group. But hers is a different path. And now if you're ready?"

"A moment, Seamus. Miss Jones, thank you for your help. It was a pleasure fighting at your side."

"Likewise, Michael."

"Give Leda my love. Maybe one day …"

"Maybe. One never knows. Goodbye, Michael."

"Goodbye, Miss Jones."

In a New York tavern, many years away, two women again met in a secluded booth.

"He's safe then," asked a woman in black.

"As safe as anyone who does what he does. And from what I've read …"

"One never knows, Bianca. The past at times is as fluid as the future. But for now he's safe back then. And I owe you."

"Damn straight you do. I just pray I never have to call in the debt."

A smallish man who looked very much like his cousin came over to their table. "Excuse me, ladies."

"Yes, Paddy?"

"Many, many years ago a man dressed in black with a wicked laugh came to me at closing time and begged a favor. He asked that if two deadly and beautiful women should ever come twice to my bar I was to give them these," he handed them sealed envelopes, "and serve them this." Paddy filled their glasses from a bottle that was old when he was young and the Irish had first learned what to do with the juice of the barley. "Drinks tonight are on Michael Shaw."

Bianca's message was simply "With all my thanks."

Nemesis's message was simply "With all my love."

And for that moment and many more, the laugh of the Nightmare echoed in their minds.

After the Fall

The Great Ape fell. In an instant, what had been the Eighth Wonder of the World was nothing more than four tons of soon to be rotten meat lying on 5th Ave. Naturally, the entire city came out to gaze upon the now dead god.

This included Lieutenant Jerome Easton of the NYPD Homicide Squad. He had been working a gangland slaying in Brooklyn the night before so had missed the previous evening's excitement of a chained beast breaking free, the town in panic, a beautiful woman in peril and biplanes to the rescue.

Finally off duty and much too tired to sleep, Easton joined his fellow New Yorkers in gawking at the fallen wonder. Using his badge, he got a place in the front of the crowd in time to hear the Great Director's pronouncement.

"No," Easton said to himself, "I'm fairly certain it was the bullets from the biplanes." And then aloud to no one in particular, "I'm just glad I don't have to clean up the mess."

"As am I, Lieutenant," a familiar voice answered. Easton turned to see Michael Shaw standing behind him.

"Mr. Shaw, I'd like to say what a pleasant surprise, but it's no surprise to find one of your kind involved in a matter like this."

Shaw feigned puzzlement. "One of my kind, Lieutenant? You mean one of the idle rich with nothing better to do than join the curious in staring at this week's once in a lifetime event?"

"You know what I'm talking about."

While Shaw's only reply was a smile, he did know to what Easton was referring. The lieutenant suspected Shaw of being the Nightmare, one of several cloaked vigilantes who preyed upon the city's underworld, dispensing justice when the law failed. Good detective that he was, Easton was correct. Not that Shaw would ever admit it. It was enough for both men that Shaw knew that Easton knew, and Easton knew that Shaw knew he knew, and so forth. It was how the game was played.

The two men stood and watched as city workers discussed the disposition of the twenty-five foot long corpse, with the Department of Sanitation arguing that it was the responsibility of Animal Control and that bureau being adamant that since the Army Air Corps brought it down it should clean it up. But the Army, having done its job, was long gone from the scene. However, all were united in the decision that whatever the ultimate fate of the gigantic primate, the Great Director should bear the cost. That individual, however, was nowhere to be found.

"Well, Mr. Shaw, have you seen enough of the big dead monkey?"

"It's more ape than monkey, Lieutenant, and in answer to your question, yes, I have. The beast is starting to smell. May I suggest we go someplace and raise a glass to its memory?"

"A bit early in the day, isn't it?"

"From the look of your suit, you've been up most the night. As have I. Since neither one of us has been to bed, well, our own beds, our day has not yet started. Moran's sound good?"

"Moran's sounds great."

Named after its owner, Moran's was a quiet bar in the east end of the city. A taxi ride later and the two were in one of its back booths, each enjoying an Irish Coffee.

"So what do you think will become of that thing we just left, Mr. Shaw?"

"This is New York, Lieutenant. Right now there are more than a dozen entrepreneurs with at least two dozen ways of making money off the corpse. I suspect there's going to be a surplus of fur coats this winter and I for one will be avoiding steak for at least six months. But let's talk of something more pleasant, such as murder. What kept you out so late last night?"

Before Easton could answer, a shorter than average man came over to their table.

"Can I get you gentlemen anything else?"

"Two more of your excellent Irish Coffees please, Seamus. And given the hour, a little more coffee than Irish this time."

Even as the mighty one fell, his spirit soared, searching for a host. Since time began, that was the way of things. The body of great ape was not immortal and eventually weakened and fell prey to disease or one of the other beasts of the island. Then his freed soul would search out a worthy successor among the jungle's lesser apes. This new host would then grow stronger, faster, smarter, and most of all bigger than its fellows until it was able to challenge the largest of the land's reptiles and once again rule as king.

But New York was not the jungle home with which the spirit of the ape was familiar. It was instead an island of stone and steel and the freed soul could sense none of its kind anywhere near. No worthy ones that is. There were kindred creatures close by, cousins to those of the island. But they were caged and held in servitude by the hairless ones, and so none were worthy of kingship. With other choice save that of oblivion, the mighty one's spirit sought refuge in the only place it could.

It was nine-thirty in the evening. Jerome Easton had been on duty for roughly three hours and awake for slightly more than four. Surprisingly he was suffering no ill effects from that morning's liquid breakfast. "That Irish dwarf must have used the good stuff," he thought as he two-fingered typed his report of the Brooklyn shoot out.

He was pulling the finished product out of the roller when, "Lieutenant, call for you."

It was one of Easton's dockside snitches, sounding more excited than he had in years.

"Ya gotta get down here, Easton." There was panic in the man's voice.

"What is it, Langan?"

"Somethin' big, and somethin' bad. Just get down here."

Easton took his time. Snitches – it was always the end of the world with them. Always playing up whatever they had for a larger payoff. Of course whatever Langan had was bad, there was no money in reporting good things. And however important his information, it could not be any bigger than what was still lying in front of the Empire State. Nor could it be badder.

It was then that Easton remembered that the docks to which he was headed were the same ones at which the Great Ape had been received. Easton had been on hand for the unloading. A giant cage, one built to size for the monster within. The creature had been gassed or drugged but even so remained on its feet and seemed aware of what was happening to it. The look in its eyes was one of anger and hatred for the pale puny things that had dared to confine it. "If that thing ever escapes," Easton remembered saying, "there will be Hell to pay." He had taken no satisfaction when he was proven right.

Something big. Something bad. The docks. The ape. Suddenly and against all reason Easton knew what Langan had to say. He hit the gas and his siren both at the same time.

"But it's dead," the logical part of his mind told him. "It's dead and as soon as they can figure out how to lift it off the pavement there will be discount fur coats and monkey steaks for everyone."

"What about the Dead Man?" Easton asked the logical part of himself. An assassin who could not be killed and who reeked of rotting flesh, the Dead Man was stopped only after the Nightmare intervened.

And with that thought Easton knew that before driving to the docks he had to stop at Moran's.

The night was clear, the air crisp and cool. *There should be fog*, Easton thought as he arrived at the docks. As if on cue, a ship's horn blew. *At least there's that.*

Three men were waiting for him, Langan and standing by his side an older man in a navy pea coat. The third, who stood slightly apart from the others, was barely dressed and had the blackest skin Easton had ever seen.

"Dis here's Capt'n Young," Langan said as Easton approached. "And dis one, hell, I don't know if he even has a name. But you gotta hear what he has to say. As for me, I'm outta here."

As the informant turned to leave Easton reached for his wallet. "Forgetting something, Langan?"

The man shook his head. "Forget it, Lieutenant. After all that happened last night, dis one's on me." Langan all but ran off.

"Captain." Young shook the extended hand as Easton asked, "Who's our friend and what can he tell me about the giant ape?"

"How do you …"

"I had my suspicions, but I wasn't sure until I saw him. He's a native from that island, isn't he?"

"Yeah, stowed away on the ship that stole his god. Had some crazy idea he could rescue him. Made it ashore last night just as "his god" hit the pavement. Someone found him on the docks jabbering, whistling and clicking. I used to sail the waters around his island so he was brought to me. Since I speak his lingo I got the job of telling him that the king was dead. That's when he really panicked."

"The death of one's god will do that."

"Wasn't that. D'wan here said something about … what was it?"

Young turned to the island native, and spoke in a language totally foreign to Easton. The reply came in the same tongue, accompanied by guttural sounds Easton didn't think he could reproduce on a bet.

"D'wan says that his island is home to many great beasts, each of them a god. When one dies, his spirit, D'wan calls it his 'ka'ng,' seeks out a worthy successor."

"Of which there are none on our island."

Young shook his head. "Except for some chimps in the Central Park and Bronx zoos, and D'wan says that being locked up they don't count."

"So we got this ka'ng loose in the city looking for a home .What happens when he doesn't find one."

Young relayed the question to D'wan who answered with clicks and whistles and a shrug that needed no translation.

A voice suddenly came from the darkness. "Captain Young, is your ship ready to sail?"

"Who ..."

"Answer the question, Young," Easton ordered.

"Uh, yeah. The Endeavor's leaving in the morning. Cargo to pick up in Harbor City then across to Africa."

"It will do," said the voice. "Take D'wan aboard, you will need him."

"Do what he says," Easton commanded at the captain's hesitation.

As Young made for his ship, a figure separated stepped from the shadows. It was a man dressed in the color of night – trenchcoat, suit, hat and gloves, all black, as was the mask that hid his face.

"I got your message," the Nightmare told Easton.

"I figured if anyone could find you it was that Irish dwarf."

"Moran's a lubrican."

"A what? No matter. You heard?"

" I did."

"Then from what you told Young I'm assuming you have some kind of plan to head off whatever's going to happen before it's too late?"

"I have a plan, Lieutenant, but it's already too late."

Unable to find a suitable host, the ka'ng of the great ape took refuge in the only place it could – the carcass in which it had last dwelt. It was that or fade away forever. Having existed for millennia, the ka'ng was strong in power and used much of it to reanimate the lifeless corpse. Slowly the ape's body rose.

"Look out!"

"My God!"

"It's still alive!"

"Call the army!"

"Frank, watch it!"

These cries and more were heard as the dead beast lumbered to its feet. Cables securing the body snapped and whipped through the air, decapitating two men and crippling several more. Then the panic of the crowd did its work. As onlookers ran from the revived creature, many were crushed beneath the feet of the fleeing crowd.

The body rose slowly, its senses slow to respond. Sight returned first, then hearing and finally the smells of the city. Bright lights hurt its dead eyes. The screams of the hairless ones below deafened it to the sounds it needed to hear. Too many foul odors blocked the scents the ka'ng sought. No matter. What it sought was not here and so the ka'ng would walk to where it could be found or until the corpse that housed it could no longer continue. Only then would the ka'ng be truly dead. Blindly choosing a direction, the spirit of the beast headed north on 5th Ave.

Futilely the police tried to stop the undead ape. Fired bullets had less effect than they had the first time, as one cannot kill that which is dead. The army arrived and armed with machine guns and rifle grenades bravely confronted the beast. And while the bombs and .50 caliber bullets blew away parts of it body, they could not stop the creature's advance.

Straight on it came, stopping for nothing, its massive paws crushing all in its wake. Light poles were felled and benches shattered. Fortunately it moved slowly enough that those on foot could easily escape but those foolish enough to remain with their cars did not fare as well. Caught in the mass of fleeing vehicles they found themselves hurtling through the air as their cars were kicked and pushed aside.

The planes came in, those fragile powered kites that had done the job the first time. Flying low through the buildings as if in a concrete canyon, they riddled the ape with bullets but to no effect. This beast could not feel the sting of the leaden missiles and the ones that did penetrate its thick hide had no effect on non-functioning organs. Still the brave pilots flew close and strafed their target, pulling up at the last minute to circle and attack again.

One pilot mistimed his run. Crashing into the lifeless yet moving body his plane flipped and fell apart, killing him instantly and showering what few people were still below with debris. Still the other planes and the army continued their attack, hoping to slow the ape until the bombers could be brought in from a distant airfield. The creature would be stopped, even at the cost of part of the city.

"Aren't we going a bit out of our way?" the Nightmare asked Easton as the detective took them on a circuitous route to the place the masked man said they needed to go.

"Do you know what midtown's like right now? The ape heading north, people fleeing in all directions. Trust me, this way we'll at least get close to the park. But why bother? Sooner or later, the army will blow enough holes in that thing to bring it down. Dead or not, take out its legs …"

"And it will crawl. I have studied the undead, Lieutenant, and this one's ka'ng will not be stopped until there is nothing left that can move."

"The radio says that bombers are being called in. They should do the trick."

"Which is why we must act before they arrive."

"If machine guns and grenades won't stop it, what makes you think a spooky laugh and twin .45s will?"

"And what makes you think I want to stop it?"

A surprised Easton almost ran up on the sidewalk. He did stop the car. "What the hell are you talking about? You mean to say you want that thing …"

"What I want, Lieutenant, is justice, and it was not just to take that ape from its home, to take a god away from its followers simply for one man's profit and our amusement. And to allow the spirit of this magnificent beast to perish because of our greed and ignorance would be the ultimate injustice. Now please, will you drive to the park or must I make my way alone?"

Easton looked at the dark shape that was his passenger. He knew what the man was capable of, had seen the bloody results of his crusade against crime. Easton had no illusions that should he refuse, a large caliber gun would suddenly appear in the man's fist and that the detective would be given one chance to vacate his car. Would the Nightmare shoot him to save what might be the ghost of a giant monkey? Easton did not know, nor did he want to find out. Putting the car in gear he drove even faster.

"Mind telling me your plan?"

"The ka'ng is heading to the park. So are we. With luck we will arrive first. Then we give it what it wants."

"According to that D'wan, what it wants is a host, but the native said that caged chimps were not worthy."

"Which is why, Lieutenant, we're going to free them. Now please, as fast as you can, to Central Park and Mr. Moses's Zoo."

They entered the zoo from the east side of the park. Finding the apes was easy, they followed the sounds of screeching, chattering and what seemed to the men to be cries of delight mixed with fear.

"They sense its coming," the Nightmare said. "They just don't know just what it is."

There were no gorillas in the zoo – not yet. Most of the chimpanzees were smaller members of that species. Only two or three were of any decent size.

"Do you think it's true?" Easton asked the Nightmare. "That we're descended from things like this?"

"You've seen what passes for muscle in most of the city's gangs. What do you think?"

"When you put it that way, Darwin was right. Now how do we get these beasts out?"

The Nightmare approached the cage door, did something to the lock. "You have a key?"

"Not exactly," the dark clad vigilante replied. "Step back."

There was a hiss, a spark then a small bang as the explosive powder the Nightmare had put into the keyhole ignited and blew the lock apart.

"Now what?" Easton asked as the door cage door swung open.

"Now wait to see if any of them are worthy."

At first the chimps were frightened, the noise of the explosion having driven them to the back of their cage. Then one of the larger ones came forward to investigate, stopping at the swinging door but going no further. It bared its teeth at the two men but did not leave its cage.

Another joined it, also baring her teeth, but she too remained in the safety of the only home she had ever known.

It was one of the smaller ones who dared to venture forth, but as soon as he approached the door he was batted back by the large one. Just for a moment did he cower back then he ran forward. Ducking under the paw of the bigger ape, the small chimp made his break for freedom.

"Now what?"

"We follow the best we can, Lieutenant. Not that there's any question where the little one will end up."

"What about them?" The detective indicated the rest of the chimps, all still in their cage.

"They'll either leave or they won't. It doesn't matter. All the ka'ng needs is one worthy soul."

The two men took a path south following a path to where the ka'ng should bring the great ape's body.

Easton looked over at his companion, or tried to at least. The Nightmare's all black clothing rendered him invisible in the darkness. "What if you're right? What if this crazy idea of your works? What then? Do you just plan on letting this ka'ng run free in the city? Or do you plan to ask it nicely to follow you to the Endeavor?"

"Don't be silly, Lieutenant. I don't speak chimpanzee."

They stood in the darkness, waiting for the undead ape to appear at the edge of the park. Soon it did and with it came the planes and the soldiers and the police, all still trying desperately to halt its progress. They had had some small success. Pieces of the corpse had been shot off or blown away. But there was still enough of the beast to allow it to move forward. But as it came to the park all firing stopped. The biplanes flew away and the army and police dispersed. In the quiet one could hear the drone of the approaching bomber planes.

"They herded it toward the park. Less damage to buildings when the bombs drop."

"They didn't herd it anywhere, Lieutenant. They just let it go where it wanted to, not that they had any choice."

"Doesn't matter. It will all be over when the planes get here. Which means we should leave before they do."

"Leave if you must, Lieutenant. I'll stay and see this through."

"Look, Shaw, or Nightmare, or whoever you are. There's no sense getting yourself killed over an already dead monkey. We tried, you tried, we just ran out of time. It wasn't in the cards."

The Nightmare's only reply was to point to where the great ape was entering the park.

The ka'ng felt itself weakening. Too much damage had been done to this body. Hundreds of years of life force had been spent in animating it and decades more in keeping it moving forward. Soon there would be nothing left. No ka to invest a new host with its power. Better to give up now and drift with the wind then to use up the last of itself in a futile search. Then suddenly the things that had been annoying it went away and all noises ceased. From in front of the body there came a faint scream of challenge. The ka'ng focused its vision downward and saw a small form standing in its way.

It was not one of the apes from its island home. Nor was it brother or sister to them. No, this tiny one was something of a lesser cousin. Still, it was closer in being than the hairless ones. And as it stood in defiance of the great thing that dared to invade what it had just claimed for itself, the ka'ng reached out and found it worthy.

The bombers were getting closer. Time was running out. The Nightmare and Easton watched as apes large and small, living and dead confronted each other. Finally, the body of the great ape wavered just as the smaller one raised its arm, beat its chest and let out what only could be a roar of triumph. The Nightmare would have joined it by letting loose the laughter that terrified the city's underworld, but it was not yet time to celebrate.

"Now, Lieutenant." Pulling something from his coat, the Nightmare ran toward the chimp.

The chimp turned at the approach of the men. Giving out another cry, he prepared to meet this new challenge. But at his growl they stopped short. Then the dark one threw something toward it, something much like the balls he and his fellows were sometimes given to play with. Only this ball emitted a noxious green gas, one that dulled the chimp's senses and soon caused it to totter and fall to the ground.

The two men quickly picked up the unconscious chimp and awkwardly started carrying it out of the park.

"We're not going to make it!"

"I don't think we'll have to. Look!"

No longer animated by the power of the ka'ng, the corpse of the mighty beast stood for a time, swaying back and forth on lifeless legs. Then for the second time, the great ape fell.

Seeing the prostrate form of the intended target, the bombers' flight commander ordered his planes to circle until further instructions could be received. They were soon in coming. "Take no chances. Proceed as ordered."

The bombs fell in a precision pattern and when they had done their work, there was little left of the Eighth Wonder of the World.

By that time Easton and the Nightmare were well on their way back to the docks.

Captain Young looked incredulous as Easton told his tale. "I don't know. He looks like any other monkey to me."

"He might be, Captain, or he just might be destined to become the king of all apes. Just see him safe."

"I doubt if I could find that island of his, even if I ever do get to those waters."

"The coast of Africa will be fine, Captain. A new start for a new king. Just give him a nice comfortable cage on the voyage over."

"The way that D'wan fellow treated him, you can count on it. That native will probably insist on a cabin for his new friend. What's its name, anyway. Can't keep calling it, well, it."

"He's on your ship, Captain, you get to name him."

"Well, he looks a little like my brother Joe."

"Joe it is, Captain. Have a safe voyage and take good care of him."

"Like one of the family, Lieutenant."

As Captain Young boarded the Endeavour, Lieutenant Easton walked over to the shadows.

"Zombies and Monsters. Chimps that host gorilla gods. My life was a lot less interesting before you came along. How about the next time you just fight some gangsters?"

His only answer was a laugh that gradually faded away in the dark.

NOT QUITE IN TIME

The man in black stood in the shadows of a darkened hallway and looked out into the street. He was waiting for armed men to arrive. They would come to murder a family hiding in the apartment he was guarding. He was the only one who could stop the killers, the only chance a husband, wife and two sons had.

Several weeks ago the Dorseys, tourists on their first day in the city, had gotten lost and driven into the wrong part of town. They had also driven into the middle of a gang rubout. None of them were hurt, but all of them had gotten a good look at the hitmen.

Now their lives were in danger. One try at assassination had already failed. And it was only by chance that the man who was called the Nightmare had heard about the coming attempt.

He had been in a waterfront dive called Dago Mike's. Mike's was a dirty place frequented by the lowest of riffraff. The Nightmare had learned long ago that by ordering a bottle and sitting quietly in a corner he could learn much about the doings of crime and criminals.

"The Wolf is getting nervous," said one rough looking man to another. "That family's still alive and can finger Jake Green and Charlie Heywood for bumping The Welshman."

"Thought the Dead Man was taking care of them."

"Somebody got the Dead Man – one of *them*."

"Them" were the city's dark protectors, avengers in black who haunted the night and struck for justice when the law failed. The Nightmare was one of their number and had, in fact, stopped the Dead Man.

"Which one?"

"Does it matter? Anyway, Wolf is worried that if Green and Heywood go down, they'll turn yellow and put him in as ordering the hit."

"So why hasn't Wolf tried again?" asked the second mobster.

"Ain't like he hasn't tried. No one knew where the cops had the family holed up, until yesterday I hear."

"Somebody squeal?"

"Nah, some janitor at the precinct found a receipt from a boarding house in a trashcan. He's in the know and thought it'd be worth something. It was. Word is the Wolf's sending a team tonight, just in case."

The Nightmare wanted to rush out, find a phone and call his police contact for the Dorseys' current address. He knew better than to try. A sudden departure after hearing such news would give his game away. Instead he sat patiently and watched the door. When a particularly dangerous looking gunman came in, the disguised Nightmare uttered an oath, did his best to hide his features and furtively left the bar. Those who saw him leave thought only that he was hiding from the newcomer, a not uncommon occurrence.

A phone call later, the Nightmare was on his way to the Finley Apartments.

As he waited in the darkness, The Nightmare wondered who would arrive first, Wolf Hopkins's mobsmen or the Flying Squad Lieutenant Jerome Easton was supposed to send.

His answer came minutes later when two black touring cars pulled up in front of the building. As he expected, armed men got out, one with a Tommy, two more with shotguns and the others carrying revolvers.

Time to play, thought the man in black as he stepped outside to meet his foes.

The laugh froze the gunmen in place. With the Nightmare's challenge coming from nowhere and everywhere the eight men at first did not know which way to turn. It was only when the Nightmare fired from the doorway with twin .45's that they knew from which direction the attack was coming.

The man with the Tommy went down first, catching two in the chest. A bullet each for those with the shotguns. Then the Nightmare ducked back inside to avoid a hail of revolver slugs.

A moment of silence as the remaining five men wondered what to do. Rushing the door meant death. Remaining might mean the police. Fleeing would only earn them the wrath of the man who sent them, and Wolf Hopkins was not a forgiving boss.

Taking advantage of their hesitation, the Nightmare again emerged from the building. Another rain of death from his guns, three more fallen crooks. And again there was silence.

The Nightmare counted the fallen. *Six*, he thought, *"not a bad night's work. Maybe the other two ...* Whatever thought he had faded when it occurred to him that maybe the other two had been smarter than the six now lying dead or dying on the sidewalk.

The man in black rushed into the building to find that one of the two had entered through the back door. Fortunately there was only one set of stairs and the gunman was only halfway up the first flight when the Nightmare's bullet took him in the back.

That left one remaining foeman. *And if I were he ...* thought the Nightmare. Leaping over the body on the steps, he ran up to the third floor in a race against death.

He almost lost. On reaching the top floor the Nightmare heard a gunshot come from the rear apartment. Though winded from his climb, he managed to kick open the front door. Without thinking, without aiming, he loosed shot after shot at the dark figure standing at the fire escape window. A scream, a fall and the threat was ended.

When he heard the gunfire come from below, Walter Dorsey had been certain that the end had come. *Why did we have to drive? Why didn't we take the train into the city,* he thought, not for the first time. Rushing his family into the bathroom, he prepared to defend them as best he could. A butcher's knife from the kitchen was small protection against guns, but it was all he had.

He wasn't expecting the shot from the window. Somehow it merely grazed his arm. Before a second shot could be fired, the front door burst open and hell was unleashed on his attacker.

Dorsey looked at his savior. A tall man dressed all in the color of night, his face fully covered by a black mask. "Are you all right?" the man asked him.

"Uh, yeah," Dorsey looked at his arm, "just a scratch. I'm okay."

"And your family?"

A quick check in the bathroom found them frightened but unharmed.

"Thank you," said Muriel Dorsey, "Mr. ...?"

"I'm called the Nightmare, Ma'am." He looked at the knife Dorsey was still holding. "You're a brave man, sir."

Dorsey dropped the knife, collapsed on the sofa. "I can't be brave anymore. None of us can. Tell them, please, the cops and crooks, they'll listen to you. Tell them that it's over. We won't be testifying, none of us. We want to go home and we want to be safe."

"I'm afraid that won't help, Mr. Dorsey. As long as you and your family are alive, you're a threat to this mob, whether you testify or not."

"Then there's no hope. You saved us tonight, but what about the next time, or the time after that."

"There won't be a next time, Mr. Dorsey. I've thought about this and decided that tonight, I did not arrive in time to save you."

They're somewhere safe," was all the Nightmare told Lieutenant Easton when they next met. "But put the word out that they're dead. Meanwhile they'll be on a private island and can stay there until the trial. Anyone who finds them there is going to hear a whole lot of laughing before they die."

WOLF HUNT

The Nightmare Falls

Michael Shaw gave his life for the woman he loved. She was trapped in a hotel heavily guarded by armed men, with many more in a casino in the rear. There was only one chance to save her. Dressed in black and voicing a laugh that chilled the heart and promised death and vengeance, Michael Shaw, who was called the Nightmare, attacked the gambling den. This drew away the gunmen and allowed his companion to save his love.

The Nightmare did not expect to survive. He was but one man and his foes were many. Keeping to the shadows as best he could, he unleashed his powerful .45s and took down as many of his foes as he could.

When bullets struck him, he fought on. When his guns were empty, he picked up the dropped revolvers and pistols of the dead and continued the fight. But it was a hopeless struggle. As the final shots found him, as he passed into darkness, he prayed that his sacrifice had not been in vain, that his love, his Leda, his own woman in black was safe.

And then – the Nightmare died.

The Nightmare is Dead.

"The Nightmare is dead."

That was the news that reached mob boss Wolf Hopkins following what the press was calling "The Coast City Massacre."

"If it's true," Hopkins snarled to an underling, "it's the best news I've had all week. Hell, it's the only good news I've had all week. The Jersey mob seems to think it's my fault the Nightmare was in Coast City in the first place."

"It's true, boss," said one of his mob, Archie Travis, who quickly added, "about the Nightmare being dead and all. The kid who worked the desk at the hotel said that he saw a couple of dames carrying out his body. And ain't nobody heard from him since."

"Don't mean nothing," countered Bull Evans, another of Hopkins's mobsmen, "It ain't like there aren't a dozen other guys in black out there gunning for us and breaking up our mobs."

"Thank you for those words of encouragement, Bull," Hopkins snapped, then sighed as the large man grinned at the perceived compliment. *Sarcasm*, Hopkins thought, *is wasted on this bunch. But they're loyal and good in a fight.*

"Yes, there are others out there," the gang boss told his assembled lieutenants, "but so far none of them are concentrating on us. It was that damned Nightmare who thought we were involved in that protection scheme. It was the damned Nightmare who broke up our bank job. And it was the damned Nightmare who was protecting the witnesses who can send Jake Green and Charlie Heywood to the chair. Three times I ordered the hit, and three times … hell, he killed a dozen of my best men, he even killed the Dead Man."

"I thought we got the Dorseys."

Hopkins shook his head. "Yeah, so did I. Turns out that they were stashed on some island. And the trial's next week. Then it'll be a quick verdict and death sentence for Charlie and Jake."

Hopkins let that hang for a moment then added,

"Unless they talk. Then it's the hot seat for all of us except them."

"They won't talk, Boss," Travis said, "not after … well, they know what you'd do."

Indeed they did. Everyone in Hopkins's pack knew how he insured loyalty. Betray him and someone you loved died – your mother, your sister, your child, your dog. Sometimes just one, sometimes all. It might be a bullet to the head, it might be in a manner designed to make hardened men weep openly. It all depended on the nature and depth of the betrayal.

"Yes, they do, Archie. But I've never known either of them to be overly sentimental. And if came down to your lives or the lives of anyone else, the choice between you being strapped in a chair with the death current racing through your body, smelling your own flesh cooking just before waking up in Hell or it happening to someone else – anyone else – which would you choose?"

There was no answer. Everyone in the room knew what choice they'd make.

Hopkins broke the silence. "So who do we kill?"

"Hate to say it, we take out Jake and Charlie. With them dead, there's no case, and they can't rat us out."

Polecat Johnny spoke up for the first time, "Shaky Jake and Charlie been with us a long time, Archie," he countered. "I say we take another run at the Dorseys. If that fails …" He didn't have to finish.

"Any reason we can't do both?"

Hopkins smiled. "Bull, sometimes I like the way you think."

The Nightmare is dead.

That was the news that reached Homicide Lieutenant Jerome Easton from his contacts in the Coast City Police Department. After laying and successfully executing a trap for Hopkins's men in that Atlantic resort town, the Nightmare and an "unidentified pink-clad vigilante" somehow became involved in a gang war that left two buildings burning and dozens dead. Among those believed to have perished was the black-garbed crime fighter himself.

"His kind have been thought dead before," Easton told himself. The cop recalled other tales of the city's mysterious defenders where one or the other was proclaimed dead only to reappear and strike down their opponents.

"But what about The Whispering Monk?" a nagging voice inside the lieutenant's head asked. His death was confirmed. "And the Black Judge?" Easton shook his head at that question. The Judge's existence was no more than a rumor, his death even more so.

Rumor, that's all it was. Easton tried very hard to believe that. But good cop that he was, he felt the need to investigate.

There had been no sightings of the Nightmare since the Coast City Massacre. No word on the street. More importantly, no word from the man himself.

Jerome Easton was the Nightmare's police contact. All the champions of the night seemed to have one to varying degrees. Easton had his suspicions as to why the Nightmare choose him, and who the Nightmare really was.

It had been a ritual. A series of crimes would occur. By "chance" Easton would run into wealthy man about town Michael Shaw. They would discuss the crimes, Shaw with questions he had no business asking and Easton giving out information no cop should supply. Shortly after that, the Nightmare would appear and the crimes would end in a barrage of gunfire. Sometimes Shaw would initiate the meeting, sometimes Easton would seek Shaw out. Only rarely did the cop see the Nightmare himself.

There was no proof of the Nightmare's true identity, rather, Easton corrected himself, no *evidence* that Shaw was the Nightmare. Both men knew that the other knew and that was enough for them. Why ruin a good thing?

But now the good thing might be ruined. Easton looked for Shaw, hoping to find the Nightmare. He hunted the Nightmare, seeking Shaw. He found no trace of either. He did discover that Shaw and a "blonde companion" may have been in Coast City at the time of the massacre, but he'd already suspected that.

So, in desperation, the lieutenant went to Moran's.

Moran's was a bar on the city's Eastside, owned and operated by one Seamus Moran, a diminutive fellow who always seemed to have a twinkle in his eye and his mind back in the "old country." Shaw had once called the bartender a leprechaun and at times Easton thought he might be right.

More than once the detective had met and "discussed crime" with Shaw in a booth at Moran's. That was always during the day. At night, after hours, things were different. It was then, Easton believed, in the brief time before darkness gave way to day, that the Nightmare and his kind met to relax and compare experiences before going back to their lairs, dens, sanctums or wherever they hung their capes and cowls.

Easton had gone there in the daytime, asking for Shaw. All he got from the barkeep was an "I haven't seen him" and a drink on the house. He went at night, after Moran's was supposedly closed. Before he could knock on the door, the shadows spoke to him.

"He is not inside, Lieutenant."

It wasn't the Nightmare. This voice was deeper, more somber, more eerie. Any questions Easton might have had were suppressed by,

"Seek him no more."

Easton did not feel inclined to argue, or to remain any longer than he must.

That had been two weeks ago, a week after the Coast City Massacre. Three weeks and no word. Sitting in his office, Jerome Easton slowly and reluctantly came to accept the fact that the Nightmare was indeed dead.

Sadness filled him, the same sort of sadness he'd feel for a fallen cop. Michael Shaw had fought and given his life to the good fight. But there would be no hero's funeral, no twenty-one gun salute, no piper playing "Amazing Grace" by his graveside.

After resolving to go to Moran's one last time and lift a glass in memory to he who was the Nightmare, Easton happened to glance down at the morning paper. An article caught his eye and changed everything.

The Nightmare is dead.

That's what Michael Shaw told himself. He had died on the floor of a Coast City casino. Everything afterwards – the rescue, the healing, the confrontation with a self-proclaimed god, the recuperation at a very private resort – all that had happened to Michael Shaw.

The game was over, for him at least. There were others who would gladly play the never ending game of cops and robbers. Let them, the cost for him was too great.

Physically Shaw was in great shape, the best he had ever been in. Mentally though, he was tired. He thought of what hung behind the hidden panel in his bedroom closet – the black suit, the mask, the gloves, the guns – and resolved never to wear them again. He thought that maybe he'd take them to his upstate cabin and bury them next to the remains of the Dead Man. Give the Nightmare a proper funeral. Or maybe he'd pack them up and mail them to Lieutenant Easton.

For the first time in three weeks a genuine smile came to the lips of Michael Shaw as he thought about what the detective might do with the regalia of the Nightmare. Keep them as a souvenir? Submit them as evidence? Maybe he'd don the mask and gloves, wield the .45s and go join Gordon in Chicago. Call himself Dark Justice or the Black Badge.

The thought almost made Shaw laugh. Almost. It will be a long time before I laugh again, he realized. Too many memories.

Shaw got up from his easy chair. Whatever he had planned to do was put on hold when Taft, his house manager, came in.

"Excuse me, Mr. Shaw. There's a Lieutenant Easton to see you."

"Thank you, show him in please." Thinking about the article in the morning paper, one that announced that he was back from a long, restful vacation and was now receiving visitors, Shaw wondered what had taken the good lieutenant so long.

"I thought you were dead," was Easton's abrupt greeting when he was shown into Shaw's library.

Gesturing the detective to a chair, Shaw replied with, "Apparently not, Lieutenant, although I must confess there have been times I've felt that way."

"So have you been keeping busy, Mr. Shaw?"

"Hardly, Lieutenant. You know us idle rich – so little to do, so much time to do it. That's why I took a nice long vacation, so I could do nothing with different people."

"Were you doing nothing in Coast City about three weeks ago?"

"I wouldn't call it nothing, Lieutenant." Shaw gave Easton a "we are both men of the world" look. "I was after all in a hotel with an attractive lady. Fortunately it was nowhere near where all that fighting occurred. Terrible business. I understand quite a few people died."

Easton nodded his head, glad to be playing the game again, even if it might be for the last time.

"Maybe one less than believed. Rumor has it that the Nightmare died in that 'terrible business.' What do you think?"

Taking time to answer, Shaw finally said, "I don't normally listen to rumors, but I believe that this one might be true."

"You … think?"

"Let's say I'm reasonably sure."

"You don't think there's a chance of a … resurrection?"

Looking directly into the detective's eyes, Shaw asked, "Lieutenant, may I be frank?"

"It would be a change," Easton replied, wondering if he was about to hear a confession, and if so, what he was going to do about it.

"Imagine yourself, or me, if you'd prefer, as one of this city's vigilantes. They, we risk our freedom and our lives and for what? Destroy one gang, another forms. Bring doom to a would-be conqueror and another takes his place. What's the point? Maddened scientists. Walking dead men. Creatures from beyond. They have to be stopped, each and every time."

"I'm a cop, Mr. Shaw, you don't have to tell me. I've been around longer than you … well, longer than certain parties have been giving us unofficial, unsanctioned but sometimes very welcome help."

"I appreciate that, Lieutenant, I do. And let no man say that this city's finest could not do the job on their own. And they will have to it without the Nightmare. He's tired, I think, and maybe has lost too much. Maybe he's looked five, ten years into the future and doesn't want to be alone in a darkened room, without friends or family, leading other men's lives. Doesn't want to be so afraid of exposure so as to deny himself the comforts of wife and family? Maybe he just doesn't see the good of it anymore."

"And maybe," suggested Easton, "he's tired of the killing."

"It could very well be, Lieutenant, it could very well be."

Suddenly and without asking permission, the detective stood and walked over to the sideboard. Pouring them both a drink, he handed one to Shaw. Lifting his own he said,

"To the Nightmare, may he rest, no, may he live in peace."

"Amen to that, Lieutenant, amen to that."

Plans are Made

In life, Owen Davies was nothing special. A low ranking thug who never graduated past stick ups and muscle jobs. One day he made the mistake of robbing a speak that was under the protection of Wolf Hopkins. It was his last mistake.

Under normal circumstances, the death of Owen Davies would have passed unnoticed, his murder making the papers only on a slow news day, and even then it would have been pushed to the back and used merely to balance a column. Except that when Davies saw his fate approaching in the forms of Jake Green and Charlie Heywood, he turned yellow. Instead of being a man and taking his bullet, he ran, ran into the street, ran past a car driven by Walter Dorsey, a tourist lost in the big city.

The shooting of Owen Davies took place in front of Walter Dorsey, his wife Muriel and their two sons. Being from out of town and unaware of the rules, Dorsey did the decent thing – he drove until he found a police station and reported the murder. Once he described the shooters and later identified them, he and his family were in dire peril, their lives at risk, their freedom curtailed so as to keep them safe.

And so the evidence of an out-of-towner who had done what he believed was his civic duty (and regretted it ever after) elevated the death of a nothing like Owen Davies into a major case. Dorsey's testimony could convict Green and Heywood. Their conviction could lead to them spilling all they knew about Wolf Hopkins. In turn, this could lead to the dismantling of one of the city's up and coming gangs.

If the Dorseys lived long enough to testify.

The start date of the trial was not advertised. Only those who had to know were informed. That of course meant that by the day in question everyone knew. Realizing this, the police took every precaution in conveying the Dorseys to the courthouse.

"This is what we're going to do," advised the captain of the Tactical Squad in charge of the Dorseys' security. "Court starts at 0930. At 0830 the Dorseys are scheduled to land at the South St. Docks. The subjects will immediately be placed in a Brinks Armored Truck for transportation to the courthouse. The truck will arrive at the courthouse at 0915 pulling as close to the front as possible. When the subjects emerge they will be surrounded by a squad of police wearing armor. The subjects will also be wearing armor and will be taken immediately to the courtroom. Everyone understand?"

As all the heads in the room collectively nodded, the commander looked at Jerome Easton. "Any questions, Lieutenant?"

Easton had only one, one that he could not, dared not ask. Looking around the room, he wondered how many of the officers present were on the payroll of Wolf Hopkins.

The detective had cause to worry.

Ninety minutes later Wolf Hopkins held his own planning meeting.

"The docks are too iffy. The cops will be too alert."

"What about taking out the truck, Boss?"

"We might be able to do that, Archie, but there's no guarantee that we'd kill those inside. Here," Hopkins pointed to a well drawn map of the courthouse and the streets surrounding it, "this is the best place. Just as they're climbing the front steps. They'll still be on guard, but their journey will be almost over, and so they will be just a little relaxed. It's the best time to strike."

"How we gonna get through all those cops?"

"There are ways, Bull, there are ways."

Wolf Hopkins was not a stupid man. He tried not to make the mistake of underestimating the intelligence of an opponent. His briefing over, he reviewed his plans several times, trying to find a flaw. He couldn't. Then, setting his plans aside, he studied the map of the courthouse and asked himself,

"How would I do it?"

The Best Laid Schemes

The trial date arrived. As planned, an armored car picked up its passengers from the ferry dock. Escorted by motor officers, the truck made its way up closed streets to the courthouse. Once it arrived, twenty uniformed men covered the back door before it opened.

Then Hell was let loose.

From the west came a ten ton truck with a large steel wedge as a bumper. It forced its way past the blockading patrol cars. As the police guard took up defensive positions another truck came from the east.

"Scatter!" came the order from the Tactical captain just as death rained from portals cut into the sides of both trucks.

Within seconds the air was filled with leaded hail as shots were exchanged by both sides. Officers struck in their legs and heads fell to the mobs' Tommys. Shots fired by cops who stood their ground and refused to flee riddled the cabs and sides of the trucks, one bullet piercing the window of the east bound truck and mortally wounding the driver. Unmanned, the heavy truck rode up the sidewalk crashing into a wall. Their transport now immobile, crooks came rushing out of the back. They knew that today there could be no surrender, no mercy, not with fallen cops pouring their life's blood out on the street. With weapons blazing they sought to sell their lives dearly and were cut down to a man.

What seemed like hours was over in minutes. Only as the survivors were tending the wounded and cuffing the guilty did they remember their original purpose – the safe transport of the Dorseys to court.

"Where are they?"

"Are they all right?"

"What about the kids?"

"Did they get inside?"

A search was made for the witnesses but the Dorseys were not to be found.

"Where the hell did they go?" a sergeant asked. "Did the other truck get them?"

"Maybe they're still inside the Brinks truck?" an officer suggested.

"Maybe."

The sergeant opened the door to check. As he did, a hissing noise pierced the air, one recognized by those who had been in the Great War.

"Down!" the sergeant shouted even as he tried to close the heavy armored doors to protect whoever was in the truck. It was the last thing he said.

Across the street, in the upper floor of a mostly vacant office building, another veteran of the war pulled the trigger of a rocket-powered recoilless weapon, sending a shaped charge into the back of the Brinks truck. Armored against bullets, the back of the truck was no match for the explosive missile. The sergeant, the truck and anyone who may have been it were blown into tiny pieces.

Standing at an upper window in the courthouse, Lieutenant Jerome Easton had witnessed the massacre. He had known it was going to be bad. Gunfire, even death had been expected. But not on this scale. He wanted to lean out, count the wounded, see how many of his fallen comrades were moving or lay still. He turned away from the window. He had a job to do and it was time to do it. As he took the elevator down to the holding cells he grimly wondered if it was all worth it.

The night before the Dorseys' supposed arrival at the docks an old touring car drove into the city from the north. Its driver was Lieutenant Easton's most trusted man. Its cargo was the most important to him. It consisted of four people – mother, father and two sons – the Dorseys. Maybe one of the officers on the protection detail had been corrupted by Hopkins's money or promises, maybe not. Easton could not take the chance. The South St. pickup, the escorted convoy, the arrival at the courthouse – it was all a charade, one that Easton knew would likely result in gunfire and death. It was a risk and a sacrifice he felt he had to make.

The Dorseys arrived at a hotel in the quiet of the night and were quickly ushered out the back door and into a waiting patrol wagon. From there they were taken to the holding cells of the city courthouse.

The cell block had been cleared out for the night, the prisoners taken to the nearest precinct station. Each of the boys had their own cell with Muriel and Walter sharing one. With no one else present, Easton left the barred doors opened.

"Sorry about the accommodations," Easton apologized. "But it's only for one night and then it will all be over."

"You're sure about that, Lieutenant?" Muriel Dorsey asked.

"Yes, Ma'am. Once your husband testifies the damage to the gang will be done. His word will forever be on record. There'd be no point, no profit in Hopkins going after you. And Hopkins isn't the kind of man to do things that don't profit him."

A glance from Walter Dorsey reminded Easton that this was not quite true, that Hopkins was capable of striking at the Dorseys even after the trial, if not out of revenge then as a warning to other potential witnesses. Both men knew this, neither wanted to worry Mrs. Dorsey about it. Arrangements had been made for their protection after the trial, but no plan is perfect.

Giving what assurances he could, the lieutenant left the family to spend their night in jail.

At 8:45, just a quarter of an hour before the shootout in front of the court building, a uniformed officer went down to the cellblock.

"I'm here to bring the Dorseys up to the courtroom."

"Are you nuts?" asked the lone guard to the cell block, "They're coming from the docks ... Oh, is that who I'm guarding? Easton said no one was to come in here."

"And now he says that I'm to take them up to the courtroom."

The guard shook his head. "The lieutenant said not to open this door unless he was here. I'm gonna wait for him."

"Too bad."

Before the guard could react, the man in the police uniform drew a long bladed knife from behind his back and used it to lethal effect. The guard fell silently as the man, a killer hired for this one job, entered the mostly empty cell block.

He wasted no time. Drawing a silenced pistol he shot down Walter Dorsey in front of his wife and children. The boys screamed, the wife cried. Inside the thick walls of the cell block, no one could hear. He gave them their moment of grief then,

"If you don't want your boys dead, tell them to shut up."

Leaving her husband's body on the cold floor of the cell, Muriel ran to her sons and quieted them.

"If you want your sons to live, you will testify in your husband's place. You will swear before God and the people of this city that the two men on trial are not the ones who shot Owen Davies."

Tears filling her eyes, Muriel Dorsey nodded her head in agreement.

"Good, and to ensure that you do so, your sons will leave with me."

Muriel's scream of refusal was quickly cut short.

"Do so, or," the killer pointed his gun at the oldest boy, "your youngest son will be the sole survivor of his family."

It was all Muriel could do to say, "Go with him, boys."

The two clung to their mother. She pushed them away and into the care of the man who killed their father. Handcuffed together, the boys were led them out of the courthouse through a route previously prepared by money and threats.

So it was that after watching his fellow officers fall in defense of an empty truck, Jerome Easton went down to the holding cells of the courthouse to find Muriel Dorsey cradling the body of her dead husband and already mourning her lost sons.

No trial was held that day. Over the objections of the defense, it was postponed for forty-eight hours, after which the prosecution would have to present their witness or the case would be dismissed. The mood in the District Attorney's Office and Police Headquarters was black. Five officers and a witness had been murdered. Two boys had been kidnapped and were still missing. Two killers were about to be set free thus allowing their boss to escape justice.

Crime had triumphed, and there was nothing anyone could do about it.

For the fourth time that day, Jerome Easton checked the security of Muriel Dorsey's hotel suite. Two cops at the door, a police woman inside, men in the lobby and outside the hotel.

"This is what I should have done," Easton told himself for the fifth time that day. "No, I had to get clever. Well, I was clever enough to get six people killed. I was clever enough to cause two kids to go missing. Damn me."

Easton knew his future – someone had to pay for the debacle and it was going to be him. He'd be disgraced in the papers, broken in rank, assigned to the worst beat in the worst part of the city. He didn't care. Whatever happened to him he deserved it. It would be a small payment on the enormous debt he owed. He'd stick it out as long as he could and if the guilt didn't go away, if he didn't stop seeing the faces of the fallen officers and the Dorseys in his dreams, then one day he'd turn in his badge, walk down to the South St. docks and keep walking. Maybe after the water filled his lungs and before his final judgment he'd have the chance to tell the brave men he'd gotten killed how sorry he was.

But that was for later. Lieutenant Jerome Easton still had one job to do, and that was to see to the safety of the woman inside the Hotel Lafayette. To see her safely to the stand then safely home again.

Easton didn't bother asking Muriel Dorsey how she would testify. He knew. In her place he would do the same. In less than two days she would take the stand and in a desperate attempt to save her sons, lie and set two killers free. Maybe her perjury would buy her sons' freedom, maybe not. It was more likely that she would never see her boys again, that they would be killed right after the trial, their bodies dumped some place where they'd likely be found, leaving a grieving wife and mother as a warning to all those who would go against the city's mobs.

And there's not a damn thing I can do about it, Easton thought.

Then two men passed him in the lobby, two men whose only

connection to the case was that they happened to be staying in the same hotel. One told the other a joke and both laughed.

This caused Easton to think of a different kind of laughter – darker, more sinister. This brought thoughts of a man in black with blazing .45s, a man with a passion for justice and a disregard for the law. A man whose death Easton had toasted.

"What the hell," he said aloud to no one in particular. "It's worth a try."

A Plea For Help

Michael Shaw sat thinking of the afternoon papers and trying his best to ignore what he had just read. Sports, the financial pages, the national news – none of those mattered. It was the massacre at the courthouse, the murder of Walter Dorsey and the abduction of two children that he had trouble chasing from his mind. That Jerome Easton was featured prominently on every front page didn't help. He seemed destined to be the scapegoat of the whole affair.

Maybe he should be, Shaw thought. It was his plan, his mistakes that had gotten those people killed. But in his heart Shaw could not blame his friend. The lieutenant had done the best that he could. Was it his fault that Hopkins had out thought him?

"Maybe it was your fault," said the part of Shaw that still remembered the nights, the forays against crime, the masks and mayhem. "If you had been there, if you had not given up, you could have found a way into the cells without being seen. You could have been hiding in the darkness to strike down the gunman. But you're not in the game anymore. No more dressing up and playing with guns. The Nightmare is dead, remember?"

"The Nightmare is dead," Shaw assured himself with some resolution. He'd find others ways of helping the police, of helping them to do their job without actually doing it for them.

Nodding to himself, Shaw looked at the empty glass on the table next to his chair and wondered if he wanted another drink. Before he could decide …

"Lieutenant Easton to see you, Sir."

Shaw stood and raised his hand to greet the detective.

"Good evening, Lieutenant, let me just say how sorry I was to read …"

"Save your sympathy, Mr. Shaw. Whatever happens to me I deserve and it won't do the Dorseys or the families of the dead cops a damned bit of good."

"I see. In that case, have a seat and tell me why you've come."

Easton almost snapped that he preferred to stand. But he'd come to ask, no, to beg this man to do his job for him. And so he sat.

"Mr. Shaw, the last time I was here we talked about the Nightmare. You asked, or rather, you imagined him asking if there was a point to what he had been doing. What good it would do."

"I remember, Lieutenant. It was right before we toasted the Nightmare's death."

"As I recall, we toasted his life."

Easton bent down and picked up one of the papers scattered about Shaw's feet. Finding the front page, he folded it so as to show only a picture of two missing boys. He held it up for Shaw to see.

"You asked what the point is. These boys are the point. They're missing and they have less than two days to live."

A familiar surge of excitement started to run through Shaw. He did his best to suppress it. "Surely the police are looking for them?"

"We are, but as you know, the police are limited by law to where they can search and how. Others may not be so limited."

"Lieutenant, I don't think …"

Standing, Easton threw the folder paper into Shaw's lap. The millionaire looked down at the faces of the missing boys.

"Less than two days, Mr. Shaw. If they're not found by then, the responsibility for their deaths is on me … and on anyone else who could have helped but just didn't see what good it would do. Now if you'll excuse me, I may only have a few days left of my career but I'm going to spend them doing my job, protecting a widow and trying to find her sons. I'll leave you to …" He looked pointedly at the half empty bottle on the table next to Shaw. "… do whatever the idle rich do for fun these days. Goodbye, Mr. Shaw."

After the detective left, Shaw just sat and thought. He waved away the servant who asked him about dinner. He ignored the bottle on the table. Occasionally he would glance down at the paper still in his lap. He sat there until late afternoon gave way to evening. When he once again glanced down at the paper and found that it had grown too dark to see it, he nodded and stood.

"Damn it," he whispered to the shadows gathering around him.

Moments later Michael Shaw was in his bedroom. An antique wardrobe was pulled from the wall, a false panel in the back removed.

From a hidden compartment he drew a suit of all black, then a mask, gloves and, finally, a brace of matched .45s.

Slowly, deliberately, Michael Shaw dressed for work. Looking at his image in a full-length mirror, he let out a sigh of regret.

"Time to play."

The Nightmare had returned.

The Nightmare Lives

Two young boys missing, less than two days to find them. There was, the Nightmare knew, no time for subtlety. No lurking in the darkness hoping to hear a stray word, an unguarded conversation. No time to trail a suspect in the case, hoping that the one he picked would lead to where the boys were being kept. This was not a time for following clues. This was a time for bold moves and quick action. It was a time for violence and terror.

It was the time for the Nightmare to announce his rebirth.

Dago Mike's was just one speak in the city. It was not a place for the average couple out to spend an evening getting cheap thrills, drinking watered booze and wondering who among them was a gangster. Mike's place was for hard drinking men on the wrong side of the law, men who didn't have to wonder if any of them were gangsters because, in some way or the other, they all were. They came to the Dago's to talk and to drink, to see who in their number was on the lam, who had been locked up and who had taken their final ride. It was not a place for the average couple or for cops or informers.

An hour after the Nightmare was reborn a dark shape lurked in the back of Dago Mike's. It did not try the back door. It knew from past visits that that portal was locked, barred and alarmed. It lingered in the yard just a moment, then climbed a pole, trusting to its own quickness and in the knowledge that people seldom looked upwards.

A few minutes after the shadowy figure left the back yard a ragged looking man passed through the front door. His face was dirty, his hair looked unwashed and his clothes had the look and smell of the charity bin. The bartender was about to order a bum's rush when the derelict slapped enough coin on the bar to pay for several drinks.

Nodding, the bartender handed the rummy a glass and a half a bottle. "Over there," he said, indicating a vacant corner. "Drink up and get out. And don't bother the others."

Muttering what might have been "thanks," the shabby looking man stumbled to his place, sat down and began to enjoy his cheap booze.

At least he pretended to.

"You'd think they'd learn by now," the disguised Nightmare said to himself and prepared himself for what was to happen.

Outside, there was a small bang at the top of a utility pole as a low level explosive separated an electric cable from the city's power grid. Inside, the speak went black as the lights suddenly went off.

Then came the laughter.

Every hood in the place knew it for what it was, a laugh that signaled pain and death for their kind. It meant that one of the dark ones, one of the hunters of the night, was in their midst.

One man started for the exit. A shot aimed at his footsteps stuck the door just inches away from him and stopped him in his tracks. Two others who remembered the rummy who had just entered fired their own shots in his direction but their lead slugs hit only the plaster of the wall. The bartender wisely ducked under the bar, silently swearing at Mike for not taking his advice and putting a man at the door to check would-be patrons.

The laughter came again, echoing around the room so that no one could get a fix on it. The voice followed.

"Two boys are missing, the boys from court. Where are they?"

The room stayed quiet. No one moved, no one spoke. Each man listened for soft tread of footsteps, the rustle of a coat or cape. No one heard anything until,

"Scared to speak, cowards?" The voice came from nowhere, from everywhere, bouncing around the room as if coming from several men at once. "Know this – one name, one place, one hint of where the boys are will spare you all."

A shot rang out in the dark, shattering the mirror behind the bar.

"The next one strikes flesh, maybe yours."

Each man felt that the voice was speaking to him. Many were tempted to speak up, to say what they knew, what they heard, what was rumored. Several would have but for …

"Afraid of the Wolf? Don't be. His days are numbered. He will soon be caged or killed. But if those boys die …" Two shots, two cries of anguish as bullets fired low stuck legs on either side of the room. "… so will many of you."

"Tomas," screamed a frightened voice in the darkness.

"Hannibal," yelled someone else.

"Keep quiet" and "shhhh" and "shut the hell up" were heard and quickly quashed by,

"Silence, they are saving your miserable lives. Who is this Thomas Hannibal?"

"Hannibal Tomas," came a correcting whisper. "Hired gun out of Harbor City. In town yesterday. No one knows why?"

And another. "Word is one of Hop… someone met him at the train."

Others might have spoken. More information might have been obtained. But just then the bartender reached out from his place on the floor behind the bar and found an electric torch. Quickly standing he swept it across the room until its beam found the Nightmare.

The situation changed. Cowering rats found their courage. Guns and knives were brought out as the roomful of crooks advanced on the masked crime fighter.

The Nightmare's first bullets took out both the torch and the man who wielded it. Covered again by darkness, he then loosed a fusillade of death into the front row of hoods. Then he ducked down and faded away just as revolvers and pistols, along with a thrown knife or two, answered his shots.

"Did we get him?" asked one hopeful gangster once the shooting had stopped.

"Who the hell knows?" replied another. "It's too damned dark to see."

The answer came from near the front. With the door open and his form blocking most of the light from outside, the Nightmare called out,

"Tell Hopkins that the Nightmare lives."

He was lost to the night before the first bullets struck the door.

A name, that was all the Nightmare had, the name of a single man in a city of millions. The name of a man who might be involved with Hopkins, who might have stolen the boys and killed their father, who right now might be awaiting word to kill them. A man who might this instant be on a train back to Harbor City.

But it was more than the Nightmare had before going into Dago Mike's. A name and a connection to Wolf Hopkins. And Hopkins soon would know of the Nightmare's reappearance and learn that Tomas had been exposed.

So why not let everyone know?

A promise on a train

"Telephone call for Lieutenant Easton! Telephone for Jerome Easton!"

Having finished yet another inspection of the outside security, the detective entered the lobby to hear the hotel page calling his name.

"I'm Easton."

"Outside call for you, sir. You can take it at the desk."

"Hello, Easton here."

"You'll want to put out a citywide alert for Hannibal Tomas," came a whispered voice Easton had doubted he'd ever hear again.

"Who's this Tomas? Is he involved with …"

"A hood from Harbor City," interrupted the voice. "Make his name public. Find him for me, Lieutenant."

"To Hell with that. If he's in the city we'll pick him up .We'll use the dragnet if we have to."

Laughter. Laughter that could strike fear into an evil heart but this time only brightened Easton's heart.

"You might pick him up, but what then? Can you make him talk in time? Are you willing to do what is needed to force him to tell what he knows? If so, then you have no need for me. Otherwise …

"Drive him to me."

Easton made a call. Within a quarter hour late-night newsies were pedaling headlines screaming Tomas's name. Radio programs were interrupted asking one and all to be on the lookout and to call in with any information. Police bands broadcast bolos and wires were sent south asking the Harbor City PD for any information on the man.

All this, the Nightmare hoped, would leave Hopkins with only one option. And it was reliance on this hope that had the dark clad avenger lurking in the shadows of Pennsylvania Station.

There were many entrances to the vast train depot but there was only one track from which the early morning train to Harbor City departed. From the darkness beneath a stairwell the Nightmare watched this track.

He watched as the eastbound train pulled in. He watched as two men who had been lingering at a newsstand rushed over to it. He watched as one of them got on. Then, just before the train pulled away, The Nightmare jumped aboard and watched Polecat Johnny leave the station.

With his mask in his pocket and his coat over his arm, no one looked twice at Shaw as he walked though the train looking for the man he hoped was Tomas. Finally, in the second car nearest the front, he found him.

Tomas was sitting alone, reading a magazine he had picked up at the newsstand.

Finding a seat midway up the aisle, Shaw waited. Ten minutes later, the train entered a tunnel.

In the brief blackout, Tomas felt someone sit next to him. "Hey buddy, why don't you …"

As the train emerged into the early morning light Tomas saw the mask, felt a prod in his ribs.

"Yes," came an icy whisper, "that is a gun in your side. And yes, I will shoot you as many times as I have to. You're Tomas?"

It was less a question than a statement, and the coldness with which it was uttered him told the Harbor City crook that lying would be useless – and fatal.

"Yeah, what of it? You from Hopkins?"

Tomas's hand crept toward the inside of his jacket. The gun pressed into his side and he dropped his hand into his lap.

"Where are the boys you took from the courthouse?"

Tomas's answer quickly, without thought. "What boys?"

"The first shot won't kill you. Neither will the second. None of them will, not right away. You'll be hours dying, days maybe. Days of agony, Tomas. Where are the boys?"

"I tell you and what? A quick death instead of a slow one? Why don't I just take my chances that you won't shoot me while we're on a train and there are people around?"

Quiet laughter told Tomas what those chances were. Then,

"Try it. I'll be off the train before anyone knows you were shot. And you'll still be hours dying. But if you want to live …"

"Living is good. I'm listening, mystery man."

"Give me the boys. Tell me where you left them and you will live to see Harbor City once again."

"What if I lie to you?"

Another laugh answered the folly of that question.

"Okay, what the hell?" Tomas mentioned a street name, described a building, gave the Nightmare the layout.

"There were three guys there when I left. That Johnny guy might be going back."

"Why were you still there?"

Tomas shrugged. "I got hired for the full job. If the dame talked, well, some of Hopkins's boys are squeamish, about kids you know. I don't care who I pull the trigger on. Still gonna let me go?"

The gunman asked this half mockingly, half in fear.

"I gave my word. If what you said is true, you are safe from me, unless our paths cross again."

Before Tomas could reply to that, the train entered another tunnel. The gun eased from his side. When he could see again the Nightmare was gone.

Michael Shaw got off at the next stop and immediately caught the next train back to the city. He had done what he had to do, what the police could not have done. He had not liked doing it but to save those boys he would have let a dozen murderers go free. No, not free exactly. All he had promised Tomas was that he would reach Harbor City alive.

Quiet Work

A single corner home in a quiet residential neighborhood. No outside guards that Shaw could see. He had not expected any. They might have drawn too much attraction. He did not discount the possibility that there might be watchers in other houses on the block.

As Michael Shaw the Nightmare had slowly walked past the building, his route taking him along the side and then the front, all the while looking for possible entry points.

It would be difficult. He would have to enter without being seen then go room to room without attracting attention or gunfire. The latter would bring reinforcements and might lead to the deaths of the children. Then, once he found them, the Nightmare would have to get himself and the boys out safely.

It was, the Nightmare decided, a night for quiet work.

Mostly quiet that is.

His reconnaissance over, Michael Shaw turned when he got to the end of the block. After he donned his mask and gloves, it was the Nightmare who crept past the rear of the houses.

There were streetlights in the back, ones that cast cones of brightness that offered the illusion of safety.

It was the spaces between the cones of light that offered the Nightmare safety. Weaving through them he easily made his way down the block and into the back yard of the corner house.

The rear door was well made with a good lock. The vigilante, however, paid it scant attention. Instead, he descended an outside stairway to the basement door.

Peering through a dirty window, the Nightmare saw nothing but blackness. Five strips of strong tape, a quick tap with a gun and the glass silently shattered. After carefully picking it out he reached though and unlocked the door. The hinges squeaked slightly when he opened it.

Pausing in the darkness, the Nightmare listened for any noise that might be someone coming down to investigate. Hearing nothing, he chanced his torch, memorizing the layout of the basement after a quick scan.

The electric box was on a side wall. Going over to it, he unscrewed a random fuse. Above him he heard,

"What the hell? Eddie, go down and check the fuses."

"Why the crap do I have to go?"

"Because I told ya. Now get down those stairs before I throw ya down."

"Okay, Frankie, I'm going. Jeez."

The basement light came on. The Nightmare hid in a corner. As Eddie passed him, the avenger drew a long bladed knife.

Quiet work. Quiet and bloody.

As Eddie's body spurted out its life's blood, the Nightmare screwed the fuse back in.

"That's got it, Eddie."

How many upstairs, the Nightmare wondered. Tomas had said three, maybe four. With Eddie lying dead at his feet that meant there were three left.

At least three, he reminded himself, *with possible outside reinforcements.*

Memories of Coast City came unbidden. Alone in the casino with a roomful of gunman between him and the exit with more on the way. He had fought as best he could but had still fallen.

That could not, would not happen tonight. Then, the Nightmare knew that his death was the probable result and the price of his lover's life. Tonight, however, he could not fall. To do so would cost two young boys their lives.

Slowly, carefully, the Nightmare ascended the stairs. Throwing knife in hand, he came up into the kitchen.

The three were in the kitchen, cards and coins on the table.

"About time," Frankie complained, "what were you doing down there, playing with ..." Looking up, saw the dark shape in the doorway. "What the ..."

A thrown knife took him in the throat. Then the Nightmare went after the other two. Not daring to fire the gun in his left hand, he beat one foeman down with it. The other he stabbed with his long knife just as that crook was pulling a revolver.

One dead in the basement, three in the kitchen. Would they have left the boys alone? Was there a fourth? Were the boys even in the house?

The answer came with a pop as a slug buried itself in the wall near his head. So much for quiet work, the Nightmare thought as he brought up his left arm and fired at the two men who had come down from the second floor. He was up the stairs before they dropped.

Three rooms. Which room would the boys be in? The door of the left rear bedroom was partly open. He tried that first.

He found the boys in bed, huddled against a corner of the wall. The younger one was crying. The older had put himself between his brother and whoever might be coming through the door.

The oldest would have screamed, but the Nightmare's whispered command of "Quiet!" silenced him.

Mindful of his frightening appearance, the vigilante was about to assure the boys that they were being rescued. But then he heard the sound of a door being broken open followed by the shouts of angry men.

"Quickly" he told the boys. "Under the bed. No noise."

Without waiting to see if he was being obeyed, he switched off the hallway light.

Peering down from the darkness of the second floor, the Nightmare watched as two men came through the front door. He heard at least two more swearing at what he had done to their fellow mobsmen. Standing at the top of the stairs, he waited for them to figure things out.

"Find anything in the basement?'

"Yeah, back door broke open and a dead Eddie."

"That leaves the second floor."

"Think he's with the kids."

"Yeah, but he ain't gonna leave with them. Let's go."

The Nightmare waited until a hood was on the bottom step.

Time to laugh.

With the laughter came gunfire raining down on the two men just below him. As they fell the Nightmare descended the stairs. Turning and looking down into the living, he fired from above. The third man fell even as the fourth turned yellow and fled though the basement.

He'll call for help, the Nightmare thought. Maybe I should do the same. But first...

The boys were still under the bed.

"It's safe," he told them and waited until they found the courage to come to him, the oldest first, still the protector, then came his brother.

"Who are you?" asked the youngest.

"A friend," the Nightmare said simply.

"Are you the guy on the radio?"

This caused the man in black to utter an honest laugh and not one designed to terrify the wicked. He'd have to tell Kent.

To the boys he said, "No, but sometimes I work with him. Now what are your names?"

The youngest was Kevin who was five. Wallace Jr., "Wally," was older by two years.

"You boys ready to go back to your mother?"

They nodded, then Kevin asked, "My daddy's dead, isn't he?"

"Yes," the Nightmare answered solemnly.

"Will you kill the men who did it?"

The Nightmare thought back to a promise made on a train. "As many as I can," he promised the boy.

Jerome Easton sat in the lobby of the Hotel Lafayette and watched the clock tick over from one day to the next. The trial was less than eight hours away. No word on Hannibal Tomas. Nothing from the dragnet or the flying squads. And no news from the Nightmare since the phone call about Tomas.

It was all about to end, the detective thought – *the trial, his career, the boys' lives*. He was about to say to Hell with it all, find a room and catch up on some sleep when,

"Another outside call for you, Sir."

The voice on the line whispered one word, "Outside." The lieutenant ran out the door onto the sidewalk. Minutes later two boys exited a dark sedan. As the car pulled away quickly Easton was sure he heard the sound of triumphant laughter.

"This Damned City"

"You found them!" Muriel Dorsey shouted as her sons ran into her arms. Before Easton could explain otherwise Wally said, "A man in black saved us, Mommy."

Muriel knew about whom her son was talking. She had met "the man in black" when he had last battled to save her family. That time her husband had only been wounded.

The look Mrs. Dorsey gave the cop said more than words. It told him that her low opinion of him and the police had reached greater depths. With some control she told her sons, "Get washed and into bed. Then you can tell me all about the man in black."

She turned on Easton as soon as the boys were out of the room.

"Maybe he should have been guarding us." There was acid in her voice. Worry over her sons had not given her time to mourn her husband and now she lashed out with bitter anger.

"He's one man. And he's done more for us than your whole department. And even then ... why doesn't he, why don't you just kill them all? You know they're guilty, so does he. So why let them live? What good will this trial do? To prove that two gangsters killed another gangster? And only so you can try a bigger gangster? What's the point?"

Easton remembered that not so long ago the Nightmare, Michael Shaw rather, had asked that same question. The detective had answered with newspaper pictures of the two boys now noisily taking their baths. Now that they were safe, he didn't have an answer for this grieving woman.

Still, he tried. "If we all did ... what you suggested ... took our own personal vengeance ... where would we be?"

Muriel Dorsey looked at him as if he were a fool that understood nothing. "I'd have a husband, my sons would have a father and we'd be far away from this damned city."

And with that she broke down in tears and would not be consoled. Feeling every bit a coward, Easton left her in the care of a police woman and fled the suite.

One Move Ahead

Driving away from the Hotel Lafayette, the Nightmare stripped off his mask and became Michael Shaw again. *It was good,* he thought, *to be "alive" again.* He had, he now realized, missed it – the gunplay, the thrill of battle, the knowledge that thanks to him there were a few less predators in this world. Maybe one day he and his kind would not be needed and if that day came he hoped that he would have the good sense to retire. But until then he'd continue to play the game and do what little good he could manage.

"You did little good for the Dorseys," said that nagging voice inside his head he'd come to hate.

"I saved them twice," he countered, thinking that arguing with oneself was not a sign of sanity, then realized that dressing up and fighting a bar full of bad guys wasn't either. "It's not my fault. I was 'dead' at the time."

"And if you hadn't been, you might have reasoned that Hopkins would be a move ahead of Easton."

"Hopkins always seems to be a move ahead, that's why ...."

Shaw's inner dialogue came to a quick end as he suddenly pulled to the curb. If Hopkins was always a move ahead that might mean...

An abrupt curbside U-turn filled the night with horns and curses as Shaw headed back to the Lafayette, trying to think a move ahead of Hopkins.

From the darkness the man in black studied the hotel. He was sure that Easton had men in the lobby, on the stairwells and on every floor. There would be a cop working the elevator and at least two in the suite.

"If I were Hopkins ..." he mused. The Nightmare knew of at least two ways that he could enter undetected, another three ways of finding and getting to the right floor unmolested. But Hopkins had not been taught to walk the shadows as the Nightmare had. He had not been trained to watch men's eyes to know when their attention was elsewhere, to walk without sound so as not to attract their attention. No, Hopkins had studied under less subtle, more vicious masters.

The Lafayette occupied the corner of its block. Other hotels abutted its side and rear with no room for adverse action. But that left two sides exposed and any number of buildings and windows from which a shot could be fired. Surely the police had thought of that. But had they planned for everything?

Another phone call to the lobby, Easton's tired voice coming through the line.

"Lieutenant," the Nightmare whispered, "the Dorseys, what room, what floor?"

Mindful of a ruse, Easton replied, "Only if you buy me a drink when this is over. Say Scotch at McFinn's?"

"Agreed, Lieutenant, but let's make it Irish at Moran's, shall we?"

"Okay, it's you. And to answer your question, fourth floor rear. And we're not entirely as stupid as the press thinks we are. We already thought of that. The suite's on the middle of the floor and the only view is a brick wall. I've got men on the roof, in the alley and on the fire escape. But thanks for checking."

After the detective hung up the Nightmare should have felt relief, but the nagging sense that he and the police had missed something bothered him. There was a move Hopkins could make and if the Nightmare could only figure it out, then perhaps another massacre like that of the other day could be avoided.

Yes, the Nightmare thought suddenly. *That could be his only move, for tonight that is.*

Even though the security around the Hotel Lafayette was as tight as possible, Michael Shaw had no trouble finding a room at the Lanvale, which was in the rear of the Lafayette. Checking in with only one bag, he asked for and received a back room on the third floor.

Looking out his rear window, Shaw found it was as he suspected. For privacy's sakes, the two hotels had staggered their windows, so that none would offer a view into the room opposite. With no direct line of sight, it would be difficult for even the best marksman to hit a particular target. Still, if Shaw was right, Hopkins would have no need for any kind of marksman.

With the lights out, Shaw peered out his window. The Dorsey's room was easy to spot. It was the only one with a guard on the fire escape. Studying the angles, he determined that Hopkins's men would have their best chance if they, like the Dorseys, were on the fourth floor.

One flight up. Moving carefully, The Nightmare silently let himself into one of what he had determined to be the three most likely fourth floor rooms. All asleep. He closed the door behind him.

About to trick open the door to the second room, he heard noises that strongly suggested that those inside were not interested in anything but themselves and their mutual satisfaction. Laughing quietly to himself, he came to the third room.

I hope I'm right, the man in black thought while standing outside the door. Drawing his pistols, he kicked open the door.

There were two men in the room and two rocket launchers on the bed, the same type rocket launchers that had been used on an armored truck just a few days ago. There was a brief pause as the three just stared at each other. Then as the Nightmare smiled behind his mask and said

"Checkmate" one of the men made a dive for the bed.

He was the first to die.

The second tried in vain to draw his revolver. Two blasts from the Nightmare's powerful automatics cut him down.

The shots were heard but thanks to the solid construction of the Lanvale, could not be pinpointed. The two would-be assassins were not discovered until later that day, when the maid finally decided to check the room. The rocket launchers were not found, the Nightmare having decided that one day he might have need of them.

Lieutenant Easton never learned that Wolf Hopkins had again out planned him, or that the Nightmare had been a move ahead of Hopkins.

Talking In Court

"I've decided not to testify."

This simple statement from Muriel Dorsey as Easton and his team were preparing to escort her and her sons to court surprised everyone.

"Without your testimony those two men will go free," Easton explained calmly. Then he added the guilt. "Your husband will have died for nothing."

There were tears in the woman's eyes but she held them back. "And if I testify he will still be dead. And for what? So that two gangsters go to jail. What about the man who killed Walter? Is he dead? Will he go to jail? And what about this Hopkins? What will he do after I get off the stand?"

"Once you testify you and your boys will be safe. Hopkins won't have any reason to harm you."

"Not even as a warning to others?" To that Easton has no honest answer. "No, Lieutenant, you can put me on the stand but I won't answer any questions."

Easton could have said more. He could have reminded Mrs. Dorsey of the men who died trying to keep her safe. He could have told her that her silence would not buy the safety of her family. He could have assured her that with her testimony Hopkins would not be a threat anymore. But he knew that nothing he said would matter. He had been married long enough to know when a woman had made her mind up.

So he sighed and shook his head in defeat. "Okay, get your things together. I'll call the judge and the D.A. then we'll slip you out of the city as quietly as possible. There's no point in even putting you on the stand."

No point in anything, the detective thought. Maybe what Shaw was doing was right. Let the cops police the honest people while the dark ones stalked the night hunting and killing the ones who used the rules of the Law to protect themselves from it. Maybe when he got kicked off the force he'd join their ranks, if they'd have a failure like himself.

"Mister Easton?" The lieutenant felt a pull on his suit coat. Looking down, he saw Wally Dorsey standing next to him. The boy had a strange look to him. Well, why not after the hell he and his brother had been through.

"Yes, son?"

"If mommy doesn't talk in court the bad guys will go free, right?"

So the boy had been listening, the lieutenant thought, *boys do that. We should have made sure the bedroom door was shut.*

Wishing he could think up a believable lie the detective merely nodded and said, "Yes, they will."

"And the man who killed my daddy, and the man who had it done, they'll go free too?"

Another nod of the head. This time it was Easton who was close to tears. How to explain to a young boy that those who were supposed to take care of him had failed?

Wally Dorsey had been through much in his young life. On the move, running, hiding, staying in strange places, although the island was fun. There his family was sometimes happy. Through it all, he had heard his father say, "It's the right thing to do." But now everybody – his mommy, the police – was giving up. And if they did, that would mean his father had been wrong.

Wally Dorsey loved his daddy; he had trusted him and believed in him. And that meant that his daddy could not be wrong. And that meant the others had to be. So he had to be brave, brave like the Man in Black. Brave like his daddy. And that meant there was only one thing to do.

"I saw those men, Mr. Easton. I'll talk in court."

"No!" Muriel Dorsey ran over to her son. "No, Wally, you can't."

"I have to, Mommy."

"But why?"

"Because Daddy said it's the right thing to do."

And as a mother hugged her son and cried over him Easton felt some of his despair leave his soul and a little bit of hope enter.

After taking his witness through the events of that fateful trip into the city, the D.A. turned, and looking at the jury, asked,

"You said that you saw two men gun down another in the street. Do you see those two men in the courtroom today?"

"Those two, right there," Muriel Dorsey said, pointing to Jake Green and Charlie Heywood.

Despite the defense attorney doing his best to shake her testimony, Mrs. Dorsey stayed firm in her identification.

The jury was out for less than three hours. The verdict was guilty.

They Can Only Fry You Once

Shaky Jake Green and Charlie Heywood faced the biggest decision of their lives. After that woman had fingered them, after their guilty verdicts, they had been led to separate holding cells and left alone. No food, no water, no human contact until an assistant D.A. had come in with the expected offer.

"Give up Hopkins and you live. Keep quiet and die." And after letting each man think about this for a minute he added, "We only need one of you."

It was all Heywood could to keep from laughing in the man's face. Life or death, neither mattered to him. The life he'd chosen, no way did he expect to live to get old. He had hoped for a few more years of the good life, however. Still, he'd rolled the dice and the snake looked back. He'd take what was coming to him and go out a right guy. Besides, he had a sister and a couple of nieces upstate and he didn't want anybody paying them a visit.

Jake Green didn't want to die. Not in the chair. He didn't want the lighting to run through his body and burn away his life. Nor did he want to spend that life locked up behind bars. *Either way,* he thought, *the only way out was in a box.* The only question was when.

Parole, he decided, he'd ask for parole. He could do fifteen, even twenty if there was a chance of getting out at the end. But could he rat out Hopkins? Green thought of his brother, a construction worker down in Maryland. Marvin had a nice wife and a couple of kids. Green knew what Hopkins would do to them. He weighed their lives against his.

When the ADA came back, Heywood spit in his eye. Green, however, offered up Hopkins in exchange for parole and a new name once inside. He didn't mention his brother's family.

Despite being the target of a major police investigation, Wolf Hopkins felt secure in his eastside home and headquarters. He had reason to be. Despite their suspicions, the police had no proof of any criminal activity on his part. Through his informers, he would know if they had and would be given warning of any coming raid.

"So do you want us to hit the dame and her brats, Boss?"

Hopkins thought for a moment then said, "No, not yet, Bull. Let's let her start feeling safe. Then we'll take a kid, the oldest I think. Then we take the young one. Then we take her, get her hooked on junk and put her to work on her back. But that's for later. Right now we gotta take care of Shaky Jake and Charlie."

"They ain't talked yet, have they?"

"Do you see the cops here, Johnny? I'll know when they talk, if they talk."

It would take three days. Three days for papers to be drawn up. Three days for Heywood and Green to be transferred to The House of Detention to await sentencing. Three days before a deal for Jake Green's deposition could be finalized and approved. It only took one day for a clerk in the D.A.'s office to send word to Hopkins that one of his men planned to turn rat. On the second day, Heywood's lawyer came to see him.

"Our mutual friend is not happy, Charlie."

"Not my fault, Mr. Randolph. I'm holding up my end. I'm keeping my mouth shut and taking the jolt."

A shake of the lawyer's head told Heywood that this was not good enough. "Our friend needs *everyone* to do his part, Charlie, not just you. I know you're concerned about your family. So are we. Rest assured they'll be taken care of. The question you have to ask yourself is ... in what manner? Good day, Charlie."

Heywood considered his options. He didn't have many. If he talked, his family was dead. If he did nothing, they were still dead. That only left him once choice. *What the hell,* he thought, *they can only fry me once.*

On the third day, Heywood and Green were placed in a transport wagon for their transport to the House of Detention. They were shackled hand and foot. There was a guard present with them in the back of the wagon. Sometime along the way, Heywood got loose. Taking the surprised guard out first, he then turned on the helpless Green. He worked quickly and quietly so that even as the truck drove through the inner door of the sally port, nothing seemed amiss. However, he was the only one alive when the back door was opened. Despite threats, despite offers of clemency, despite beatings so severe that they threatened to cheat the electric chair, he never revealed from whom he had received the key to his handcuffs or the blade with which he had cut two men's throats.

A Favor in the Dark

With a sigh, Shaw put down his evening paper. Once again, Wolf Hopkins had outguessed, outthought and outplayed the police. *That's why,* he thought, *people like Kent, Richard and I wear the black and haunt the night. When the law fails, when justice is thwarted there is always vengeance and we are the ones who can mete it out.*

Tonight was the night for vengeance. Vengeance for the cops who fell outside the courthouse, vengeance for Walter Dorsey, vengeance for the prison guard whose throat had been cut, and yes, even vengeance for Shaky Jake and Owen Davies. Tonight there would be no games. Tonight was a night for forced entry, laughter and blazing guns. Tonight a rabid wolf would be put down for good.

It was a determined Michael Shaw who entered his bedroom. There he donned the black suit, the gloves, the hat and the mask. With a double brace of .45s in their holsters, it was the Man in Black who prepared to go out.

The telephone rang. Not the house phone, but a special line that Shaw had had installed shortly after his crusade began. Few knew the number.

"Yes," he said in a voice that was halfway between his normal tone and the Nightmare's whisper.

From the other end of the line came Seamus Moran's brogue. "There is a gentleman here to see you."

"And is that gentleman somewhat bald, a bit overweight and wearing both a cheap suit and the cares of the world on his shoulders?"

"That he is, lad. That he is."

"And which of us did he ask for?"

"Now who do you think? He'd come to your home for the one but not the other."

"Give him a mug of Paddy's best brew and tell him that I'll be there by the time he finishes it."

"Do hurry. He's much too obvious and he's frightening my less honest customers."

Knowing what the drinks were like in Moran's, Easton took his time enjoying the best ale he had ever been served. He enjoyed it so much that he ordered another, thinking, *why not? Shaw, or someone very close to him, was paying.* And after draining the last drop of the wonderful nectar from the mug the detective reluctantly stepped outside.

"Well?" he asked the night.

A voice from the darkness. "You wanted to see me, Lieutenant."

"I'll settle for hearing you. First of all, thank you for the boys. I imagine that coming back was difficult."

There was regret and a sense of loss in the whispered reply. "Far too easy, I'm afraid."

It was only weeks ago that Easton had wished the Nightmare to "Live in Peace." It was he who had pulled him back into the night and now he had to ask something even harder of the man.

"I need to ask another favor."

"No need to ask, Lieutenant. Tonight, all that Wolf Hopkins has – his men, his allies, his organization, his life – will be taken from him."

"That's not what I want, that's not what I need. I want, I need, no, this city needs Hopkins alive. This city, its people need to see him led out of his headquarters in chains. They need to see him tried and convicted and thrown into prison like the common crook he is. They need to see him get what he deserves."

"What Hopkins deserves is death. What the city needs is an end to his criminal ways. Mine is the quickest way to that end. You ask me to spare his life, Lieutenant. Why should I?"

"Because Hopkins does not deserve a quick death. Because it would restore faith in the police. Because the people need to see that the law works. But mostly because one man risked his family and gave his life in its name. Because Walter Dorsey said that it was the right thing to do."

"It will not be easy."

"Nothing worthwhile is."

There was a pause, one long enough to make Easton think that the Nightmare had departed. And then,

"Your way this time, Lieutenant. But should it fail ..."

"Then it's your way, and may God help us all."

"Goodnight, Lieutenant."

"Goodnight, and thanks again."

Not expecting a reply, Easton turned to leave. But the Nightmare spoke one last time.

"Evans, Travis, Polecat Johnny – do you care what happens to them?"

"It's Hopkins I want."

A whispered "Good, wait for my word" was followed by departing laughter.

I should go home, Easton thought as he stood alone in the darkness. Thoughts of a soft bed warred with the memory of the fine ale served inside Moran's. Sleep, the detective finally decided, could wait.

As Easton walked over to what had been his booth he saw that it was already occupied. About to turn away he heard,

"Lieutenant, come join me."

"Mr. Shaw!" Somewhat confused, the cop asked, "How did you ..."

"Get in? Through the front door of course. You were busy, apparently talking to yourself so you must not have noticed."

"Or there's a back door to this place?" Easton offered, taking his seat.

"Several," came the enigmatic reply. "And I think we'd both be surprised as to where they lead. So how goes the wolf hunt?"

It was back on, the game of pretend that both played so that serious work might be done.

"Slow, Mr. Shaw, but with the full resources of the law now after him, Hopkins won't stay free for long."

"So you have some evidence against him?"

"Enough for a warrant sure, for an indictment – maybe, for a conviction ..." Easton shook his head. "I'm hoping something breaks soon." To himself he added, *before I'm kicked off the force, before your other self starts a bloodbath, before Hopkins kills more innocents.*

"So why not search his headquarters? You're bound to find something."

"You would think so, but this guy's smart. Any evidence – books, ledgers, that sort of thing – is probably kept somewhere else. If we raid his place and come up empty ..."

Easton sighed. "Anyway, if may not be my problem much longer. After the mess I've made of things ... your company wouldn't need a good security man, would it, Mr. Shaw?"

The man who was sometimes the Nightmare smiled. "I'm sure it could, if I had a company. One of these days I'll have to start one. Then again, anything that comes close to honest work would make my great-grandfather spin in his grave. Lieutenant, would it help if I dropped a few words in the right ears? I do have some low friends in high places."

"I think, Mr. Shaw, that for now I'll count on the friends I do have coming through for me."

"Start Running"

There were things the Nightmare needed to learn.

Some he got from Polecat Johnny. The Hopkins lieutenant was sweating out his pores in a Turkish bath when the steam gave way to a black shape. Questions were asked. Caught without his gun, indeed, without even a pocket in which he could have kept a gun, Johnny had no choice but to answer. The alternative was to be locked in the room as the Nightmare slowly turned up the heat, higher and higher, until it passed the point of human endurance and Polecat was boiled like a lobster.

"Hopkins will kill me," the mobster protested after he had spilled all.

"He might," came the whispered warning, "if he learns that you talked. So might I, if I see you on the streets of this city after tonight. Either way, Johnny, you're a dead man. Start running now and pray that your past is slower than your fears."

The man in black next sought out Bull Evans. He found him in a crowded poolroom, which after some laughter and a shot into the ceiling ceased to be crowded.

When the Nightmare asked his questions, Evans's reply was a short two word answer. Answering the vulgarity with an amused laugh, the Nightmare then surprised the gangster.

"I could end your life now, Bull Evans, but that would do neither of us any good. I offer a deal." The masked man picked up cue stick. "We will play a game. If I win you will tell me what I need to know."

"And if I win?"

Another laugh. "You get to live."

Evans nodded. "Seems fair." Not that he any intention of playing fair. The minute the Nightmare was distracted by the game, the very instant he was bent over the table to strike the ball, Evans planned to take out his rod and end the vigilante's life.

"I'll break," the Nightmare's whisper. Then he cracked the pool cue over Evans's head.

He followed this up by ramming the thick end of the broken cue into his foe's stomach. The thin end he whipped across the face of the surprised crook.

"Do you like my game, Evans? If you want to win, if you want to live, you will tell me what I want to know."

From the corner of his eye, the Nightmare caught movement. A few of the braver patrons were trying to sneak back in. Whipping out a .45 he fired in their direction. As they scattered into the street, he then turned toward the counter where the attendant was reaching for something.

"Don't," he warned.

Foolishly, the man failed to follow the warning and brought out a shotgun. The cost of this folly was his life as the Nightmare shot him in the chest.

By now Evans was on his knees, trying to recover, trying to draw his gun so as to put paid to the Nightmare. A hard slap to the face drove Evans back to the floor. A fresh pool cue pinned him there.

"I have all night, Evans. You, however, have only so many limbs and joints. How many must I break before you answer my questions?"

The answer was one.

With Bull Evans cradling a broken arm, the Nightmare turned to go. Standing in the doorway he said, "Hopkins will know you talked. He will hunt you down, or I will. See a doctor, Evans, then start running."

Archie Travis was last. The Nightmare found him at home. Looking in through a window, he saw the gangster listening to the radio with his family.

More innocents that will be harmed, the masked man thought. Not wishing to break in on the woman and child, the Nightmare laughed loud enough to be heard.

Travis came out. Standing at his front door, he saw the Nightmare appear briefly beneath a street lamp before ducking into an alley. Resigned to his fate, Travis followed.

"Far enough," came a voice from the dark.

"I wondered when you'd come for me. Am I the first?"

"Evans and Johnny were before you."

"They rat out Hopkins?"

"Yes."

"Then it doesn't matter what I say. The Wolf will blame us all. Unless you plan to kill him."

It was with regret that the Nightmare answered, "No."

"What about the others? Are they dead?"

"No."

Travis thought for a moment, then, "Here's the deal. You ask me what you need to know. I tell you then ... then ... then you kill me."

Few things surprised the Nightmare. This did.

"Why?" he asked.

"With those two alive and me dead, Hopkins will figure that I was the one who didn't talk. My family will be safe."

Even though he knew that Travis could not see him, the Nightmare shook his head. "Hopkins has already caused a wife to lose her husband and children to lose their father. I could give you time to escape."

"And Hopkins would find me. Somehow he would find me. This is the only way. Ask your questions."

The Nightmare did. Travis answered. Then, because to him it was the only way, he drew his revolver and fired into the alley to keep his family safe.

Amanda Travis had heard the laughter and knew why her husband had left the house. Gunshots told her that he would not be returning. Archie Travis had not been a good man, this she knew. But he had been a good husband and father. Putting her daughter to bed, she wept silent tears until the front door opened.

Archie Travis entered. "We have to run," he told his wife.

"Strike Now"

None of Wolf Hopkins three lieutenants knew all of what the Nightmare needed to know. Each knew some, together they knew it all – records, entry and exit. The man in black went after the records first, before the gang boss could learn that he had been betrayed.

He was almost too late. Just as he arrived at the small Southside accounting firm, a touring car pulled up. Caught in its headlights as he was picking the lock, he just had time to escape the beam before the shooting started.

As bullets hit wood and shattered glass, the Nightmare drew his .45s. I had so hoped to get through the night without killing anyone, the man behind the mask thought.

First he took out the headlights. Then came the laugh. This drew gunfire. As he dodged out of its way the Nightmare fired towards the muzzle flashes. Cries of pain told him that his lead had found its marks. Still on the move, he hopped on to the running board.

"There he is, ram him," he said in a rough voice.

In his excitement the driver hit the gas, the Nightmare jumping free just as the car crashed into the front of the building.

With the front window now just shattered glass, there was no need for the Nightmare to pick the lock. Once inside, he quickly found was he was seeking. Using the phone on the desk, he called Easton.

"How did I know it was you?" was the lieutenant's reply to the Nightmare's whispered greeting.

"There's been a shooting." Ignoring the cop's "Of course there has" the masked man gave an address then added, "The top shelf of the bookcase. There are several unmarked ledgers that should give you what you need."

The line clicked. Easton was dressed and out the door in record time.

An hour later the detective had the books stored safely in his trunk. When he got back into his car he found a note.

"Strike now."

Accompanying the brief message was a floor plan of Hopkins's home and headquarters.

After leaving his note, the Nightmare raced across the city to the wolf's lair. Passing it by, he went straight to the last house in the block.

Up the fire escape, in through a second floor window, down to the basement and even lower. Travelling beneath the houses, he soon came to a ladder. This he ascended and found himself in what he believed was the building next door to Hopkins's.

There were two bedrooms that shared a connecting wall with the house next door. Each had a closet in what would be the right place. To be sure, the Nightmare used the hammer and nails he had brought with him and nailed their doors shut.

Then he waited.

It didn't take long.

Soon there were the shout of "Police" followed by the sounds of revolvers, shotguns and Tommys. He heard the thud of falling bodies and the cries of wounded men.

It was hard not to join the fray but still he waited. Soon, his patience was rewarded as from the hallway he heard the pouding of fists on a nailed-shut door.

The back room. Standing off to the side in case Hopkins tried to shoot through the door, The Nightmare laughed just loud enough to be heard by his captive. Then,

"You've lost, Hopkins. Even if you managed to break through this door I'd gun you down as it opened. I'm very tempted to empty my guns into this closet but I made a promise to a man I respect. Now if you want to live you'll listen."

There was silence. The Nightmare went on. "You're not looking at the jolt. You're good, the cops can't pin a murder rap on you. But they do have your ledgers. I'm guessing there's enough in them for a twenty year stay in the Graybar Hotel. So here's your choice – surrender to the police and live. Fight them and you may die. Or say the word and I will kill you."

A brief silence then through the double closet doors and the panel between them the Nightmare barely made out,

"It's him, it's Hopkins."

"Don't shoot, his hands are raised."

"Against the wall, Hopkins. You're under arrest."

It took everything the man in black had to suppress a laugh of triumph. He would give this victory to the police.

Aftermath

With the evidence of his own records against him, Wolf Hopkins was convicted of extortion, pandering, bootlegging and bookmaking both in the city's Supreme Court and later in Federal court. His aggregate sentence was a little less than twenty years.

"He'll be back," predicted Jerome Easton over much delayed celebratory drinks in Moran's.

"Probably," agreed Michael Shaw, "but not for many years. May we both be somewhere else when that time comes."

"Amen to that."

Glasses clinked together, then Easton said, "But there's still work to be done. Somehow Hopkins's three top men got away."

"Imagine that. Still, I'm sure that now that you're back in the department's good graces you'll have no trouble rounding them up by yourself."

"By myself?" Shaw nodded. "So it's like that. I wondered how you, eh, how the information we used to capture Hopkins was obtained."

"What information is that, Lieutenant?"

"Never mind. What about you, Mr. Shaw, what are your plans?"

"Even the idle rich have loose ends to tie up. I may travel a little and maybe reach out to an old friend or two."

The streets of Harbor City. As Hannibal Tomas left a bar called Dave's Place he was confronted by a figure in black.

"It was my understanding," he said, "that we had an agreement."

"You reached Harbor City alive, did you not? And now our paths have crossed again."

"Oh Hell."

"Exactly where you are going."

A single shot avenged Walter Dorsey. With justice done, the Nightmare got into his car to drive back to his city, back to the game which, God help him, he was fated to play for as long as he could.

CURSED LUCK

First the ones in black broke in, vigilantes whose laughter and violence frightened the crowd, scattered the players, and killed a good number of her guards. She herself was disabled, a bullet to the head that was quicker than her magic. It did not kill her, could not kill her, she was not meant for Hades's realm, but it weakened her so that she lay longer than a day gathering her strength, drawing it from the casino that was her temple. And when she had recovered, after she had used most of her power so that she could walk and talk and get about the business of remodeling and reopening, then came the lightning.

Fire fell from the sky, thrown from the heavens by the hand of a vengeful god – her father, whom she had disappointed in far too many ways. He had come at her bidding to take a woman he wanted, only to be robbed and cheated of his prize by the ones in black. Angrily he had struck out, bringing storm and thunder to the coast town where she lived and worked, making sure that his bolts struck her temple to finish the destruction started by the gunplay.

So as she stood midway between the burnt rubble of what had been Coast City's finest casino and the charred remains of what was one its finest boarding houses, Tyche, Goddess of Chance, vowed that all involved would pay.

It was night in the city. The owner of an east end diner left his restaurant to make a late deposit. It was risky he knew, walking the streets with so much money, but it was even more risky to leave it in the safe – or worse, the register, for stickup men to come and take it away. Besides, it was only a two-block walk and he varied the hours he made the deposit.

When he left, a newly hired waiter took a break and made a phone call. A payphone up the street rang. "He's on the way," the waiter said. The man on the other end hung up and walked toward the diner, looking for the owner. As he did so a shadow detached itself from the wall behind him and followed.

Almost there, the owner thought just before he was pushed from behind. Stumbling forward, he fell into an alley. Cursing his luck, he hoped that the robber would take only the money and not his life.

The crook wanted both. He had decided long ago that "no witnesses" was the best way to stay out of prison. He drew his .38 and was about to fire when laughter came from deep within the alley.

The gunman knew that sound. It was the mocking laughter of one of the city's cloaked vigilantes. It was the sound many of his fellow crooks had heard just before they died. It was the sound of his own death.

Fight or flee? The gunman decided on both, firing two shots into the blackness and hoping to get lucky before running away. Laughter told him he had missed.

Maybe it was chance that caused one of his hastily fired shots to strike an outside circuit box. Maybe it was that bullet that caused the spark that sent current to a darkened street lamp near the alley's mouth. Maybe the long neglected lamp would have sputtered on anyway. Or maybe it was just bad luck that caused the alley to be flooded with light.

"Run!" shouted the man in black who was now a well-lit target, a target who could not shoot back for fear of hitting the diner's owner. The man dropped as a bullet whizzed over his head. He rolled as another shot hit the ground where he had just been.

"Run!" he shouted again then loosed a fusillade of bullets at the street lamp that had betrayed him. All his shots missed but at least this time the would-be victim listened to him. The diner's owner ran one way as he broke from the alley. The gunman, not interested in trading shots in a now fair fight, ran the other.

Alone in the alley, the man known to both foes and allies as the Nightmare looked up at the street lamp. *Damn the luck*, he thought. That the owner had gotten away was some consolation but he wished that he had been able to bring down the robber. *Another night*, he decided as sirens in the distance told him that he should make his own escape.

A week after he had dodged bullets in a not so dark alley, the Nightmare was sitting against a dirty wall in an even dirtier bar called The Jade Dragon. Despite its fancy name it was one of the city's sleaziest dives. He was, of course, not dressed in his usual black but in an oversized sweater and trousers from some church's charity bin. Nursing a watered drink, the Nightmare was listening to those around him.

A child named Toby Barnes was missing, believed to have been kidnapped. The Nightmare had been asked by his police contact to help find the boy. The Jade Dragon was the third bar the Nightmare had been in that evening hoping to overhear some word as to who had done the deed or where the boy might be stashed. He was about to give up and try a fourth place, maybe Dago Mike's, when…

"Heard there was a snatch."

It was a man on the Nightmare's right whose table companion replied, "Yeah, a D.A.'s kid. Supposedly by some new guy in town, goes by the name of…"

That's when the door to the Dragon burst open and a man rushed in. "The cops!" announced the newcomer. "They've called for the dragnet. Everybody's being snatched up." He looked over his shoulder to the outside. Behind him came the sounds of sirens and police whistles. "They're almost here. Clear out."

The Dragon rapidly emptied and while the Nightmare had no problem in evading the police sweep, he had missed his chance to discover the name of the kidnapper. With the underworld shut down for the night, he went home, hoping that someone else would have better luck in finding the missing boy.

Ten days later, in the early morning hours when no one but a paid-off watchman was about, a battered truck pulled up to a warehouse on a city dock. Inside the building were fine silks from the orient, tapestries from the Middle East and carvings from Africa. The men in the truck had no interest in any of these. They were not there to steal but instead to teach a lesson to the importer who refused to pay extra docking fees, exorbitant labor costs and protection money to the mob boss who had claimed the docks as his personal fiefdom. Their unloading of cans of gasoline and kerosene was interrupted by "No fires tonight, boys!" spoken through a bullhorn.

The men looked to see that four patrol cars, a transport wagon and an unmarked police cruiser had followed them on to the dock and that ten policemen with drawn guns were facing them.

The men were not fools. They knew that while the use of flammable liquids was against the law, the simple possession of such liquids was not. They quietly surrendered. What they did not know was that one of the cans already unloaded had been damaged during their ride and was leaking its ignitable contents on the ground. They, and the police, found out when someone discarded a lit cigarette.

The fire spread quickly and was not extinguished until a good third of the warehouse and its contents had been consumed by the flames.

Stepping away from the fire scene, Police Lieutenant Jerome Easton spoke to the shadows where he was sure a certain man in black was waiting. "Thanks for the tip. Damn shame the way it worked out. Just bad luck I guess."

Bad luck indeed, the Nightmare thought. *There seems to be a lot of that going around.*

Following the conflagration at the docks and after several other close calls with bullets fired too close, inconvenient car lamps that exposed his position and miraculous escapes by criminals who once would have fallen prey to either his guns or his fists, Michael Shaw, the man who was the Nightmare, was sitting alone in a booth at Moran's, a mostly quiet little bar on the city's eastside that poured a good drink at a fair price. Shaw was sipping the finest Irish whiskey on either side of the Atlantic and thinking that maybe it was time to give up the masked life and find another way of serving society. *I'm losing my touch,* he thought, *with all that's gone wrong lately I should stop before I get myself or someone else killed.*

He had quit once before, had even declared the Nightmare dead, but had returned to save a family and end the reign of a gang boss. Raising his glass and staring into the golden liquid, he asked aloud, "And what good did it do?" True, the family, at least most of it, was safe, but the gangs went on. They were hydras, cut off one head and two others rise in its place.

"What was that you said, Michael?'

Shaw looked up to see Moran himself, the diminutive owner of the bar, standing at his table.

"Nothing, Seamus, just reliving the past and pondering the future."

"Not that you can affect either one. Taking care of oneself in the present is enough for a man to do." Seeing that Shaw's glass was nearly empty, he asked, "Now can I be getting you anything else?"

Shaw shook his head. "Nothing more, Seamus, unless you managed to bottle some of that 'luck of the Irish' I've heard so much about. I could use some, mine's gone all sour."

"Luck of the Irish," Moran snorted. "Five hundred years of English oppression, famine driving out our youngest and finest and now a civil war that pits county against county and brother against brother. Aye, we Irish have the luck all right and none of it's good. I often wonder what great power we offended in the past to be so cursed. But that's our problem and not yours, Michael. Unlike ours, your troubles will soon pass, unless of course you've gone and incurred the wrath of a god or two. But how likely is that in these days and times?"

Later that night, as Shaw watched the sun come up through the window of his study, his mind went back to a night of pain and fire, of laughter and gunplay in a seaside casino. He had saved the woman he loved, he had been pulled from death's embrace and he had defied beings who called themselves gods. There was the Thunderer. Shaw had mocked him to his face. And there was the Lady, the one who operated the casino. Tyche, the goddess of chance and fortune, and it was her temple he had raided. It was his mockery and her failure that had brought down the lightning that had destroyed it.

Had he incurred the wrath of a god or two? Shaw thought it very likely.

He went back to where it started, not as Shaw, not as the Nightmare but as just one of the many looking for work, any kind of work, honest or not, as long as it paid. He found where Tyche's place had been and watched as men and their machines built a new boarding house on the now vacant lot.

"They hiring?" he asked another onlooker.

The reply was a shake of a head. "They were, but you're about a week too late and there's about a dozen ahead of you."

Shaw nodded, as if he had expected the answer. "Isn't there a gambling joint around here? Hear it's run by a jane. Maybe she could use someone for, well, something. Anything really."

The man pointed to the construction and laughed. "In that case you're a couple of months too late. There was a fight, some masks shot up the place then burned it down. Damn masks, legal killers if you ask me."

"The dame, she reopen anywhere?"

Another shake of the head. "Not here. She's got a racket in the city, working a joint for a fella named Boyd." The man looked away to watch a wood frame being put in place. "But if it's work you're looking for and you're not choosy, I know a juice joint that needs a bouncer."

He turned and found himself alone. "Where'd the hell he go?" He shrugged and went back to watching other men work.

Finding a casino in the city was not difficult. Finding the right one took weeks. Each night Michael Shaw visited a different gambling den – playing every game, placing small bets and losing every time. If he stood at nineteen, the dealer would have twenty. If he had a ten and a queen, the dealer would turn up blackjack. At roulette he'd bet on odd and see even come up. He'd bet red only to see black. And if he bet both the ball would fall in the green.

Each night ended in frustration. It wasn't the losing; it was his not finding the source of his ill luck. Maybe he was not meant to, maybe it was part of his cursed fortune that he would fail at whatever he set out to do.

No, Shaw would not believe that. To do so meant that his life and the lives of all those around him were ruled by nothing more than chance and fate, that they lived only at the whim or design of higher powers. That he would not accept. Luck did play a part, but only that – a part. Reason, logic, determination – these too were part of the great whole. And it would be these that he used to find the one he sought.

Night after night of methodical searching paid off. The place that he sought was on the west side, in what appeared to be just an ordinary restaurant. Unofficially it was known as Fortune's Palace. Even as his limo pulled up to drop him off he felt – something, a frisson in the air, an enchantment maybe that drew one to it and promised fulfillment if only one would come inside and take a chance.

Knowing what his chances were, Shaw stepped inside. After giving the password, he was escorted past the diners and into a spacious rear room where he found slots, tables, wheels and, best of all…

Her.

Tyche.

The cause of his ill luck.

Though he had never seen her, Shaw knew her right away from the description of others. Dressed in a green gown that fell about her like a robe, Tyche moved among the gamblers like the goddess she was supposed to be – talking to some, listening to others, granting favors and maintaining order as needed. This was her temple, where worshippers placed offerings on her altars of chance in hopes of changing their lives. She drew her strength from this place and it showed in her face each time a wheel was spun or a card dealt.

But such could be said of any casino, every casino – anywhere men and women placed a bet and called on her to be their lady that night. Why then did she limit herself to just one place? And why, if the rumors were true, did a goddess deign to work for a common hood like Emmett Boyd?

Like many others in the room, Shaw watched her, but from a distance, not getting too close for fear that she would sense his other self. And when he was not watching her, Shaw examined the room, looking at entrances and exits, places to hide and avenues of escape. For as much as he did not want to admit it, he knew that soon the Nightmare would have to pay a visit and confront the goddess in her own house.

He watched for five nights – from the front and the back, at ground level and from rooftops. He did not see her leave. That might mean that she could blend with the darkness or that she had left in disguise. However, Lady Luck was not a creature of shadows and the Nightmare had been trained by the best to see through artifice and disguise. No, it was most likely that Tyche seldom left her temple – few deities did – and she lived somewhere on the second or third floor.

Probably the third floor. More natural light came in and it gave a better view of the city. Perhaps in the past few days, in the early morning hours, just before dawn chased men like him back to their quite ordinary and unexciting lives, she had looked out and seen him. Seen him lurking, watching for her, looking for a way in. If so, did she care? Would she try to stop him, or simple rely on the bad luck with which she had cursed him?

It did not matter. He had to make the attempt, had to confront her to find out what he must do to get her to lift the curse, and if he could, in good conscience, do it. It was that or give up his crusade to bring a measure of justice to the city.

There were several ways inside. He discounted the easiest. Scale the outside? One loose brick and there would be a quick fall and a sudden stop. The fire escape of the adjacent building? A rusted bolt breaking at the wrong time would lead to the same result, only much noisier with heavy metal falling on top of him. No, his approach would have to be carefully planned and well thought out to eliminate even the slightest possibility of chance.

Even as he planned the long circuitous route that would have him entering through the rooftop door, the Nightmare realized the extent of what Tyche had done to him. Three months ago he would have thought nothing of climbing a wall or fire escape and trusting to luck and skill to see him through any difficulties. Now he was second and third-guessing himself, and unless he shook off the resultant paralysis he was a beaten man.

To hell with it, he decided. *Luck might be against him but his skill had yet to fail. To hell with rooftops and fire escapes and rooftop doors.* Leaving the darkness of the alley, the Nightmare crossed the street and approached the front door.

He did not give luck the chance to work against him. Pressure in the right places followed by a push and the door gave way.

The restaurant was empty, the chairs turned up for the morning cleaning crew. Noises came from the rear, the casino staff finishing up for the night. He ignored them. He knew from his previous visit that there was no entrance to the upper floors from the rear room. There were, however, stairs to his right and these he took.

The second floor was used for storage and supplies. She had to be on the third.

The Nightmare cautiously climbed the stairs, looking for handholds and prepared to jump aside if a tread broke beneath him. Making it to the third floor without incident, he thought about drawing one or both of this .45s. *And what good would they be against a goddess, Michael,* he asked himself. Laughing quietly, he opened the first door he came to.

There she was – Tyche, Goddess of Luck. As before, she was in green, wearing a floor-length gown that was almost but not quite transparent under an open robe that was just as sheer.

Goddess or no, Shaw thought, taking in her beauty, *this is a woman a man could worship.* Another time, another place, different circumstances and Shaw might have been that man. But not then, not that night, not when the game was being played for more than physical satisfaction.

"I knew you would come to me, Master Nightmare, to beg the lifting of your curse."

"I come, but not to beg. To request, to bargain, to warn perhaps; but not to beg."

Some women seem more beautiful when they grow angry, when they drop the façade society tells them they must maintain and let their true selves show. Tyche was not one of these. Her features darkened and perhaps some of her true face was revealed.

"You would bargain with me, mortal! You would threaten a god!"

"You would not be the first, Lady Tyche. And yet here I stand, asking but not begging you to lift the curse."

"Would you know why I cursed you, Master Nightmare?"

The man behind the mask smiled. "I can imagine."

"No, you cannot. You laid waste to my temple, my site of power, and your actions caused it to be burned to the ground. Despite that, and the gunshot that further weakened me, I might not have sought you out. It was fair combat and even one such as I must now and then be humbled. But it was afterward, once the fire was out and I was goddess of a smoking ruin, that a curse fell on me. The curse that was and is Reuben Sol.

"I owe this Reuben Sol. It was from him that I leased the buildings that housed the casino and hotel. It was he who provided the liquor and who paid off the authorities. And it was he who provided the men you fought and killed. And because of this, because of you, I was in debt to this … mortal, a debt which I had no means to pay."

"You could have walked away."

"How little you understand my kind, Master Nightmare. There are few rules that bind us, but Obligation is one of them. So to pay what I owe I work here. Sol arranged it with an associate of his, one Emmett Boyle. Boyle gets a house cut of sixty percent. Sol gets half of the remainder to settle my debt. Much of that covers what is called 'vigorish,' interest on my debt that accrues faster than I can pay it off."

That doesn't leave you much to live on."

"If it did, would I be living in this…hovel?"

The Nightmare looked past Tyche at her apartment. It was neat and functional, nicer than what most people had those days, but nowhere near worthy of a goddess.

"Why don't you just use your power over Chance to affect the play in your casino? Have the dice roll and the cards come up your way. The more money you make the quicker your debt is paid off."

Tyche shook her head. "The players, whether they know it or not, are my worshipers. I cannot cheat them. There must be balance. The bad luck with which I cursed you comes from others' good fortune. No, I am bound to Sol and through him to Boyle. And as the cause of my misfortune, you shall suffer as long as I do."

"My Lady Tyche, my actions were the result of your own doing. You took the woman I loved. I saved her. It was as you said, 'fair combat.'"

The goddess laughed in disdain. "Of those rules that bind us, none say that my kind have to be fair to mortals. You may go, Master Nightmare. May this first visit be your last, or this city will become the luckiest in the world, for all of its ill fortune will fall upon you, and you will not be safe even in your own home."

The Nightmare bowed, exaggerating his movements so as to make a mockery of the courtesy and the person to whom it was directed. "Let it be as you wish, Lady Tyche," he said as he again stood straight, "my skills against your curse."

With that the Nightmare left. As he did, Tyche heard his laughter coming from the stairway, full of confidence and promising doom.

Even as he issued his parting challenge to the goddess of Chance, the Nightmare asked himself, *But can you deliver?*

Outside, he changed back to Michael Shaw and hailed a taxi. Given his current circumstances he thought it best to let someone else drive, figuring their luck would be better than his. In the back of the cab he reviewed his meeting with Tyche.

She had mentioned balance, telling him that his bad luck came from someone's good luck. Came – or caused? He would have to ask Easton if the police were catching more crooks than usual. Or maybe the ones that got away were the lucky ones. *Bad for me, good for them. I lose, someone else wins.*

Which brought his mind back to the casinos. In all of them, even Tyche's, he had lost every wager. That meant others had to win. An idea started forming. It grew when he remembered the goddess's warning:

"May this first visit be your last."

His true first visit had been as himself, as Michael Shaw. Tyche had not detected it, had not felt the curse at work. It was nice to know that infallibility was not one of her attributes.

A plan formed. And when he remembered what Tyche had said about obligation, he had to stifle a laugh that he unleashed only after the cabbie dropped him off in front of his stately manor.

Michael Shaw was no stranger to gambling. He owed his fortune to his great-grandfather, who was said to have won Shaw Manor and a great deal of money in a poker game. It was also said that his great-grandfather's winning was due more to his manipulation of a marked deck than any amount of luck. Shaw's grandfather took chances on gold mines and oil wells, most of which paid off. His son, Shaw's father, was the "white sheep" of the family – honest to a fault and loathe to take any kind of chance. It was left to Shaw to carry on the family tradition by playing the stock market, winning a game that had recently cost so many so much.

And now he played for higher stakes, risking not money but his reputation, his freedom and his life, wearing the mask of the Nightmare and standing between both sides in the eternal game of cops and robbers.

Michael Shaw knew gambling, it was in his blood, and he knew gamblers. If criminals were a superstitious lot, then gamblers were even more so. He was counting on this knowledge.

As Shaw, he became a regular at Fortune's Palace. Each visit he placed more than token bets, placing 100 dollar chips first on the dice tables and then on blackjack, wagering more in an hour than most men made in a year.

It did not take the other gamblers long to notice his play, both his betting and his losing. They latched on to him, watching where he placed his chips then betting against him. Every night he played. Though he could afford it, every night he lost a fair sum of money. Everyone else won, except the house.

Begging the ghost of his great-grandfather to be forgiven the sin of deliberately losing, Shaw played and lost for a week. No one noticed him. Pit bosses are trained to watch the winners and encourage the losers. Tyche walked the floor and ignored him.

It was on the fifth night that he began to feel a certain tension in the air and noticed added security around the tables. Someone, maybe Tyche, possibly Boyd, had begun to suspect that they were being cheated but could not figure out how. On the sixth night he saw the goddess talking to two men, cheap looking hoods in expensive suits, ones no doubt designed to give them sophisticated airs. Boyle, and probably Sol, Shaw thought. Behind the men, their eyes watching the crowd, were even cheaper hoods, gunmen whose ill-fitting clothing did nothing to disguise the bulges of their weapons.

Shaw watched the group from a distance. Tyche was shaking her head, the two men were nodding theirs. None of the three looked happy. *Do they know with whom, or rather, with what they are dealing?* Shaw could not help imagining Tyche losing her temper and calling down godlike wrath on them. That just might solve her problem and his, and if not for the possibility that more or less innocent people would be injured, he might have looked for a way of causing it to happen.

Something was said. The argument ended with the goddess, Boyle and Sol – accompanied by the thugs – leaving the casino and going up to her apartment.

I am glad that I don't have my working clothes with me, Shaw thought. The temptation to listen in might have been too much. I'd be caught and that would end the whole deal. Or else I'd try blasting my way in and thanks to the curse I'd be killed along with everyone but Tyche, leaving her the only winner.

Instead he imagined what was happening. Boyle explaining to Tyche the need to increase revenues – or else. Sol outlining what the "or else" might entail. Shaw wondered if Tyche would try explaining things as simply a run of bad luck.

Smiling at the possible irony, Shaw left the casino. It was time for part two of his plan.

He was back in the Jade Dragon, again dressed in charity clothing, a mostly empty bottle in front of him. Apparently drunk, he talked loudly to anyone who would listen.

"I tell you it's a sure thing. I got it from one of her dealers. This dame Tyche is tired of turning most of her jack over to somebody else. She's fixing to bring Boyle down by busting her own joint. The fix is in for Friday night and there's heavy sugar to be had."

The Dragon was the Nightmare's fourth stop. There was just one more to go.

Shaw's last stop was Moran's. He arrived just before closing time and took his usual booth in the back. As he sat down he was greeted by the tavern's diminutive owner.

"Michael, it's been a while, for either of you. I thought perhaps you had retired your friend in black – again."

"No, Seamus, my other self is here to stay as long as he's needed."

"Then your luck has come back, has it?'

"No, Seamus, it's a bad as ever, but I've found a way to work around it. And I'd like your help in doing so."

The "fix" as the Nightmare had put it, was set for the following Friday. That Wednesday, a few men and women recruited by Moran got to the casino early.

"I'll stake them, Seamus," Shaw had explained to the bar owner, "and we'll split whatever they win."

"And if they lose?"

"Then the losses are all mine. And to be honest, I hope to lose a lot."

Shaw did. It was as he had hoped. Playing with his money, the men and women sent by Moran lost it all.

"What now?" Moran asked after Wednesday night had drifted into Thursday morning.

"They used my money and so my luck followed them. Same thing Friday night, Seamus. My money, my risk. I'll be there as well. And call everyone you know. Tell them to call everyone they know. I will as well. Tell them to be there and make sure that they know who our players are and to bet big against them. My bad luck is going to break the bank at Fortune's Palace."

That Friday, the Palace was crowded and there was anticipation in the air. The usual crowd was there – the bored, the compulsive, the reckless – all looking for the momentary thrill that gambling provided. Others, those who had heard the planted rumors and believed them, were there as well. Shaw and Moran's recruits were present as were dangerous-looking men brought in by Boyle and Sol in the event that the stories they had heard were true.

Shaw played recklessly, making wild bets that he had little chance of winning even without his curse. Other gamblers followed, playing against him and raking in the chips. Men and women at other tables, using Shaw's money, also lost while those in the know won big.

Looking around, Shaw did not see Tyche. The hostess of Fortune's Palace had yet to make an appearance. He did, however, see Boyle and Sol walking the floor, watching the play, checking out who was winning and losing and no doubt trying to figure out how they were being cheated and by whom.

Dice were changed, decks of cards were exchanged, dealers and croupiers were replaced. Nothing stopped the steady drain of the house funds. Finally, the hoods gave in. The word was given and one by one the gamblers were paid off and the tables closed. Fortune's Palace was closing several hours early.

Shaw was one of the first to leave. Going to his hired car, he removed a bag he had left in the back seat then released the driver. The car drove off. Shaw found a dark alley, opened the bag and examined its contents – black mask, black coat, black gloves, a brace of .45s – his working clothes. Donning them, he let Michael Shaw give way to the Nightmare.

"Time to play," he said. Taking a length of rope from the bag, he made his way back to Fortune's Palace.

It was not the night for the direct approach. It was the night to pit his skill against the curse. Entering the house next to the casino, the Nightmare cautiously made his way to the roof. There he tread carefully, feeling for weak areas and soft spots. Soon he was atop the Palace.

A new rope, the best and strongest he could find. The chimney looked firm, all the bricks in place and no loose mortar. Tying the rope tight, he lowered himself down.

The Nightmare had been prepared to slip or jimmy the rear third floor window. Instead he found it open. He nodded then, laughing to himself, slipped through it.

A quick flash of his torch showed him that he was in Tyche's bedroom. Memorizing the position of the furniture he made his way to the bedroom door. Turning the knob slowly, he eased it open.

Men were talking.

" …trying to pull," one was saying. "We heard the rumors, the talk on the street. You're running a game on us."

"I assure you, gentlemen, the only games I am running are downstairs."

"Well you ain't running them so good," said another man. "This last week you've lost more than all the other joints together. Explain that. No, don't bother, there's only one explanation and it's what we think it is."

There were scuffling sounds, then a slap, then a woman's cry. The Nightmare prepared himself for Tyche lashing out but nothing came. *Of course not,* he realized, *Tyche's still in debt to these hoods. Obligation may prevent her from harming them.* He listened, waiting for the just the right moment.

"This ain't working, sister. You did good on the shore but that's when you were making all the dough. So we're gonna try something else."

"What's that, Sol?"

Tyche's question drew lecherous chuckles from both men. "Emmett here's got other places, other – houses. A classy, good-looking broad like you, you could entertain a special client or two, maybe three, each night. A couple of months, maybe more, you'll be in the clear. You know, on your feet and off your back."

"How dare you!"

Here it comes, the Nightmare thought. But instead he heard a slap then the sound of a body hitting the floor.

Then the other man, Boyle, said, "There's a bedroom back there. Why don't we let her start tonight, just to make sure she's got the goods. Rubes, she owes you more than me. You go first. I don't mind seconds. You boys can hold her down then take your own turns. All three at once if you like. Let's break her in right."

Drawing his .45s, the Nightmare stepped back to allow the door to open. When it did he let loose a laugh, a laugh designed to reach into the souls of those who heard it and draw out their fear and terror, a laugh that told them that their sins had been found out, a laugh that warned them that this could be the last night of their lives.

The Nightmare stepped through the door, for the moment the master of the room, his cold voice announcing, "This lady is under my protection."

Sol and Boyle moved back. The guards stepped forward, their hands going beneath their coats.

"This is private business, Mask," said the shorter of the bosses. "Now get out of here before there's trouble."

"It's my business now, Sol. And there won't be any trouble if you and your friends leave now and promise not to bother the lady again."

"She owes us."

"Yes, she does, Boyle. But there's lots of money downstairs. Take it all. Leave her with nothing then leave her alone. Do this and we all walk away."

As he talked the Nightmare slowly lowered his guns, wondering if the guards were as stupid as they looked.

"And if we don't?"

Before answering, the Nightmare quickly looked down at Tyche, who was still on the floor. "My lady, about my previous request?"

"Granted."

"I thought it might be. To answer your question, Boyle, leave or be carried out. Your choice."

The three guards were as stupid as they looked, or maybe they too were under some type of obligation. At Boyle's "Take him" they moved to draw their weapons but not before the Nightmare could raise his automatics. He shot them each once, then shot them again to be sure.

Two more shots, neither from the Nightmare's gun. The doorframe behind him splintered. He turned to see Rueben Sol aiming his revolver. Two guns went off at the same time. Sol's bullet missed. The Nightmare's did not.

"What about you, Boyle?" the Nightmare asked, his voice raised so that the remaining gang boss could hear over any gunfire-induced deafness. "We're in a casino. Care to try your luck?"

Boyle shook his head. "I know when the game's gone against me. I'll take the deal. The money and she walks."

This time the Nightmare's laugh was one of mockery mixed with amusement. "That was before. Now you get half and she keeps half." Raising his .45, he pointed it at Boyle. "Or she can take it all."

Reluctantly Boyle agreed. "Done."

"Now go before we change our mind."

Boyle fled, leaving the Nightmare alone with the goddess.

"Your obligation to this one," he looked at the body of Rueben Sol, "is at an end. Just as you planned."

"What do you mean by that, Master Nightmare?"

"Goddess, I'm human but not stupid. Your curse was not all it could be, more inconvenience than mortally dangerous, nothing my skills could not overcome. And given the curse, I could not have found you had you not wished me to. Nor do I believe that you did not sense me playing and losing every night this week. You permitted it, perhaps tipped the scales just slightly out of balance. And my finding the window open was just too – lucky."

"And my plan was?"

"As you said, you could not move against Sol because of your obligation to him. So you set things up so that this" – he indicated the dead bodies on the floor – "would happen. You used me."

Tyche shrugged. "What of it? We gods have been using mortals for millennia. Your curse has been lifted. You may go."

"I am not so easily dismissed. I saved you. Or rather, by killing Sol I freed you. I now claim what was his, your obligation to him. You owe me."

The look on Tyche's face told the Nightmare that he had guessed right. Her nod confirmed it.

"I acknowledge the debt. What do you want?"

The Nightmare thought about this wide open offer. What did he want? Eternal good luck? No fun in that and it would only mean that his future bad luck would fall upon others. He looked at Tyche. She was one of the most beautiful women he had ever seen. But that would make him no better than Boyle and Sol. And he had briefly seen behind her human mask. Money? He had more than enough.

But these were just fancies. He had already decided what his demands would be.

"What I want is what I first offered Boyle and Sol. You leave this city, leave with almost nothing, with just enough to get started somewhere else. The rest of the money goes to the Police Widows and Orphans Fund."

"Is that all, Master Nightmare? Nothing for yourself?"

"I may take some of the money to cover recent gambling losses, but… no, wait, there is one other thing."

"And that is?"

"Should anyone approach you and say that the Nightmare sent them you will help them if you can do so without upsetting the balance."

"That I can and will do."

"Then we are quits, Lady Tyche. You should leave now. I'll contact the police about this mess. I would wish you good luck but that would be pointless. So I'll just say safe travels."

"Thank you, Master Nightmare, and may you be a little luckier than you were before we met. By the way, have you any suggestions as to where I might go?'

The Nightmare smiled. "There's a city in Nevada called Las Vegas. It sounds perfect for you and you for it."

The Fabulous Egg

The home of Parker Avery was filled with the stuff of myth and legend. Or so he claimed. It was Avery's boast that in his sixty years of travel and adventure he had amassed wonders the likes of which had only been dreamt about or told in stories, fables and ballads. Excalibur, a dragon's egg, the lamp of the genie, Hippolyta's girdle, the chain that had bound the Fenris Wolf, a flying carpet, Joseph's coat, a Valkyrie's spear and a battered cup that might be the Holy Grail – all of these and more were said to be in Avery's possession.

No believed him, of course. But that didn't stop the cream of New York's society from turning out when Avery announced that he would be displaying his wonders for their delight and amusement at a party to be given on the first Saturday of the new year.

Among those attending the fete was Michael Shaw. Outwardly Shaw was part of the city's idle rich, one of those who had, by good fortune or cunning design, escaped the Crash of '29. It was commonly believed that he spent his days in leisure and his evenings in bars and fancy nightspots, dressed in a tuxedo with a drink in one hand and a beautiful girl in the other. This was not strictly true. While Shaw admitted to sleeping late whenever possible and was more than wealthy enough to enjoy whatever creature comforts could be had, at night he was more often clad in dark clothing, his hands holding blazing .45s which he used against gangsters, mobsmen and other denizens of Gotham's underworld. For Michael Shaw was one of the city's unofficial protectors, a shadowy vigilante called the Nightmare.

This evening, however, Shaw was off duty. He had left his black trenchcoat, mask and gloves at home along with his well used .45 semi-automatic pistols. There would be no crime fighting for him this night, for Shaw wanted to see what treasures his friend Avery had collected and join the rest of the city's elite in trying to guess which, if any, might be the real thing and wonder if Avery truly believed they were all genuine or if he was having a good laugh at their expense.

Also present was police lieutenant Jerome Easton, the current hero of the city for having recently brought to justice Wolf Hopkins, the former crime boss of the city's Eastside. Easton had done it the hard way, collecting evidence sufficient not only to arrest Hopkins but to convict him in a court of law. There was talk of promotion and some of

New York's dailies openly wondered why, with men like Easton on the force, the police department continued to depend on cloaked and masked avengers to insure that justice was properly meted out.

Easton could have told them. He could have revealed that for every two or three good cops there was at least one crooked one, that the great experiment of Prohibition had made more criminals than it had saved souls and that it were it not for brave men and women like the Nightmare and the Pink Reaper, who nightly risked their lives with no thought of reward or even thanks, the gangs would have long since divided the city into their own separate fiefdoms and bled its citizens dry.

He could have also told them the true story of how Wolf Hopkins was brought to justice, but that would have broken a promise he had made to a certain masked man.

Like Michael Shaw, Easton was at Avery's party because of the mythic treasures. But while Shaw was there to stare and wonder, Easton was attending in his official capacity. In those days of unemployment and long bread lines, the rich and influential required protection from the underclasses and for a man like Parker Avery, no one but the city's most celebrated cop would do.

Easton had brought with him a team of ten officers. These he stationed outside the Avery mansion. Inside, security was handled by a private firm paid for by Avery and vetted by Easton. No one would be admitted without a numbered invitation. The wait staff had been hired from a very reputable service and they had all been searched before the evening's activities had begun. It was, Easton thought, the best protected gathering the city had seen in a long time.

Still he was worried. He was a cop, it was his job to worry, to assess a situation and wonder how things might go wrong. Again and again he reviewed the security layout – were the windows secure, should he shift men from the second floor ballroom to better protect the first floor, could twenty men with revolvers and pistols hold off determined gangsters armed with shotguns and Tommys? Could every one of those twenty men be trusted? And what was Michael Shaw doing there?

Casually, Easton walked up to the man he suspected of being the Nightmare. "Mr. Shaw, I'm surprised to see you here?"

Shaw smiled. He knew of the lieutenant's suspicions, and knew that the lieutenant knew. It was part of the grand game of good guys and bad that they both played.

"Where else would I be, Lieutenant, on a night where the wonders of the world are on display?"

"Nowhere else, Mr. Shaw. It's the why that has me worried."

"Ease your mind, Lieutenant. While I will allow that these types of gatherings tend to attract an unsavory sort that care only for the monetary value of the items on display, were I the man you think I am, I would be outside making sure that none of that crowd came close to testing the excellent security measures you have in place. Rest assured, my purpose this evening is to gawk and guess along with everyone else."

"So you don't expect any trouble?"

"I didn't say that. Despite being some distance from the city proper, this is still New York, and that means one should always expect trouble. But I'm sure your security is more than adequate. So let's get ourselves some drinks and view the exhibits. You can use your trained policeman's eye to tell me which are genuine and which are fakes."

Easton was on duty and took only plain soda to Shaw's whiskey and water.

"So what do you think, Lieutenant?" Shaw asked as they passed the battered cup. "Fancy taking a drink from that?"

"Real or not, it would seem somewhat sacrilegious. Maybe a flight on that carpet. What about you, Joseph's coat looks like it might fit you, or is it too bright for your tastes?"

"You know I prefer darker clothing, Lieutenant. Besides, that coat looks more like it came from the garment district than the holy land, just as that egg looks too small to have been laid by a dragon, or even an ostrich."

Easton looked the egg over. It was mostly white, with faded streaks of yellow, red and orange running through it. "It looks something like an old Easter egg."

"Which makes me suspect that it is one of the few genuine articles in this room, and that includes most of the Avery's guests."

"You might be right, Mr. Shaw," Easton agreed as they passed by the egg to view a so-called magic lamp and a piece of driftwood said to be from Noah's Ark. They then turned toward the center of the room where, in a place of honor, stood a large rock with a sword sticking out from it.

"Will you be trying your luck later tonight, Mr. Shaw?"

"I think not, Lieutenant. With my luck, I'd draw out the sword and what would I do with all of Britain to command?"

The two men parted company, Shaw to play his role as the bored millionaire out for any kind of diversion and Easton to continue his duties, checking on inside security both upstairs and down and then on the outside. As made his way around the mansion, he could not help but stare into the night and wonder who might be lurking in the darkness.

Against all expectations the evening proved uneventful. No one got too drunk, and no woman's virtue was threatened unless she specifically asked it to be. There were no fights or even loud disagreements and the one person who got sick had to decency to do in an upstairs bathroom. It was, despite the treasures on display, one of the most boring parties Shaw had ever attended.

Then came the grand finale. Several times the lights of the ballroom flickered on and off, a signal for all to be quiet. Then Parker Avery's voice was heard.

"I want to thank all of you for coming tonight. I hope you enjoyed the mementos of my travels. Now I know some of you, hell, I know that all of you are wondering which if any of them are truly what they seem to be. A good question, one I used to ask myself. Then I realized that it doesn't matter. They are as real as we want them to be, just like the myths and legends from whence they came. Seeking proof only robs us of our dreams and in the end, dreams are sometimes all we have."

Avery paused, "But you did not come here for a philosophy lesson. So let's get down to the final portion of tonight's activities – which of you, if any, is worthy of claiming the throne of England. Step up and try to draw the sword from the stone. Should anyone succeed, they shall be deemed the rightful king of Britain."

Except for a few people at the bar, and two or three couples who had found private corners in which to be alone, all eyes were the on the stone. Even Easton's, Shaw realized. "A perfect distraction," he thought.

The Nightmare stared from Michael Shaw's eyes, watching not the crowd but the treasures the crowd was now ignoring. As so it was that only he saw the slim young man in waiter's livery creep slowly along the wall, passing the cup, passing the coat, passing all the treasures save one.

Moving as stealthily as the young man, the Nightmare approached Easton without attracting any notice. It was, however, Shaw's voice that spoke.

"It seems, Lieutenant, that we are not the only ones who think the dragon's egg might be genuine." He pointed to the waiter, who by now had seized the egg and was running toward the nearest exit.

Easton's cry of "Stop" did nothing to slow the young waiter. It did, however, bring two security guards into the room through the door towards which the thief was running. The young man quickly changed direction and headed for a pair of French doors that led to an outside porch.

Easton drew his revolver.

"Lieutenant, don't, he's only a boy," Avery protested. "Besides, it's a steep drop out there. He won't have a chance."

"He doesn't have a chance now," Easton replied as a third security man stepped in off the porch.

"Give it up, son," Easton advised and moved forward, as did his men. "It's only a fake egg, not worth dying for."

Trapped in the middle of a shrinking triangle, the waiter paused and shrugged as if in surrender. Then he threw the egg at the man by the French doors who instinctively raised his hands to catch it. With the guard thus distracted, the thief ran past him, through the doors and off the balcony.

Men gasped, women screamed. Brushing past the guard holding the egg, Easton hurried to the edge of the porch. Looking down, he could see nothing in the darkness.

"Somebody get down there," he shouted to no one in particular. "I want to know if we need to call an ambulance or the coroner."

Just then two men of the outside security detail appeared below with electric torches. With the body of the thief illuminated, one bent down, felt the fallen man's neck. Looking up at Easton, he shook his head.

"The coroner, then," Easton said more to himself than anyone else as he walked back inside. To the guard still holding the egg he snapped, "Give that to Avery. And don't drop it, it cost a man his life."

"There was nothing you could have done, Lieutenant," Michael Shaw said coming up next to Easton.

"I could have been doing my job instead of watching the show. Thanks for catching it, although ..." The detective glanced at the still open French doors, "... part of me wishes you hadn't. That young man, dying for a fake egg."

"You gave him every chance, Lieutenant, he made the choice."

Shouts from below drew both men's attention. Together they rushed to the edge of the balcony. Looking down, they saw that something was happening to the body of the thief.

It was moving, just a bit, as if there was something inside trying to get out. Shimmers of heat, quite visible in the cold January air, began to radiate from it. Easton was shouting "What the hell did you do?" at the guards whose gestures indicated that they were innocent of doing anything.

Smoke began pouring from any open orifice – mouth, ears, eyes, nose, a head wound and from beneath the body. "Get away," called Shaw from the balcony. The men obeyed just as the dead man burst into flames caused by the fire that had come from within him.

"I think, Lieutenant, you might want to call the Fire Department before notifying the coroner."

Glaring at Shaw as if the whole thing was his fault, Easton muttered, "Let's get down there." To the security guards he said, "Make sure nothing else goes wrong," and to Avery, "Sorry about all this."

"Nonsense," the party's host replied, "the dragon's egg has been returned, my guests are safe and they've all had a bit of excitement with no harm done. Good job, Lieutenant."

Muttering a "Thanks" he didn't feel he had earned, Easton excused himself to view the probably still burning body, thinking that the rich had a strange idea of what constituted "No harm done."

Outside in the night, Skeets Terrell waited in the darkness with his men. Skeets was a low level gang leader looking to move up now that Wolf Hopkins was in stir. To do this he needed two things – funds and a rep. He had figured on getting both by knocking over the Avery house. The treasure itself would get him the much needed cash, either hocked or sold back to Avery. And robbing the joint under the nose of the cop who put Hopkins away would take case of his second need. Skeets would be a big man and all the top guns would want to be part of his crew.

Skeets was playing it smart. His men were in place, ready to storm the mansion at his signal. However, this signal wouldn't come until the gala wound down and the guests went home. That's when security would start relaxing. All was safe, they'd be thinking. No problems, no worries, an easy night that was almost over. They'd be relaxed, tired and not ready for armed men who'd come in shooting. Maybe that cop Easton would catch a bullet or two. That would be the cake's icing.

Such was Skeet's plan. But his plan didn't factor in the possibility that a young waiter whose theft of an egg had been thwarted would jump to his death from a second floor balcony or that his body would spontaneously combust.

"Jeez, you see dat, Boss?"

"Yeah, I saw it, Polecat. Tell the boys it's off for tonight."

"To much heat, eh Boss?"

Skeets ignored the joke. Something about the way that the body had burst into flames intrigued Skeets. Watching from the darkness that hid him it took Polecat Johnny several tries to regain his attention.

"The boys got de word, Boss. What now?"

"Wait a while, Polecat. I want to see what happens. There'll be other parties, other loot. Maybe we'll just knock over a bank or three. But something tells me that maybe we won't have to."

He moved closer so as to hear what might be said.

But for the prompt action of the detectives standing by the body, the fire might have spread to the house and surrounding grounds. No sooner had the dead man started burning than one detective ran into the house and rallied the staff into forming a bucket brigade, quenching the fire before the Fire Department could be called. By the time Easton and Shaw had gotten to the body the fire was out and the waiter was a blackened husk.

"Something strange about this," muttered Shaw.

"About what, Mr. Shaw?"

"I've seen burnt bodies, before, Lieutenant. In the war. I'm sure you have as well. This one looks … different."

"How so?"

"It's less like burnt skin and more like a coating, some sort of shell, a chrysalis if you will," offered Shaw.

"What?"

"A chrysalis, Lieutenant, is …"

"I know I'm just a dumb cop, Mr. Shaw, but I'm not that dumb. I know what a chrysalis is. What do you think, moth or butterfly?"

"God only knows, Lieutenant. Just make sure to keep it under guard."

"New plan, Polecat," Skeets whispered in the dark after overhearing Shaw and Easton's conversation. "Tell the boys to gather near the morgue. We got a body to steal."

Two motorcycle cops escorted the morgue wagon back to the coroner's office, with another mounted officer following in the rear. It did little good. Skeets and his men were waiting for them. As the wagon backed into the loading dock, the Terrell Gang opened fire with shotguns and Thompsons.

The officer who had followed the wagon died first, cut in two by the spray from a chopper. The two remaining cops took refuge in front of the wagon, returning fire as best they could. One mobster fell, then another, but there were too many foemen. At Skeets's direction his men slowly encircled the besieged cops and then at his signal cut them to pieces with a withering crossfire.

As the battle raged, inside the morgue wagon cracks began to appear in the burnt skin of the body. The cracks spread and soon, like a chick escaping from its egg, a young boy emerged. Unaware of the massacre occurring just outside, the naked youth quickly grew into young manhood. Memory returned and he recalled his most recent death and his life – and the death and life before that one, and the one before that and all the times he had died and lived since that fateful day in a forest of Germany.

The flood of memory was too strong, the pain of living and the agony of dying time and again too much. As he did each time, the young man cried out against his rebirth and prayed that the gods would pity him and somehow make this his last.

The cops dead, the driver and morgue attendant slain in their seats, Skeets and his men had little time to waste. "Open the back," he ordered Polecat. "You others, get ready to grab that things and get it the hell out of here before the cops or one of the freaks in black get here."

"Boss," Polecat said seconds later, "you gotta see dis."

"Dis" was a naked young man lying amid large pieces of what had once been burnt flesh.

"What the hell are you?" Skeets asked.

Then came the sound of sirens in the background. There was no time for questions. "Take him," growled Skeets and he, his men and the formerly dead man fled the scene.

It was hours later. The bodies of the crooks, cops and morgue workers had been taken inside. "At least they didn't have far too go," quipped one rookie who thought he was being funny. The next day he would learn that no one else did, that dead cops are not a laughing matter and that he would have plenty of time to make up jokes on the midnight beat in Queens.

Hours later, Jerome Easton walked the now mostly empty crime scene. The police photographer was still taking his photos, the lamp flash from his bulky Speed Graphic briefly turning night into day. One detective was sketching a diagram while another was picking up shell casings for the police scientists to examine.

Easton looked back at the morgue wagon "An egg worth dying for," he said to himself. "A body worth killing for." The two were connected but how? Easton's thoughts turned back to Shaw.

"It was your idea to guard that thing. Why didn't you put on your outfit and follow it down? You could have stopped this mess; you could have saved these men."

Easton had not realized he had spoken aloud until a voice from the shadows replied.

"Even we can't be everywhere at once, Lieutenant."

Easton studied the darkness, trying and failing to pinpoint from where the voice had come. It was Shaw's voice – maybe. It was the Nightmare's voice definitely.

Shaw or not, the lieutenant had no time for recriminations. He had a body to find and cops to avenge. He'd take what help was offered.

"You know what's going on?"

"I know."

"Yeah, your kind always does."

"Have you identified the gunmen?"

Easton nodded. "Two low level hoods, used to work for Hopkins, now maybe working for some wannabe named Terrell, Skeets or Skates or something like that. Any ideas?"

"As to finding Skeets Terrell, I'll put the word out. As to your missing body, yes, I have an idea, one that I hope is wrong. But if it's not …" The voice of the Nightmare faded. "Leave word at Moran's when the fires start."

Moran's was a place where the first drink of your first visit was on the house and the ones after that well-poured and at a reasonable price. Moran was on the smallish side, all his family was. And if you glanced his way when he wasn't busy you'd swear he was in another world. In that you'd be right, but you'd never guess which one.

Just a neighborhood tavern on the Eastside of the city. Until it closed for the night that is.

It was just after Moran locked up for the evening when Jerome Easton knocked. There followed loud cursing and swearing in a tongue the lieutenant suspected to be Gaelic but was actually much older as the front door swung open. Looking down at the little man Easton said, "I'm expected."

"That you are, otherwise I wouldna let you in." The tavern owner pointed to a darkened booth in a corner. "He's over there. Don't disturb the others."

What others? Easton wondered. The bar was dark and seemed empty.

But as he walked to the indicated corner there were flashes of pink and scarlet, and some of the darkness seemed to move. There was laughter, both men's and women's.

"It's where we can be alone, Lieutenant," came the Nightmare's whispered voice from the booth. "Somewhere to relax between our days' activities and our night's endeavors."

"Don't worry, I can keep a secret."

Another laugh from across the room, one Easton was sure was directed at him, one that warned, "You'd better."

"Have a seat, Lieutenant, and a drink."

Easton took the place opposite the Nightmare. Despite being only a table away, he could barely make out the man's form. "I'm on duty, make it coffee."

"This is an Irish bar and it's a cold night, so why not make it an Irish coffee?"

"Who am I to argue with such reasoning?"

No sooner had he said this than Moran was there with the desired brew. From past experience Easton knew that his drink would be made from the finest beans, the sweetest cream and the smoothest whiskey and he'd never find the like of it any place else. He paused just a bit to let it cool, took a sip, then another and reflected that for that brief period of time life was good. Then it was to business.

"How did you know? About the fires?"

"How many have there been?"

"Four – a roadhouse, two speaks and a brewery. All were once owned by Hopkins, now they are, or were, in dispute."

"And what do your arson experts say started them?'

"They don't. They tell me there's no trace of flammables and that the fires burned too hot to have been caused by paper and matches."

"Witnesses?"

"You know these guys don't leave any. But a couple of people who were on the outside claim they heard gunshots just before the fires started."

"And the victims, any of them shot?"

Easton shook his head. "Burnt up or smoke strangled. This is leading somewhere. What do you know that I don't?"

"A young man dies, his body combusts and burns to a husk. Then his body is stolen, leaving behind his old skin. What do you know of myth and legend, Lieutenant?"

Easton thought of all he had experienced since meeting the Nightmare. "More than I care to. What is it this time?"

"A phoenix, a fabulous creature that dies in flame and is reborn in fire."

"I thought that was a bird."

"So did I, Lieutenant. Perhaps our missing waiter is akin to one. He was trying to steal an egg. Perhaps our new friend Skeets is using him, killing him again and again to start fires meant to intimidate or eliminate the completion."

Easton snorted, then said an impolite word or two. "More likely our waiter was part of his gang and the fire was some kind of explosive he had on him. Skeets snatched the body so we couldn't link things back to him."

"Perhaps," the Nightmare allowed as Easton took several more sips of his excellent brew and again experienced rare moments of peace and contentment before returning to this less than perfect world.

An honest cop who almost always paid his own way, Easton stood and threw some bills on the table. "If that's all you've got, Nightmare, I've a got a cop killer and a firebug to catch."

"And if I should find them first, Lieutenant?"

"Wrap them up and leave them on the precinct steps."

"Dead or alive?"

"Your choice. Dead means less paperwork for me."

There were nights when Michael Shaw did not don the black of the Nightmare, when he left behind the black coat, gloves and mask of his other self. On these nights Shaw dressed in old, shabby clothes and went to dingy bars and after-hours blind pigs. There he would find a table against a wall, sit and drink and let the conversation flow around him. By doing this he learned much of what was happening in the underworld – who was hiring gunmen, who was planning what heist, who had supposedly killed whom. In this manner the Nightmare could learn of crimes that had yet to happen and plan vengeance for those not yet come to light.

This was not one of those nights. There had been four fires in three weeks. Two of these had spread to adjacent buildings not involved in crime. There had been significant property damage and some loss of life. The Nightmare could not afford to wait for word of planned arson to reach him.

Instead, in the privacy of his room, Michael Shaw put on the darkness of his trade – black suit and trenchcoat, black mask and gloves, a brace of death dealing .45s. Taking a non-descript yet powerful coupe into the city, the Nightmare went out looking for information.

He was not gentle. Outside of the dives frequented by gangsters and mobsmen the Nightmare lurked in the shadows, waiting for a man alone.

Rusty Davis was one of these men. Rusty had just returned to the city after pulling some out of state jobs. He was flush and willing to spread his luck around. He was also looking to join with a local mob so as to keep the green flowing in. He was leaving The Junction where he had picked up a couple of tips, gotten some good leads and had been warned off a place or two. He was in a good mood when he left the bar.

That was when the man in black grabbed him.

Thrown hard against a wall, Rusty heard a whispered voice, "Skeets Terrell, where is he?"

Rusty's first reply, "Who?" got him thrown again into brickwork and his second, "I don't know," caused him to be propelled face first into a rotting pile of waste and garbage. When he was dragged out by his feet and roughly turned over he found that he was under a sputtering light. Looking up all he saw was a large dark figure holding an even larger gun. That's when he knew he was in the grip of one of Them – the terrors of the night that warred on crime, who showed little mercy and took few prisoners.

Again came the question. "Skeets Terrell, where is he and what is he planning?"

In that instant, Rusty Davis's whole world contracted to the black hole in the barrel of the big gun that was pointing right at him.

Rusty Davis was no coward. He had traded shots with the cops of three states and once had battled the G's. Several times he had stood up against the third degree and taken beatings without turning rat. But that night, alone in an alley with a being he could barely see, Rusty felt his bowels loosen and his bladder let go. Lying in his own waste, seconds away from being shot to death, he searched his mind for something to tell this terrible specter.

He had nothing. Then, as he readied himself for the laugh, the bullet and the end, he remembered – something. When Rusty had asked for a reliable knock shop One-Thumb Louie had told him, "Stay clear of the one on the docks tonight. Word from the Polecat is that something's going down, something hot."

"The docks!" Rusty shouted to save his life. "The whorehouse down at the docks!" He hoped it would be enough.

A minute passed, then another. "He's gone," Rusty thought but then Rusty heard low, mocking laughter from the mouth of the alley.

"Rusty Davis," came the sepulchral whisper, "because I wish it you are alive. Leave this city tonight if you want to remain so."

Bruised and battered, lying in garbage and his own waste, Rusty decided to do exactly that. He wondered if the boys in Chicago needed another gunman.

"Finally," Michael Shaw said to himself as he briefly put aside the Nightmare for the drive to the docks. "It took four hoods but I got want I wanted – I hope." Shaw knew that Davis's information was reliable; the man was too scared to tell anything but the truth, but was it what he needed? Shaw knew the place to which Davis had referred, a house of ill repute not so cleverly called the Wharehouse. It was at the far end of the docks in what once had been offices and a ship's chandlers. The two-story building had been converted into a bar downstairs and small cubicles upstairs for the girls to ply their trade. It did a good business with arriving and departing sailors as well as those in the city who craved paid gratification in a clean place at a reasonable price. It was, Shaw thought, ripe for a takeover attempt and according to Davis, something was going to happen there that night. The Nightmare planned to be there.

In her office, Katrina Royce, the owner and "manager" of The Wharehouse, laughed in Skeets Terrell's face. "Twenty percent? You must be off your nut. Why should I pay you anything?"

Skeets shrugged. "To stay open. To stay healthy." He turned to the two men he had brought with him. "Right, boys?"

Grinning, Polecat Johnny nodded his agreement. The other, a pale young man who used to be a waiter, just grew paler. He knew what was coming, wanted to shout a warning. He had tried that the last time. It had only brought the end that much quicker.

He thought of running, of braving Skeets's and Polecat's guns. Maybe this time he could make it out of the building before being gunned down, maybe he could escape the gunmen Skeets had posted on the outside. He had tried that before as well. And failed. And when he returned, Skeets had him killed again – slowly.

In a hell of his own making, the young man prayed that this woman would accept Skeets's offer. Instead he heard,

"Get lost. I'm connected."

"You were connected – with Wolf Hopkins. He's gone and so's your juice. Pay up or burn down."

Royce's face darkened. "So you're the one?" Skeets smile was all the answer Royce needed. "I can go ten."

"You'll go twenty like the others."

"Then you can go to Hell." Not trying to hide her action, Royce hit a button on her desk. "In a minute there'll be two bruisers in here to give you and your boys the bum's rush. And if you try coming back to torch my place you better bring an army, because that's what you'll be facing."

Skeets pulled a revolver from his pocket. "I don't need an army."

For an instant Royce thought he was going to plug her. Instead he calmly rose, turned toward the pale young man and shot him in the head. Leaving, he told Royce,

"You have about five minutes to get everyone out. And if you reopen, I'll want twenty-five percent."

Alone in her office with a dead man, Katrina Royce wondered what Skeets's game was. Call the cops, have her arrested for murder? He had to know that by the time John Law got there the body would be gone and the blood cleaned up. This wasn't the first dead man that had to be removed from the Wharehouse. It was, however, the first that spontaneously burst into flame.

The old wooden structure caught easily and quickly. So fast did the fire spread that Royce knew there was no chance of putting it out. Instead, she hit a button on her desk that sounded a general alarm. Meant to be used in the event of a police raid, it warned her employees, girls and customers to vacate the premises immediately.

"I'm gonna rebuild, you son of a bitch," said to herself as she fled down the stairs, "but not before I give you one hundred percent of a knife in your back."

Outside, Skeets and Polecat watched and waited for the fire to claim the building. "How we doing, Johnny?"

"Five fires, seven paying off, Skeets."

"Not enough, we need to send a bigger message."

Skeets looked at the Wharehouse. Flames were spreading; people were fleeing the burning building.

"Tell the boys, no one leaves the place alive."

"What about the cops and the fire department?"

"By the time they get here it'll be all over."

The Nightmare had arrived too late to prevent the fire. Pulling up in his coupe, he saw that the second floor was already ablaze and that people were evacuating the building in an orderly fashion. With the Wharehouse on a concrete piling, there was no danger to the rest of the dock area. Things would be stay safe until the Fire Department arrived. He could concentrate on looking for Skeets and the rest.

As he got closer, the Nightmare noticed a ring of gunmen all facing the building. In their hands were choppers, shotguns and automatics. Sure of their intent, he knew that whatever the risk to himself, he could not allow them to open fire on the growing crowd.

Stepping from the shadows, the Nightmare announced himself with challenging laughter. Mobsters turned and saw the menacing form with his guns drawn and offering battle. They knew not what dark avenger faced them but they knew what had to be done. As a man they abandoned their given task of slaughter and decreed death to the Nightmare.

The night-clad crusader struck first, firing shots into the foemen closest to him. As they fell, he faded into the shadows from whence he came. Gunfire followed him but none of the deadly missiles found their mark. Instead, the flashes from the weapons that had discharged them gave the Nightmare new targets.

Even with more of his opponents down, it was still too many against one. Soon the Nightmare would have to choose between fighting on and possibly falling or retreating and letting the remaining mobsmen turn their fire on to the crowd from the Wharehouse.

Help came from an unexpected source.

Not all the patrons of the Wharehouse were sailors on leave or gentlemen from the city out of a bit of the strange. Some were members of the same under-culture to which belonged Skeets and his crew. Additionally there those on which Royce had relied for security.

All these men were armed. It was not in them to go anywhere without a weapon. And when they heard gunfire and found themselves surrounded by armed hoodlums, they did that which their nature demanded. They drew and fired on those they perceived as their enemies.

Skeets Terrell had ordered a slaughter. And a slaughter he received. But it was his own men who were cut down from two directions. Soon only he and Polecat were left standing.

Having hung back from the crew, the mob boss and his lieutenant were in a place of relative safety. Or so they thought.

"Boss, we should go," were Polecat's last words before a shot rang out and he fell at Skeets's feet, moaning and clutching a shattered kneecap. Skeets would have abandoned his henchman but for a dark shape that stepped out of the night and blocked his way.

"Which one are you?" he asked the masked man.

"Does it matter?"

"I like to know who I'm killing."

Both men were armed, guns at the ready. Skeets was fast but the Nightmare faster. His first shot crippled the gangster's shooting hand, the second and third dropped him along side Polecat. Still game, Skeets's left hand reached out for his fallen pistol. The Nightmare's fourth shot ruined his elbow.

It was the end. Skeets knew this. Still, he had no intention of going out yellow. With a resigned smile on his face, he said, "I'd also like to know who's gonna give me the works."

"I am the Nightmare, but it is not your time to die. You will live to stand trial for murder and it will be the State who will avenge the deaths of the police you killed."

The smile faded from Skeets's face. Going out in a gun battle was one thing. The hot seat was another. "Kill me now," he begged.

Mocking laughter was his only answer. Soon there came the sounds of sirens.

Back in the shadows, the Nightmare waited. Waited as the police, fire and ambulances arrived. Waited as the wounded were treated and the dead counted. Waited as the decision was made not to enter the smoldering husk that had been the Wharehouse, to leave it to a wrecking crew to tear it down and haul out any corpses that still remained. And when all the onlookers and reporters had been cleared away and the last of the official responders had gone, the Nightmare still waited.

It was by then daylight, a time when the colors of the night no longer hid him. So it was Michael Shaw who saw the naked boy emerge from the rubble. With every step the youth seemed to age and by the time he got to where a lone man holding a black coat was waiting, he was once again a young man in his twenties.

"Those others," the still dazed young man asked as he took Shaw's coat to cover his body, "the one called Skeets and the rest, are they …"

"Dead or gone," Shaw replied.

"Thank God." But for Shaw's support the young man would have collapsed. "Who are you?"

"A friend. I think we need to talk."

Shaw took the young man back to his estate just outside the city. Once dressed, fed and rested, he told his story.

"My name is Ira Knox and I am 237 years old. Immortality is not the boon you would think it is. I grow old and die, or I die by accident, or I am killed. Dying hurts, more than anyone can imagine. There is a brief moment, just before the blackness, when the soul leaves the body. You feel it as it rips away from the flesh. For me, each time is worse than the last, and I have died many times. Every time I return, I pray that it will be for the last time. So far, God has not answered my prayers.

"I have lived the life of a saint, hoping that by doing so I would be judged worthy of Heaven and spared from returning. For the same reason I have committed unspeakable evils so as to be condemned to the Pit. As you can see …" Opening his arms, Know indicated himself then shrugged in eternal frustration.

"How did you come to this state," Shaw asked, handing Knox a glass of wine, "or is fiery rebirth your nature."

Know shook his head. "I was born human, in what is now Germany, as I said, a long time ago. As a youth, my grandfather would tell me tales of the lands around us. One was of the Firebird, who dies and is reborn in its own flame. He claimed that it lived on a mountain not far from our home. At times I would stare at this mountain, wondering if such a tale could be true. Then one night a bright light appeared on the mountain side. Being relatively young and mostly foolish, I resolved to discover the truth of the legend. The nest day I climbed the mountain."

"And found the phoenix?"

Knox laughed. "Oh no, Mr. Shaw, nothing as simple as that. I found burnt trees and scorched earth, and the remains of what might have been eggshell. For the simple young man I was, it was enough to confirm my grandfather's story, yet not enough for me. I began to haunt the woods of the mountain, searching for the firebird, hoping for, well, wonder I guess. From time to time I'd catch a glimpse of – something. Something that flew by too fast to spy clearly, something yellow, orange and red, the colors of the flame.

"I stopped haunting the woods and began living there – my camp, my home, close to where I had found the eggshell and the burning. From what my grandfather said, I knew the fire on the mountain appeared every year or two, so if I waited long enough …"

"Obviously you did."

"Would that I hadn't, Mr. Shaw. Would that I had given up, or gone mad, or had been killed by a wild beast. But no. One night I was awakened from sleep by a loud cry. Looking out from my tent I saw what was and still is the most beautiful sight ever. The size of an eagle, the bird was resplendent in gold, orange and red. It was as if her feathers were already aflame. As I watched, she gave out another cry, then stepped away, leaving behind an egg. A third cry, this one seeming to be one of triumph, of a job well done.

"Her feathers grew bright, then brighter still, then glowed until they burst into flame. To me it was clear what was happening. As she burned, the heat of her immolation would warm the egg until it hatched. Then her chick would hatch, or maybe she would be reborn, one soul passed on through many bodies.

"I had found the wonder I had sought, yet it was not enough. Yearning to be part of this great miracle, I rushed forward to bathe in the heat of the flame. I reached her just as she died."

As the man paused to drain his glass, Shaw asked, "What happened then?"

Knox gave a rueful sigh. "I caught fire. Death by fire, Mr. Shaw, is an agonizing way to die. You feel each layer of skin as it is burnt from you, your nerve endings constantly sending out signals of pain. I did not pass out but instead remained conscious until I felt that tug that I later learned was my soul leaving my now charred flesh.

"I awoke in my village. Others had seen the flames and came to investigate. They found me, naked and asleep, and brought me home. Since then, I have not remained dead."

"What happened to the egg?"

"I do not know. I went back but found nothing that looked like eggshells. Perhaps one of my rescuers took it.

"Somehow. Mr. Shaw, I stole the fire, the life force of the firebird, that which returns me from death and without which the egg cannot hatch."

"And when you heard that Avery's collection …"

"The funny thing is, Mr. Shaw, is that I did not hear of Avery's collection. It was simply a job. Finding the egg, finding that egg, the one I last saw on the mountain before I died the first time, was simply chance."

"Or maybe Fate."

"Could be," Knox allowed. "When I saw it … well, you were there."

"You waited for your chance and tried to steal the egg."

"And died yet again, and woke up in a Hell on Earth. Until you saved me. What was that you called yourself?"

"The Nightmare, but not by choice. Had you succeeded in stealing the egg, what would you have done with it?"

Knox thought for a moment. "I … don't know." Then, hopefully, "Any ideas."

"Just one. But first we have to have that egg."

As Shaw, the Nightmare had been in Parker Avery's home many times. He knew all the ways in and out, knew which windows were likely to be locked and was familiar with the mansion's security. He knew that, when not on display, Avery's treasures were stored in his basement, which the adventurous millionaire had converted into a vault more secure than most of the city's banks.

Standing in the shadows of the Avery estate, watching the house from a spot not too far from where the now jailed Skeets Terrell had first seen Ira Know burn, the Nightmare considered his approach.

There were, he knew, eight ways of getting into the house without tripping an alarm or alerting the staff. Once inside, there were three possible routes to the basement. Equipped as he was with the latest in burglary and safe-cracking tools, he had two ways of opening the safe, four if he wanted to make lots of noise and wake up the neighbors.

He could be in and out of the house with the egg inside of three hours – if all went well. If not, well, that's what made what he did fun. The risk, the danger, the consequences of getting caught – it was a challenge and one which the Nightmare was tempted to take. And yet –

In his crusade against crime the Nightmare had crept into thieves' dens and gangster lairs. He had snuck into mob hideouts and come out again with no one the wiser. He had once sprung an innocent man from the Tombs and had rescued a condemned man from death row just an hour before his execution. He had even navigated the treacherous underground maze that protected the Assassins' Guild and penetrated its Inner Sanctum.

Why then did he now hesitate? This was a house, not a guarded fortress. Those inside were average citizens, not crazed gunmen. There was no reason for the Nightmare not to burgle the house and steal the phoenix egg.

Except that it wasn't right.

As far as the Nightmare knew, the egg was the legal property of Parker Avery. There were no lives on the line, no one inside was breaking the law and no crime would be prevented by his taking the egg.

The only crime would be his.

The Nightmare had beaten men for information and killed them when it was necessary – all for the cause of justice. Taking the egg would not be justice, it would simply be aiding one man at the expense of another.

Funny how thin are the lines which we will not cross, the Nightmare thought, then as he decided there was only one thing to do he laughed out loud at himself. When he was finished, he slowly made his was toward the house.

Parker Avery was asleep, dreaming of beautiful women in very little clothing when laughter intruded upon his slumber. At first he thought his dream girls were laughing at him, but he hadn't had that dream since his teenaged years. Besides, they weren't pointing. That's when he woke up.

And found a creature in black standing at his bedside.

"Parker Avery," the being said in a scary, whispered voice, "I am the Nightmare."

In his travels and adventures, Avery had faced wild beasts and savage hordes. He had survived three firing squads and twice had been tied to sacrificial altars. He had led two revolutions and had prevented a third. He had seen the undead walk and had watched a yeti melt. He should not have been scared by this man in black.

At least, that's what he told himself as he just barely kept from soiling his sheets.

"Wha … what do you want?"

"I need something from you."

His initial shock over. Avery was beginning to awake. He had heard of this Nightmare, he was one of those weird crime fighters about which the tabloids always wrote. So it was in a much calmer voice that he asked, "What do you need?"

"That which you call a dragon's egg, that which a young man tried to steal not too long ago."

"And you need it to stop a crime or save a life?"

"There is no crime and no life will be saved, but it just may be that a soul will find peace."

Avery was not one to hesitate. "It's yours. Just let me get dressed and I'll take you to the vault."

"No need." From inside his coat the Nightmare produced the phoenix egg.

"If you already … why the hell did you wake me up?"

"Because it was the right thing to do."

The Nightmare was gone before Avery could reply.

"What happened here?"

Once the Nightmare had obtained the egg, Shaw drove Knox to property he owned upstate, where Shaw had once had a cabin. They arrived just before dawn. It was the ruins of the cabin that prompted Knox's question.

"I had to blow up a dead man."

"Did he stay dead?"

Shaw thought of a head buried in a dry well some distance away.

"I hope so. Are you ready?"

"Let's get this done."

With his back to the remains of the cabin and the phoenix egg at his feet, Knox took his stance on a concrete pad once used for parking. Standing close enough so that he would not miss, Shaw drew one of the Nightmare's .45s and took deadly aim.

"I don't know if this will work," Shaw said, "but if it does – are you prepared to face the Judgment from which there is no appeal?"

"I am."

"Then may God have mercy on your soul."

Michael Shaw fired. His aim was true and a bullet pierced Ira Knox's heart. The not so young man fell and for a time just laid there, not moving. Then, as it had so many times before, his body began to radiate heat and smoke poured from the openings of his corpse. Soon the fire inside the body caused it to burst into flames.

And as the body of Ira Knox burned, the heat from the conflagration warmed the egg that lay nearby. Small cracks appeared then larger ones. The fire grew hotter, the flames grew larger. Shaw, who had been approaching, was forced back by the heat.

He watched in wonder as both the body and the egg were engulfed. Soon there was nothing to see but a burning whose brightness rivaled the rising sun.

But that which burns brightly does not burn long. Soon the flames began to abate. And when they went out …

There was nothing of Ira Knox but ashes.

There was nothing of the egg but shells.

What there was was a young child, a girl come naked into the world. To Shaw she seemed just five or six. Her eyes were filled with the innocence and wonder of youth and her hair was a mixture of red and yellow, the colors of the flame.

She grew before his eyes – from five or six to eight and nine. When she passed from twelve into thirteen Shaw averted his eyes for the time it would take her to grow past adolescence. When he looked again, she was a beautiful young woman, still clad only in innocence and wonder.

"You are … Shaw?" Her voice was sweet and lyrical, almost a song. He could only nod. "And you are … Nightmare."

This time Shaw managed a weak "yes" then "And you are ..."

"I am myself. I have always been myself and always will be."

Was there an undertone of regret in the melody of her reply. Shaw didn't stop to wonder but asked, "What of Ira Knox?'

A scowl ruined the innocence of her face. "The fire thief is gone, but his .. humanity remains, and some of his memories. Which is how I know of you."

She paused and spreading her arms like wings, looked at her body. "I might learn to like this … humanity." Looking at Shaw. "You must teach me, show me, Shaw Who Is Nightmare. But some time other than now."

Her body became the color of flame. Feathers red, gold and orange grew, arms became wings and the phoenix appeared where the woman had been. Turning toward Shaw, she nodded, then launched herself into the sky, giving out a cry like the closing chorus of a song.

And as the Phoenix flew into the sun, it was Michael Shaw and not the Nightmare whose joyous laughter provided the coda.

CHOICE OF THE PHOENIX

He found her in an alley; clothes torn, no obvious violation, throat slit ear to ear, her left thumb missing. She was another victim of the killer the papers had started calling "The Midnight Slasher."

Not terribly original, thought the man who had found her, *and not quite accurate either*. The crimes usually occurred several hours after midnight, just as dawn was chasing away the darkness so that a new day could start. But it was, he supposed, a good way to sell papers. He made a note to ask Britt the next time he saw him.

I should call the police, let them know. But not quite yet.

Turning from his inspection of the body, the man looked around the alley, searching for anything that might lead to the killer's identity. As before, there was nothing. He shook his head.

Six victims, two men and four women with nothing to link them except that they were unlucky enough to be alone when their killer found them. That and their missing thumbs. The papers didn't know about the thumbs. The cops were holding on to that fact.

But the man knew. He knew because Lieutenant Jerome Easton of the Homicide Squad had told him. Easton had told him because the detective needed help in finding the killer, help outside his own police department. He needed the help of the Nightmare, a vigilante in black who stalked the streets hunting monsters both human and otherwise.

In truth, the police lieutenant had not said a word to the man in black. He had, instead, driven out to the manor house of Michael Shaw, reputed to be one of the city's wealthiest – and laziest – citizens. Easton correctly suspected that Shaw was also the Nightmare, although he had never taken any steps to prove that fact.

On his arrival, Easton was led into a solarium where a table had been set for three. The lieutenant had just enough time to note this fact when Shaw entered.

"Lieutenant," he said, grabbing Easton's hand and shaking it vigorously, "good to see you again. I got your message last night that you'd be stopping by. Can you join us for breakfast?"

"Breakfast?" Easton asked himself, it was just past noon. "Us?" Shaw no doubt knew why he had come and had invited one of his "associates."

Which would it be, he wondered. The girl in pink or the woman in black. He hoped for the one in pink; the one in black scared him.

It was neither. As if on cue a woman Easton had never seen before walked into the solarium. No, walked was not the right word for how she moved. Glided maybe, as if her feet were just touching the ground, or maybe hovering just slightly above it as if gravity was a concept with which she was familiar but did not accept. She was young, bright and beautiful, with hair that was yellow and red and all the shades between.

Again Easton's hand was shaken but with a touch lighter than Shaw's. Her voice, as she greeted him with "Lieutenant, how nice to meet you. Michael has told me much about you," was as light as her touch and had an accent that was almost a song.

"I'm very pleased you meet you as well. And you are …"

"She is, Lieutenant," Shaw interrupted, "and that's good enough for me."

Easton thought he understood. *Oh to be rich and idle and without responsibilities.* Then he remembered that if his suspicions were true, Michael Shaw was neither idle nor irresponsible.

Once they were seated but before the food was served, Shaw asked, "Now, Lieutenant, how can I help you?" His manner of asking led Easton to believe that he already knew.

"You've been reading the papers?"

"In my spare time, and I have lots of that." Shaw glanced at the woman and after they shared a certain kind of smile, amended his statement. "Well, not as much I used to, but I have been reading about the Broadway Slasher."

"The Midnight Slasher," Easton corrected. "I wish to hell it was the *Broadway* Slasher, then the Commissioner would put a whole squad on it instead of just me, and certain other people would get involved as well."

Shaw turned to his companion. "The lieutenant is referring to the ones in black I've told you about." Then to the detective, "I suppose they're busy, protecting the treasures of the rich from criminal gangs and supercrooks or else keeping the city safe from devil bats and maniacs bent on mass destruction."

"There is one other."

"I'm sure there are several others, Lieutenant, and that at least one of them is interested. But here comes breakfast. Let's eat while we talk. There's nothing like gruesome tales of murder to give one an appetite. Now then, about this Slasher, what aren't you telling the papers?"

As Easton spoke of things a civilian should not be told, he could not help but notice that while his plate and Shaw's had on them potatoes, bacon and toast, the woman's meal appeared to be raw meat. *Well*, he thought, *maybe she's European.*

After breakfast, as Easton was getting ready to leave, Shaw said, "You never told me why you drove all the way out here, Lieutenant."

"I had other business in the area and thought I'd drop in. For some reason I always feel better after talking to you. Well, good day, Mr. Shaw. You too, Miss."

Alone in the solarium with Shaw, the woman said, "Even with what little I know about your kind, that seemed odd. This … policeman, drove all the way out here just to 'drop in?"

Shaw shook his head. "It's a game we play. Easton knows I'm the Nightmare but if he acknowledges it then he has to take official action against me. I am, after all, a crazed vigilante who has gunned down people in cold blood. Actually, most of the ones I've killed have had warm blood, except for one and I'm not sure he had any blood at all. But as I've said, he knows, and I know that he knows and so forth. This was his way of asking for my help."

"But you were already working on the murders."

"Yes, but now I know about the thumbs."

"What do they mean?"

Shaw shrugged. "I haven't the faintest idea. But at least I'll be able to tell this killer from all the others that are out there."

"Shaw Who Is Nightmare?'

"Yes, She Who Is?"

"You said that you would teach me about humanity. These killings, they are a part of it?'

"Unfortunately, yes."

"Then I want to help, so I can learn."

The Nightmare looked down at the murdered woman, a girl really, not quite out her teens. She seemed to have been dressed for a special night. If that was so, where were her companions? It was Shaw's experience that young women did not travel alone; instead they went out with a group of friends or a male escort. Had there been a fight? Had she and her date quarreled and she went off by herself, making herself easy prey? Had she been separated from her group, either accidently or otherwise? These were questions for the police once she was identified. The Nightmare needed facts – a blood trail, a scrap of paper leading to a person or place, someone fleeing the scene. There was none of that in the alley. Unless …

The Nightmare looked up, waved, confident that he could be seen from above. His wave was answered by what sounded like a single sustained musical note as something the colors of flame descended.

A bird, somewhat larger than an eagle, its plumage all the shades of red, yellow and orange lit on a fence near him. In the darkness of the alley it shown with light that suggested it was fueled by an inner fire.

"Did you see anything?" the Nightmare asked, "a man running away, someone hiding in the shadows?"

Letting out a cry of regret, the bird flew from the fence to land before the Nightmare, changing as it did. The bird grew larger and its feathers disappeared as it took human form. Within a space of a few minutes, the brightly colored bird had transformed into the woman the Nightmare addressed as "She Who Is."

"I saw nothing." Glancing at the victim, she added, "Her body is cool." Then, "This is death for your kind?"

"It is," he answered, trying to ignore the fact that she was naked. He was not entirely successful. "I have got to start wearing a cloak," he said, smiling at the sight before him.

"You do not need one."

"No, but you do." As he took off his black coat and wrapped it around her he realized that she was waiting for something.

"We do not return as do your kind."

"I have told you before; there is no 'my kind.' There is only me."

"It must be lonely."

"It was, but it is no longer." Reaching out, she caressed his cheek. "I must go, I must hunt."

The coat fell and that which seemed to be a woman transformed and flew off, a glowing meteor returning to the sky.

The Nightmare shed his gloves and mask and as Michael Shaw sought a phone so that he could tell Easton of the Slasher's latest victim.

Shaw spent his morning – late morning – in his library, studying a map showing the locations of the Slasher's attacks. He had left the doors to the balcony of an upstairs bedroom – one he had told his staff was *her* bedroom – open should she choose to return. She did not always do so, sometimes spending days away. Shaw had once asked her what she did during those times.

"I hunt, I fly, I sing," she replied as if there was nothing else in the world to do.

And for her there probably was not, Shaw thought. The Slasher was chased from his mind as he looked back on how she came to be in his life.

There was an egg, a fabulous egg in the possession of a rich collector. It was thought to be from a dragon but proved to be so much more. It was, instead, a phoenix egg – no, the phoenix egg, its magic stolen centuries ago by a young man who sought immortality but who instead found himself trapped in a hellish cycle of death after painful death. As the Nightmare, Shaw put an end to this cycle, ending the young man's existence and freeing the Phoenix to live again, albeit with her nature changed. The essence of the fire thief's humanity had remained, as did some of his memories, allowing the Phoenix to assume human form.

"I might learn to like this … humanity," she had said to him the night of her fiery resurrection. "You must teach me, show me, Shaw who is Nightmare, but some time other than now."

She then flew away, with Shaw having no idea when or if he would ever see her again.

Some weeks later, Shaw was in his bedroom preparing to go out as his other self when he heard a noise on the balcony. He knew it could not have been one of his dark clad associates. One only heard them when it was too late to matter, and then only if they wished it. It could have been a member of the underworld who had pierced his secret and had come to make a name for himself by gunning the Nightmare. A clumsy burglar or a would-be kidnapper were also possibilities. Whoever it was, Shaw decided, he had come to the wrong house. With automatic in hand, he opened the balcony door to find …

A bird somewhat larger than an eagle with plumage all the shades of red, yellow and orange perched on the balcony rail. As Shaw watched, she flew from the rail to the ground, changing as it did into her human form.

"Shaw Who Is Nightmare, I have come to learn of humanity."

"Come in," he said, trying but failing to hide both his surprise and delight. Gesturing her inside, he closed the balcony door.

Here I am, he thought, *alone in my bedroom with an exotic, beautiful woman of legend, one who wants me to teach her about humanity. One who will no doubt do whatever I tell her to do.* It was, he reflected, the ultimate dream and fantasy. But Michael Shaw was nothing if not a gentleman. This was an innocent, one who trusted him and he could not, would not, introduce her to humanity by taking advantage of that innocence.

"And I will gladly teach you. But first, let's find you some clothes."

Over the next few weeks he showed her his world. She did not like the city. Too many people for a creature of solitude. She did like the great park. "I will hunt here tonight," she'd told him. She liked the art museums but could not stay in the one with displays of natural history. He took her to dinner – once. She would not eat the vegetables and cooked meat did not agree with her.

One night they attended the theater –Shaw had a private box. She had liked the music but could not follow the plot. On the way back she asked,

"So many people. Why do they live so close? You do not." But before Shaw could explain, "The music, it was about love?"

Shaw confirmed that it was.

"The fire thief, he had known love once or twice. It made him happy and sad. Is that what love is?"

Recalling a woman in black who had fought by his side, Shaw again agreed.

"You are most strange creatures. This love, it leads to mating?"

"It can."

"Love and mating, these are a part of humanity?"

"They are."

"Then Shaw Who Is Nightmare, you must teach me."

That night he did.

The next morning she was still beside him, awakening when he did. "I think I like this part of humanity, Michael," she said before changing and flying off.

"Mr. Shaw?"

Looking up from the map, Shaw answered his servant, "Yes, Taft?"

"The, um, lady … that is, your … guest. She's come down and is asking to see you."

I hope she's dressed this time. "Show her in, please. And we're not to be disturbed."

"Of course not, Sir." Taft withdrew, trying but failing to conceal a smile on his face at his master's affairs.

What would he think, Shaw wondered, if he knew all of what was going on? Would the smile grow larger, or would it fade and be replaced by one of fear and terror at what his employer really was?

The Phoenix walked in, wearing a dress that was as colorful as she was.

"We hunt tonight?"

Shaw shook his head. "Not tonight. The killer only strikes every three or four nights. Right now I'm trying to find a pattern in his attacks."

Looking at the map, the woman drew her finger around five of the marked sites. "These are his. This one," she pointed to the where the last killing had occurred. "This one is not."

"What makes you say that?"

"We are both, Shaw Who Is Nightmare, hunters and killers. But you are not a predator, one who hunts and kills because it is his nature. I hunt and kill because I must – to eat and to survive. This one," again she circled the locations of the first five victims, "is the same. He kills because he must."

"Agreed, my dear, but why is this last one not his?"

"We all have our hunting grounds. I have seen this," she pointed to the marked areas, "from the sky. Where we were last night, it is not his. The lights and the paths are wrong."

"He took the thumb," Shaw objected. "How did he know?"

"You know, I know, so did that policeman. Many know, most have told someone. You humans, I have observed, must share what you know. It is as much your nature as it is mine to fly and sing."

Shaw had his doubts, but if she was right …

"Then if this last victim was a copycat and the fifth death was three days ago …"

"Tonight we hunt?" she asked.

"Tonight we hunt," he agreed.

The Phoenix seemed pleased and smiled a smile that had Shaw been a rabbit, squirrel or field mouse would have frightened him into immobility.

All Shaw could think was *And Kent thinks his laugh is scary.*

That night while the Phoenix roamed the sky the Nightmare stalked the streets, alleys and areaways. He looked for those who were lost, confused or whose senses were addled by drink or drug. He kept an eye on the forgotten ones, those with no home but the streets, who had no choice but to sleep rough in the dark places where no cop patrolled. And he watched to see if any one person was being led into any of those places by another.

Once he frightened would-be young lovers, the state of their clothing telling him that they were more interested in seeking pleasure than causing harm. Twice he interrupted carnal transactions of a more commercial kind, his laugh sending the working girls to seek somewhere else to ply their trade and the men running home to their wives. He thwarted two muggings and one beating by a loanshark's muscle, drawing his .45 only once, his own scary laugh doing most of his work.

All the while he listened for music from the sky.

It was after the second mugging as the would-be robber was running one way and the would-be victim the other that he heard them, the notes that told him that his airborne partner had found what they sought.

Red, orange and yellowed swooped in front of him then flew away, slowly and at eye level. The Nightmare followed through alleys, across streets and through trash and garbage strewn lots. He made no effort at concealment, trusting that anyone reporting a man in black chasing a colorful bird would not be believed.

Two minutes went by, then three. The Nightmare began to worry that they would be too late, that the Slasher would have done his work and be gone by the time they arrived.

His fear was justified. They did arrive too late, but only just. The killer had completed most of his foul work, had plunged his knife into his sixth victim for the final time and was about to use it to remove the dead man's thumb when a cry from above drew his attention and a voice came from behind him.

"Just what do you do with the thumbs?" the Nightmare asked an icy whisper.

The man turned around to see a creature in black pointing two very large guns at him. He turned again, thinking to pit his luck against the specter's aim as he ran away only to see something that might have been a naked woman or a large bird or maybe both. Whatever it was, the look it gave him was such that he decided that he had a better chance with the man holding the guns. He turned a third time and holding his knife with a fighter's grip was about to charge when mocking laughter stopped him.

"Don't," the Nightmare finally said. "Do you want to die alone and unknown in this alley? If you do I am willing to accommodate you. And I guarantee that no one will find your body or know your name or hear of what you've done. But if you want your story told and your name in the papers and a chance at life in a secure, padded cell, put down the knife."

The man hesitated. This was his kill and he had not yet finished. He had to finish or the voice in his head would not be pleased. He tensed and was about to spring when,

"I'll shoot you. She'll eat you."

He looked back. The bright thing with a hungry look took a step forward. "Drop the knife," ordered the voice in his head. He did.

Twenty minutes later Lieutenant Jerome Easton arrived to find the Midnight Slasher handcuffed to a pipe in the alley, his mouth gagged and feet bound. At his side was the knife he had used to commit his foul murders, nearby was his last victim, his thumb cut but still in place.

"You know what to do," he told the men he had brought with him, then sought out the darkest part of the alley. But before he could thank the man he was sure was hiding in the shadows he heard,

"I wish I could have been a few minutes earlier."

"So do I," the detective replied. "But some things can't be helped. Remember, you may not have saved this one, but you did save all the ones after him."

There was no reply. Easton had not expected one. There was, however, music above him and when he looked up he saw a colorful bird whose plumage reminded him of a woman whose name he did not know.

"Oh dear Lord," Easton said to the darkness, "he's got another one."

The next day's tabloid headlines were all about the arrest of the Midnight Slasher, once again giving Easton credit for the Nightmare's work. On orders from the Commissioner, the cop allowed it. It was department policy that vigilantes such as the Nightmare were no more than rumor or legend. This was fine with the vigilantes; they did their best work in the dark.

It took the better part of two days for Milo Cole, aka the Midnight Slasher to fully confess. It was late when Easton left for home. As he was walking to his car the darkness spoke to him.

"It's not over."

No, it wouldn't be, Easton thought, *it's never that simple.* Somehow knowing what the Nightmare was going to say, the detective still asked,

"What's not over?"

"The Slasher case. Six were his, one was not. It's not over."

"How do you know? Did a little bird tell you?"

"The pattern was broken; it was the wrong hunting ground for one such as he."

"The girl from the night before, Annie Preston."

"If that is her name."

"It was." *How must this look to someone passing by,* Easton wondered. *Me standing on a city street seemingly talking to himself. What the hell, in this city that's practically normal.* To the Nightmare he said,

"Cole hesitated over that one, but in the end he confessed to all of the murders, including Preston's. As far as the department's concerned it's over. The Slasher case is closed."

"Then I'm free to act on my own."

"I suppose you'll want the files."

"Thank you but I already have them. I just wanted to let you know. Good night, Lieutenant."

"Wait, when did you, how did you get into police head…" Easton stopped when he realized that this time he really was talking to himself.

At two in the morning Easton woke from an untroubled sleep to the realization of what the vigilante's words might mean. If there was a second murderer, it was someone who knew about the left thumbs. And the only ones who knew about them were – the police, the D.A.'s office and a few select city officials. Someone had talked. Either that or … No, the "or" did not bear thinking about.

There would be no more sleep for him that night. Looking out of his window and hoping that for once his friend in black was wrong, Easton said to the night sky, "Be careful, Mr. Shaw. Be very careful."

"It may not have been deliberate," Michael Shaw explained, more to himself than to his sometimes winged companion. They were in his study, him looking over the notes he had made from Annie Preston's file, her looking out the window. The Phoenix wanted nothing more than to join the sky and sing her song, but that part of her that was human had come to regard the man as a friend and something more and she wanted to help him. She was waiting to hear how.

"People will talk," Shaw was saying, "especially about something as interesting as a dead body with only one thumb. A detective tells his wife, she tells her friend, her friend tells her hairdresser, and before long half the city knows what is supposed to be a secret."

"Then how," the Phoenix asked, looking away from the window, "do we find who told about the thumb?"

"We don't. We look for whoever wanted Annie Preston dead."

"Is this killer another hunter?"

Shaw shook his head. "No just a fool who got what he thought was a good idea to hide a murder. And if it's up to the police he'll succeed. Unfortunately for him, we're not going to let him."

"I am not going to have to eat him, am I?"

A surprised Shaw looked at his companion. "Eh, no. What I said to that man in the alley was just to frighten him."

"Good, human flesh tastes terrible."

Taking a deep breath, Shaw reminded himself that the beautiful creature standing before him was not a real girl but rather a creature of myth, that he might literally be playing with fire.

"So how do we find this fool?" she was asking.

"We start by breaking into the victim's house."

It was a quiet neighborhood, a place the usual crimes of the city seldom touched. That it, it was until the death of Annie Preston. The police chose to believe that Annie had met a random death at the hands of a madman. The papers believed the police, so did Annie's parents and friends.

The Nightmare knew that this was not the case, that the high school senior had not been engaged in any of the illicit activities the baser tabloids implied she was, that she had not been complicit in her own death. Rather, she had been betrayed, marked for death and lured to her doom by someone she trusted.

There was more to the man in black's belief than just the hunting instincts of his winged partner. The coroner's report he had obtained from the police indicated that the killer was a few inches taller than Cole had been, that the knife used was longer and cut deeper and that, unlike Cole's victims, her thumb had been cut off while she was still alive.

Annie Preston's murder had been quite deliberate and disguised to look like one of a series.

The Prestons had a dog, one that for no apparent reason started barking furiously. When Howard Preston checked he saw that the target of the dog's wrath was a brightly colored bird, one that Howard had never seen before. After dragging the dog away from his duty of protecting the house and locking him in the basement, they did their best to ignore the noises he made.

While Max, for that was the dog's name, was being dragged to the basement the Nightmare entered the house through the window of a darkened back room. Once inside he carefully and quietly made his way upstairs and found Annie's bedroom. Using briefly flashes of his torch room he searched her room.

There was nothing on her dresser – photos, notes, a date book – to tell the Nightmare why she might have been in the city the evening she was killed. *There has to be something,* he thought. He looked over her bookshelf. Mostly textbooks she needed for school but there were a few Nancy Drew mysteries along with a well-read copy of Pride and Prejudice. Nothing there, except …

There were two copies of *The Secret of the Old Clock*, one with a dust jacket and one without. It was unlikely that anyone would need two of the same book. The Nightmare reached for the covered one, removed the dust jacket and found a journal labeled "My Diary." *Clever girl,* he thought, *Nancy would have been proud.* Placing the diary in a pocket of his coat, the Nightmare exited the way he had entered, Annie's parents none the wiser.

There was nothing in the diary to help the Nightmare, not at first. Complaints about her parents, tales from school, wishful thinking about boys and comments as to which of her girlfriends had a steady. There were code phrases speculating on how far each of these girls may have gone with their beaus. None seemed to have gone past "petting," whatever that meant to kids these days. As for Annie herself, she was "keeping the bank closed" until she met "that special someone."

Later in her diary it seemed that "that special someone" had appeared. She wrote of meeting "Lawrence" and how he was "the cat's whiskers." At first it seemed that it was a schoolmate in whom she was interested, there were remarks about how much she was looking forward to seeing him in class. Then Shaw remembered something from Annie's police files – that she had attended St. Rita's Academy for Girls. The only men who would be in that building would be janitors and teachers.

He read on. "Lawrence" had become aware that Annie was crushing on him and it seemed that her affection was returned. He showed her favor in class, helping her with difficult assignments and offering private instruction. A few days later Annie's entry indicated that she had accepted his offer, although the instruction was in something other than school work. Annie wrote that she had "opened the bank" and allowed him to kiss and fondle her.

A week later Annie wrote, "I am a girl no longer but a woman."

There was one last entry, Annie writing of how she was going to speak to "Larry" of their future, and how soon after she left school would he be leaving his wife for her and how happy they would be. The entry was dated two days before Annie's death. Apparently their talk had not gone well.

Finding "Larry" was simple. A phone call, an impersonation and a school secretary who was more than happy to provide "Monsignor O'Brien" the names of all the laity currently teaching at St. Rita's, along with their addresses, marital status and religious affiliation.

"Can't be too careful these," he had explained in a brogue he'd picked up from his favorite bartender.

The secretary agreed. "I understand, Monsignor. Any lay person who works for the school must be a practicing Catholic and, if he's a man, must be married. Mother Domina insists."

"And a good woman she is too. Thank you very much, and may God shine his light upon you."

"You as well, Monsignor."

And may God forgive me for the lies I have to tell, Shaw thought as he hung up the phone. *Not that lying is the greatest of my sins,* he reflected, thinking of what he had done as the Nightmare. *All in a good cause, and none of it to anyone who was not deserving,* he decided.

St. Rita's, a good sized school that serviced a large parish, had seven lay teachers only three of whom were male. One of these was Lawrence Barr.

"This mating is new to me," the Phoenix told Shaw once he had explained the situation. "If they were capable and willing, what was the harm? Why was there killing?"

"Our society protects its young. And Barr already had a mate. If his affair with a student, one who should have been under his protection, became known he would have lost his job, and maybe his marriage and freedom. He killed to protect all that."

"To kill for food I understand. To kill in a fight as well. You kind kills for no reason. I am not sure I like your humanity, Shaw Who Is Nightmare."

"There are times, She Who Is, that I do not like it very much myself."

"Then the next time I burn, burn with me and we shall fly and sing forever."

A tempting offer, Shaw thought, but for now there is work to do, questions to ask and a killer to bring to justice.

Lawrence Barr sat alone and in silence. No phonograph played in the house. No radio was on. He sat as he had every night since before the death of Annie Preston and the capture of her killer the day after. The Slasher, the papers said, had confessed to killing seven people, Annie among them. He was safe; his secret was safe, that was what he had told himself these past few nights.

Barr did not feel safe. Others knew, the Slasher being one of them. What if he told, recanted his confession?

Barr heard his wife moving around upstairs. They had not spoken much since that night, the night he had told her all and discussed what to do. Since Annie's death they had not talked at all. Each day he went to school, wondering which girl if any Annie might have told and trying not to find any of them attractive. Each evening he came home and he and Carol ate dinner in silence. He graded papers; she cleared and washed the dishes. She went upstairs; he sat in the dark, waiting.

Barr did not know why he waited, not until the sound of laughter filled his house. It was not joyous laughter, rather it was mocking and foreboding. It was a laugh that told him vengeance had come.

A voice in the dark. "Lawrence Barr, tell me of Annie Preston."

It was one of them, this Barr knew. They were better than the police. The police would arrest him, place him of trial, tell everyone. The dark ones the radio and tabloids spoke of did not bother with such things. Barr hoped that he would not have to wait too long for the bullet in the dark.

"I seduced her," he told the unseen avenger. "I used her innocence to take her innocence. She was not the first, but the others, they knew what was what. They knew that I was married, that for them it was only an adventure, for me a fling. They were in it for the thrills, for the experience. Annie, she wanted romance."

"And so she died."

"I'm guilty. I caused her death. I deserve the same."

Mocking laughter answered him, then …

"Death will come, Lawrence Barr, but not to you, not tonight. Your sins are reprehensible – your betrayal of your vows, your misuse of your position, your seduction of the innocent. And yes, you are responsible for Annie Preston's death. But yours was not the hand that slit her throat or removed her thumb. That hand belonged to another."

There was noise from above. A switch was thrown. The Nightmare was caught in the light from the stairway. A woman years younger than Barr came down.

The Nightmare knew what they were seeing, a figure all in black – the mask on his face as dark as his clothing. One gloved hand held a .45. Seeing that the woman bore no weapon, he pointed it away from her. By his side there was a woman with fiery hair, who appeared to be wearing only a cloak.

"You were at a PTA meeting that night," he said to Barr. "I know this. You could not have killed the girl." The Nightmare turned to the woman. "Nor did you, Mrs. Barr. You are small and slender, not strong or tall enough to have committed this act. And you have faced this situation before, have you not?"

"I was Lawrence's first. It was his first year teaching, I was a sophomore. I left in my junior year to marry him. We had to move away. We have to move several times since then. I couldn't, not again."

"The girl, Annie, threatened to tell – her parents, the school, everyone – unless I left Carol and went off with her. I, we offered money. She ran off crying."

"Lawrence and I didn't know what to do. We, I called his brother Steven. He's a vice detective. We thought maybe he could scare her. He said that he'd take care of it. We didn't know how until we read the papers."

"Why?" the Nightmare asked. "Why would he risk his career, his freedom?"

"He was my brother, and there was a price."

"Steven had always wanted me. The night we asked he … took me upstairs while Lawrence waited down here. And again the next night when he said that she'd been taken care of, that she wouldn't bother us anymore."

The woman in the cloak spoke for the first time. "Who made the call?" she asked. "Who lured the prey into the trap?"

"I did," admitted Barr. "I called her, told her to meet me outside the Hotel Lafayette. Steve looks enough like me that she would have gotten into a car with him."

"Your brother will pay for all his crime against Annie," he turned toward Carol, "and against you. You too will pay. You, Lawrence Barr, for corrupting the young. You, Carol Barr, for aiding him by not revealing his actions. And both of you shall pay for your crime of silence by not denouncing Steven Barr after you knew the truth."

"What will you do with us?" Barr asked, again expecting the bullet that might end his suffering.

"I will do nothing," the Nightmare told them. He turned toward the Phoenix. "They are yours. Take what you've learned of humanity and deal with them as you will."

"Are there limits, He Who is Nightmare?"

"Kill them, free them or anything in between." Dropping his voice to whisper he added, "Just don't eat them."

With that he was gone, leaving fate of the Barrs in the hands of someone who was not quite human.

Detective Steven Barr was tired. He had had a busy night. First he led a raid on a dope shop, an all-night diner where H and snow were available if one knew how to order and tea came rolled in paper and not in a cup. After that two joy houses that refused to pay precinct protection had been closed down. Finally a late night numbers racket was busted up just before the three magic digits were drawn. Barr wanted nothing more than to go home, collapse into bed and maybe dream of his brother's sweet wife.

He almost got his wish.

Barr had just closed the door of his apartment behind him when he heard …

"Steven Barr."

Well trained by the department, Barr flipped on the light, dropped to one knee and drew his revolver all in one fluid motion. When no shot came he looked around for the intruder.

"You thought you could hide your crime among other deaths. You were wrong."

Barr tried to locate the voice without success. It seemed to come from everywhere. And with only one light on and too many dark places, he could not see the man he knew had to be there.

"You must pay for Annie Preston."

"Who are you?"

"I am vengeance. I am justice. I am the last voice you will ever hear."

"You do know that I'm a cop, that whoever you are the Department will hunt you down."

His answer was a laugh that filled the small apartment followed by, "Your department will know you for what you are, a killer of young girls. They will deny you, disown you. They will forget your name, your very existence."

"It wasn't me. It was Lawrence and his …"

"Your brother and his wife have by now met their fate. Prepare to meet yours."

In a panic Barr stood and emptied his revolver, six shots in six different areas of the room. A lamp broke, a window shattered but there was no cry of pain, no fall of a body. There was only laughter. That and a shot from a .45 pistol were the last things Steven Barr ever heard.

Lieutenant Jerome Easton was home and thinking of bed when his phone rang. A voice he had come to know too well gave him the address of Lawrence and Carol Barr. Abandoning plans for a good night's sleep, or any sleep for that matter, Easton hurried to his meeting with the Nightmare.

The Barr home was ablaze. There was no sign of its occupants. Light from the fire cast shadows everywhere. The detective picked one and waited.

"Lieutenant," came the expected whisper in the dark.

"What's this all about? What's going on?"

"Justice. Retribution. The Barrs were complicit in the death of Annie Preston."

"So you decided to burn their house down. A bit extreme, even for you. Are they inside?"

"I know not, Lieutenant. This is not my doing. I was busy elsewhere."

"Doing what?"

"Steven Barr, brother to the man who owned this house, was a detective with the Vice Squad. He killed Annie Preston. He slit her throat and cut of her thumb to hide his brother's crime."

"Tell me you didn't …"

"He will be found shot to death in his apartment."

"… kill a cop."

"He was a rapist and a murderer. Your commissioner had already decided that Annie's death came at the hands of Milo Cole. He announced this to the press. He would not have retracted this statement nor would he have taken Steven Barr to court. Mine was the only justice Annie Preston will receive."

"One day, Nightmare, you and your kind will go too far."

"We always go too far, Lieutenant, that is why you need us."

Cries of "Over here!" and "We found them" interrupted any reply Easton would have made. Turning toward the burning house the detective saw firefighters carrying two people from the flaming wreckage. They were naked and dazed but otherwise unharmed.

Easton walked back to his car, knowing that by now the man in black had left, gone back to his other life as a bored millionaire with a strange taste in girlfriends. Looking back at the rubble that was once a home he wondered just what story he would tell the commissioner this time.

No longer the Nightmare, Michael Shaw drove back to his manor accompanied by a woman with fiery hair and wearing only a cloak. Without waiting to be asked she said,

"The flame burns. The flame destroys. The flame purifies. I am reborn in its fires to start a new life. The Barrs had lost much; I called on the flame to take away the rest. You gave me the choice; I chose to give them a chance to be reborn into a new life."

Shaw thought of the diary that was on his desk at home. He had planned to send it to a reporter he knew at the Gotham Sentinel if that was the only way to bringing the Barrs to justice. He would now keep it, to protect the honor and memory of a girl he never knew and to honor the decision of the one sitting next to him.

"Did I make the right choice, Shaw Who Is Nightmare?"

"She Who Is, you made a human choice, and a better one than I could have made."

Bathed in Fire

It was dawn. Michael Shaw stood on the balcony of his bedroom and watched the sun rise. He had awakened early, well rested after a vigorous night that for once had nothing to do with crime fighting.

"Michael," came a voice from inside, "are you coming back to bed."

She only calls me Michael at times like these. Shaw wasn't complaining however. The woman who had called to him was a dream come true, a myth made flesh, an exotic creature the like of which he had known only once before.

Shaw had lost his first love, and now it looked as if …

"Michael!" The woman's voice was more insistent.

Smiling to himself, Shaw thought, W*hy not? After all, it might be the last time.* Looking toward the city he had vowed to protect he added, *for many of us.*

The night brought different thoughts. *How many times,* Shaw wondered, *have I died or should have died.* There was Eire, and Coast City. There was the time his luck ran out and he had to get by on skill alone. There were near misses and daring escapes. His mind echoed his thought of the morning, that tonight might be the last time.

He was alone in his room. The woman, She Who Is, was waiting for him in hers. In what had become almost a nightly ritual, Shaw had Barr did not put on what he called his "work clothes" – a black suit with black shirt,why he waited, not until the sound of laughter a black coat inside of which was a brace of pistols. Around his waist was a belt from which hung a long knife brought from a land outside time. There were gloves, a hat and finally a mask, all black of course. The mask he put in his pocket, to be donned when the time was right.

Shaw looked at himself in the mirror. The Nightmare was ready.

She Who Is met him in the hall. Together they left his manor house and drove toward New York and Gotham. Together they would either save the city or see it burned.

A week before. Closing time at Moran's, Shaw's favorite bar and an after-hours gathering place for the city's dark avengers. That night it was mostly empty, just him and Seamus Moran – owner, bartender and a member of the Gentry of Eire, the likes of which included leprechauns, bogarts, and other folk of Fairie.

"Quiet night," Shaw observed.

"And is this where I'm supposed to remark, 'Too quiet?'"

The man who was the Nightmare shook his head. "Just making a comment, Seamus, and not just about this place. The city's been quiet. No work for a somewhat honest vigilante to do."

"That will change, Michael, that will change. Once word gets around that most of your sort are out of town."

It was about the time that his fellow crime fighters normally arrived to take their usual seats. Not that anyone ever saw them come in. They just appeared after the night's adventures to discuss cases, exchange warnings and techniques, or to sometimes just relax among their peers.

Shaw looked around. It was past time and he and Seamus were still the only ones present.

"It does seem a little empty. Where is everyone, if you know."

Seamus topped off Shaw's glass with some more of the finest Irish whiskey in all creation, distilled only for his bar and one other. And why not? After all, the man across the bar had saved the diminutive Irishman's homeland. He was deserving of the best. Besides, Shaw, was rich beyond the dreams of most mortal men and could well afford above the top shelf.

He poured himself another as well. Taking a sip, well, more than a mere sip, he sighed in satisfaction.

"Ah, mother's milk. Of course, if it was then yours truly would never have been weaned. But to answer your question, our friend Kent was called to San Francisco's Chinatown, something about a Tong war. On hearing about the sudden appearance of giant devil bats, friend Richard left this morning for Rhode Island, taking the girlfriend, the Sikh, and that horse he calls a dog. Jethro's in Florida, something about a kidnapping and blackmail scheme. Clark and his crew are off to Brazil and the rest have scattered hither and yon on some quest or the other. The best I can figure, Michael, is that you and your pet canary are right now the city's only defenders of truth and justice."

Shaw made a point of looking at the stock behind the bar. "Don't let She Who Is hear you say that. Alcohol burns so easily."

"Point taken, Michael. Where is our little firebird?"

"Out hunting. She likes to catch her own dinner."

"Ah, I thought there were fewer pigeons, rats and stray animals around these days. But tell her to be careful around the park. I understand there's something going around. She may not catch it, but I'm sure she'd pass it on to you, you lucky devil you."

The calm in the city lasted three days more. The headlines of one of the daily tabloids announced HELL BREAKS LOOSE! in near "end of the world" type, not knowing that for once it had come close perilously close to the truth.

The first was a bank, just south of the park. Four armed, masked men burst in brandishing weapons. In a very professional manner two emptied the tellers' trays and another relieved the customers of their money while the fourth stood watch with a machine gun.

All went as it was supposed to go, to the point where the money had been obtained. Then, the man with the Tommy gun opened up on the customers. As he cut them down, the two robbers still behind the service counter shot the tellers. The bank's guard, who had been disarmed as soon as the men burst in, was the last to die. The manager they allowed to live, if only to convey the message,

"This is just the beginning."

Inside the park, a young couple was walking their dog. It was a cute, little dog; their apartment only allowed small pets. As they walked it they paid little attention to the dog, instead they made eyes at each other and plans about what they were going to do once they got back to their apartment.

There was a "crack" and the dog fell dead, a small caliber bullet tearing through its tiny frame. Three men then ran up, grabbed the couple and dragged them into the trees.

They did not harm the woman, not physically. Instead they made her watch as her husband of three months was viciously beaten. The beating was efficient and dispassionate, designed not to kill but to cripple, the only mercy shown was that it was quick. When it was over, the man who had held the woman while her husband was attacked said only,

"This is just the beginning."

That was just the beginning. Seemingly all at once, more banks and shops were robbed and more patrons and workers slaughtered. More people were abducted, held, brutalized then dumped back on the streets from where they were taken. Public institutions were vandalized and utilities sabotaged, resulting in a loss of vital services.

Panic gripped the center of the city. Some took advantage of the chaos to line their pockets. Others saw this as an opportunity to settle old scores, hoping that one more body would go unnoticed amid the many already piled up. The police did the best they could but there were too many crimes and too few of them. By the second day, midtown was deserted as people fled the crime and carnage.

It did not help, for after the looting had stopped and the guns were reloaded, crime and the criminals committing it moved outward.

"We need your help."

Michael Shaw was again in Moran's. It was the afternoon of the second day of what seemed to be a battle for the city. This time he sat in his favorite booth, accompanied by a beautiful woman whose hair was all the colors of fire and by Lieutenant Jerome Easton, a homicide detective who suspected Shaw of being the Nightmare but for various reasons had never sought to prove it. The request for help had come from the lieutenant.

"*My* help, Lieutenant? How can I help? I understand the city is in the middle of a grave crisis, but other than offering a sizeable amount of cash to defray whatever expenses have occurred I don't see how one of the idle rich can help the NYPD."

Easton closed his eyes and started counting. His wife had told him that counting to ten before speaking was a good way to reduce stress. She had read it in some magazine or the other. Easton was not sure it worked. He did know that it kept him from screaming at the man sitting across from him.

"Are you all right, Friend of Shaw?"

It was Shaw's companion who had asked. Her melodious voice, almost a song in itself, did more to relieve his stress than counting past 100 would have done. He opened his eyes.

"Yes, thank you, er … Miss." Easton had never learned her name. He had once asked Shaw only to be told that "she was who she was" or something to that effect. Taking one last, long look at the vision next to Shaw, Easton turned to him.

"I'm sorry, Mr. Shaw. What I meant to say was that we, that is, the police department could use the help of a certain friend of yours and any friends of his who may be so inclined. If you've had time to read the papers you know that crime in the city is at an all-time high. The department's doing the best it can, but with the influenza outbreak we're down to about half strength. Any and all help would be appreciated."

Shaw smiled. Easton had come close to breaking the rules of the game, the game where he pretended to be nothing more than a bored, rich millionaire and Easton pretended to believe him. It was a convenient fiction that allowed both of them to do their chosen jobs better.

"Is this request coming from you, Lieutenant? Or did someone …"

"This request, Mr. Shaw, comes from Centre Street."

"Ah, the Police Commissioner's office, then. Who is the commissioner these days, Lieutenant? I can never be sure."

Easton told him. Shaw replied,

"Isn't he the one who publicly stated that the city would be better off without, now how did he put it, 'these costumed clowns taking the law into their own hands'?"

"You're not going to let that keep you from …"

"Rest easy, Lieutenant. I'm sure my friend cares as much about what your commissioner has to say as I do. Although for the record, there's only one Clown and I don't think his gas gun would be all that effective. Anyway I think he's retired. Ask Detective Donler, he might be able to tell you."

"So you'll, or rather, your friend and his friends will help?"

Shaw sighed, a long deep sigh full of despair and regret. It was a bit too dramatic to be genuine, but it did forewarn Easton about what was to come.

"I am afraid, Lieutenant, that those 'dark paladins of the night' as that *From the Shadows* magazine refers to them, are collectively unavailable. I have been given to understand that most of them are out of town on some crusade or the other. Still, I'm sure that those left behind, however few in number they are, will do all they can."

There was a noticeable look of disappointment on Easton's face. The detective had no doubt expected Shaw, as the Nightmare, to gather an army of "dark paladins" who would, with much laughter, sweep the city streets clean of all crime and those who were committing it.

Shaw ordered more drinks – the good stuff for himself, "fortified" coffee for Easton and another beer for She Who Is. There had been a time when the fiery beauty drank only water, but that was before she had tried Moran's special brew.

"How bad is the influenza outbreak, Lieutenant?" Moran asked when he brought the drinks.

"Not as bad as the Spanish Flu – not as fatal or contagious. But bad enough. The hospitals were full enough before the all shootings, beatings, and mayhem started. Now, well, the only ones more overworked than the police are the doctors and nurses."

"Lieutenant? May I suggest that the city hire private security firms to protect the hospitals, their staff, and the patients from criminal attack?"

"A good idea, Mr. Shaw but where would that money come from?" A look from Shaw told him. "Oh, very generous. I'll pass your offer on to the Commissioner."

"It's the least I can do, Lieutenant. And never let it be said that I did not do the least I could do." After a pause Shaw added, "Has any thought been given to the idea that all this may be part of an organized plan? It's happened before, although not on this scale."

"Despite how we are portrayed in the movies, tabloids and those pulps you seem so found of, we're not stupid or incompetent. But it's taking every man we've got just to maintain order. Once that's been established then we can begin to look into the cause of it."

"Then perhaps, Lieutenant, although my friend cannot give you an army, he can investigate that aspect of this crisis? One man, or rather, two people can often succeed where an army would fail."

"As I've said before, Mr. Shaw, whatever help you can … arrange will be greatly appreciated and definitely not forgotten."

Shaw spent the third day of the what the tabloids were now calling the Battle of Manhattan arranging for the promised private protection of hospitals, clinics, schools, and other facilities that had opened their doors to help those stricken by diseased or who simply had nowhere else to go. Many of the larger agencies had already been hired by businesses and wealthy private citizens but Shaw was able to hire enough independent ops to cover the more vital areas. Some of these were little more than licensed gunmen but all were straight shooters with large guns who, once they took your money, would fight to the death, preferably the death of someone else.

"And what of us, Shaw Who Is Nightmare?" asked the woman with the fiery hair. "What is to be our part?"

"Tonight," Shaw replied, "we hunt."

"Good," she replied, smiling a predators' smile.

With Shaw dressed in black and the woman wearing only a cloak, they drove to the city in Shaw's newly purchased Chrysler Airflow, an ugly car that nevertheless, thanks to its streamlined designed and eight cylinder engine, could travel at speeds in excess of 90 miles an hour. It was, of course, black and, like its driver, blended perfectly with the night.

Ignoring police demands to stop, and smashing barriers designed more to keep citizens away from the afflicted area than to keep criminal within it, the Airflow stopped several blocks short of the Great Park.

Never had Shaw seen the city so empty. The Grand Cathedral was locked and closed to the Faithful. Prometheus looked down on an empty square. All was quiet except for the sounds of distant screams.

"That is where we need to go," Shaw said, putting on his mask and becoming the Nightmare. She Who Is did not respond. Instead she seemed entranced by the statue of the Fire-Bringer.

"Friend of yours," the Nightmare asked in his whispered voice.

"He was. There were more of my kind back then. It was said that it was they who brought him the Fire of Olympus. For this offense they became the vultures who tortured him."

More screams, just barely audible. The Nightmare pointed toward them.

"We find the source, we find our prey."

The woman who was not a woman dropped her cloak and stood naked in the street. Before the Nightmare's eyes she transformed, taking her true shape. It was sight that never failed to amaze him.

She Who Is shrank into herself, going from woman to adolescent to girl to child. Her hair grew to cover her younger body, then transformed into feathers as the creature took its true form. When it was over, where once a woman stood there sat a large bird of prey, its plumage red, orange, and gold – all the colors of flame.

"Find them," said the Nightmare and the Phoenix took flight.

It returned minutes later. Hovering, it set off again, flying slowly enough for the Nightmare to follow. Three blocks north, two west.

The screams had come from a young woman, one of many who had not been able to escape the zone of crime at the center of the city. Her companion was lying in the street. He was bloody and his limbs were bent in unnatural angles. It was his fatal beating at the hands of the three men who were now approaching the young woman that was the cause of her screams.

So intent were the men on brutalizing their victim that they failed to notice the large bird over their heads. Nor did they see the man in black as he came nearer and nearer – not until his menacing laughter drew their attention.

The thugs had used their fists and clubs on their victim but on seeing the Nightmare they drew pistols. Again the Nightmare laughed, mocking them and their threat, freezing them long enough to draw his .45s.

He fired to cripple not kill, the first crook dropping to the street with wounds to both legs. The second fell with two bullets in his arm and one in his side.

The third man had fallen back, away from the gunfight. It was his idea to flank the Nightmare, to attack him from the side as he took down the others. The Nightmare was aware of this, watching the gunman even as he dealt with the others. He allowed the man to think he had a chance.

Believing the man in back to be distracted and unaware, the gunman took careful aim. But even as his finger tightened on his trigger, a fiery figure descended from above and sharp talons raked his face and shoulders. Screaming as the flesh was ripped from his body, he collapsed on the street.

Suddenly all was quiet. The woman whose screams had attracted the attention of the man and the bird was sobbing softly over the body of her brother. The two gunshot victims were moaning and the one whose face was so ravaged that he would bear the scars for the remainder of his life had passed out from the pain.

The Phoenix rose back into the sky, keeping watch. Automatics in hand, the Nightmare stood over the men he had shot.

"Who?" he asked. "Who sent you?"

The man who had been shot in the arm and torso uttered a short, two word answer. The Nightmare shot him in the leg.

"I'll ask again, who do you work for?"

The other man, the one whose legs were spilling his life's blood on the city street said, "He'll kill us if we talk."

"I'll kill you if you don't." The Nightmare then looked meaningfully at the man the Phoenix had attacked. "Or would you rather," he looked up at the colorful bird circling the night sky and said, somewhat dramatically, "I call down your death from above."

"The Bright One," both men shouted at once.

"That what he calls himself," added the man the Nightmare had just shot. "Somewhere in the Park. I don't know where."

The Nightmare nodded. Turning away from the men he picked up their fallen weapons, placing them in pockets in his coat. One could not have too many guns in a war zone. Then he went to the still crying woman.

"You'll have to leave him," he said as gently as he could. Then he signaled his avian companion who lit on a nearby abandoned car. "Follow her," he told the woman. To the Phoenix he said,

"Lead her to safety then return." He paused to listen. In the distance there were gunshots and more screams. "There are still more people to help, and maybe more information to be gathered. We will hunt until dawn."

The fighting over for now, one victim safe, the Nightmare felt exposed. As he sought the safety of the shadows one of the men said, "What about us?"

"What about you?" he replied. "I said I would not kill you. I did not say I would help you. But if you survive, and if this Bright One does not kill you for your failure, tell him this from the Nightmare:

"The end is coming. His end is near."

The Phoenix returned. It and the Nightmare again set out in the direction of screams and gunshots. By daybreak, six more people had been saved and led from the zone. A baker's dozen of crooks were put down, some forever, in what seemed to be countless shootouts during which the Nightmare had needed the pistols he had taken from the gunmen he had first encountered. In a gunfight where seconds might mean the difference between life and death, it was quicker to drop his .45s and use those pistols than it was to reload.

During the shooting, the man in black had not had the time to inspect his confiscated weapons. Too busy protecting his life and the lives of others, he noticed only that they worked, were lighter, held more cartridges, and were more accurate than the heavy automatics he carried. It was not until dawn was breaking and he and the Phoenix were returning to his Airflow that he took the time to look them over.

The two he had left were of strange design. Instead of heavy metal, some parts were of a hard, plastic-like material. In addition, the model types of both the Colt and the Smith & Wesson were ones he had never heard of.

The Nightmare thought back to the last time he had encountered a strange weapon. It had been in a strange land and wielded by a police woman from a distant time.

A horrible thought began to settle in his mind as he thought back to the men he had killed that night. Some were just ordinary thugs. As for the others – their voices were strange, their clothing stranger, not just out of style but never in style; dungarees, sweaters, and tennis shirts rather than the suits most men of his time wore.

"No, it can't be," the Nightmare said out loud as his suspicion grew Even as the sun rose, as the Phoenix again took human form and ran naked into the Airflow, he sought and found a working payphone.

"What is it," a weary, just awakened Jerome Easton asked.

"It is I, Lieutenant," a whispered voice answered.

"I suspect you've been busy. Did you learn anything?'

"Yes, things may be worse than we feared. I need you to do something. I have left dead and wounded men behind me."

"Of course you have."

The Nightmare gave Easton the locations of where the men might be adding, "Send a detail of as many men as you need. Arrest the living, collect the dead, and have doctors examine them."

What should they look for?"

"The impossible."

They drove back to the manor, She Who Is in her cloak, Shaw without his mask. On the way he spoke aloud, more to himself than his companion.

"It all fits. The strange weapons, men out of time, the sickness, the violence. I thought I'd left him behind in Eire, but what did he say? 'There are other paths which I may trod.' Somehow he found his way here and means to bring his plague to my land."

"Of whom do you speak, Shaw Who Is Nightmare?"

"A monster who calls himself Apollonius of Tyana. I fought him once, and with help defeated him. He claimed to be the true Messiah."

"I have heard of him. He sought to replace the One from Nazareth, the son of the God over the gods. He was known in Syria, India and the Caliphate. He said to be a being of great power. For you to have defeated him …"

"Means I was lucky once and may have to be even luckier now."

But then again I am, Shaw thought, thinking back to an encounter with the goddess of luck.

"Shaw Who Is Nightmare?"

"Yes?"

"Tonight was exciting, was it not? The hunting, the fighting, the killing."

"And?" he replied, suspecting where she was leading.

"I can think of something just as exciting – Michael."

He was tired, he needed rest and sleep. But one did not turn down a fire creature with a predator's smile, especially when one did not want to.

Shaw pressed the accelerator. The Airflow hit ninety as he raced home.

It was the late afternoon of the fourth day when Shaw awoke, refreshed in mind if not in body. Leaving the still sleeping She Who Is he dressed and went downstairs to his study. There his valet Harding was waiting for him.

"There was a telephone call while you were asleep, Sir. A Mister Moran, about your appointment tonight. He asked to remind you to dress for the occasion."

"Thank you, Harding."

"Will the lady be joining you, Sir?"

"The lady does as the lady wishes, Harding."

The valet gave a shudder that he hoped his master did not see. "Yes, Sir, I have noticed that."

Later that evening, the black Airflow once again cut through the night. The Nightmare at the wheel, the Phoenix at his side. When they arrived at Moran's they found the front door locked. When the diminutive owner answered his knock, the Nightmare asked,

"Closing early these days, Seamus?'

"Sure and it's not like there's any business. With all that's going on most people are either hiding behind their own doors or making plans to flee the city."

"Can't say that I blame them."

Lieutenant Easton's voice came from the booth he and Shaw usually occupied, a subtle reminder of the game the two of them played.

"It's getting worse. We've had to pull back another five blocks in all directions. It's not the mobsters, it's that dam flu, or whatever it is. No one seems to know. The doctors at Lincoln Medical said that it's virulent as hell but can't understand how it's transmitted or why it's moving so slowly."

The Nightmare joined Easton in his booth. The Phoenix joined Seamus at the bar where she sampled his finest ale, the detective pretending that he did not recognize her as Michael Shaw's companion.

"I know," the Nightmare said quietly. It was perhaps the most frightening thing Easton had ever heard him say.

The Lieutenant was afraid to ask but knew he had to. "Then what the hell are we dealing with?"

"Exactly that, Lieutenant – Hell. What did the Coroner find?"

"It's like you said – the impossible. One of your dead had had surgery, metal screws holding his arms together. The screws were dated-stamped 1992."

Seamus came over with drinks. "It's happening again," the Nightmare told the bartender. "Here instead of Eire. The bastard found his way here."

"Would someone please tell me what you're talking about?"

Seamus answered him. "A god, Lieutenant, or a creature close enough to one. He brings plague, famine and war. His soldiers he draws from other places and times. He almost destroyed my homeland, and would have had not the Nightmare risked all to defeat him."

A god. Easton thought. *Why not? We've had zombies, giant undead gorillas and people who burst into flame over and over again. So why not a god or two?*

"Any chance he followed you home," the Lieutenant asked the Nightmare. There was no blame in his voice, not recrimination, just a cop gathering facts.

"Every chance, which makes it my responsibility."

"Our responsibility."

Both Easton and the Nightmare nodded at Seamus's words, then the man in black fell silent. After a few minutes he said,

"Seamus, call the League, call your cousin and anyone else you can think of that can help in the evacuation of the island. Maybe you can open a door into Eire or some of the other worlds. Lieutenant, call the Army Air Corps. Have them ready to bomb the bridges."

Not believing what he was hearing, Easton said simply, "And then what?"

"We, or rather you, will have to look through all the doomsday devices left by the various madmen who've threatened this city over the years. Some of them are probably in decent working order."

"Nightmare, what are you saying?"

"I'm saying, Lieutenant, that tomorrow night I'm going back into the zone and I'm going to do my best to kill Apollonius. If I fail, save who you can, but if dawn breaks and I haven't returned – for the good of the country, for the world maybe – to stop this plague of disease and violence from spreading – Manhattan must be destroyed."

It was a cold equation – sacrifice many so that many more may be saved. Seamus nodded in understanding; Easton just stared, a part of him in disbelief, the rest trying to figure out how to convince the mayor and commissioner of what must be done, if it should be done, if the Nightmare spoke the truth and had not slipped off into a dark world of delusion and insanity. He was trying to decide how to decide when,

"I can do that."

It was the Phoenix who spoke from the bar. Addressing the men she said, "Tomorrow night I will go with Sh … The Nightmare. We will battle Apollonius and his minions. If we succeed, then all will be well. If we fail, then I will ignite my fire. But this time it will not be the fire of rebirth but that of oblivion. My death, my final death will be glorious and will consume most of the island."

"But the people …" protested Easton.

"I suggest, Lieutenant, that you begin the evacuation as soon as possible."

More silence as the four contemplated the enormity of what might have to be done. A terrible deed, one for which history would condemn them should it ever discover it was they who were responsible. But it was a deed that needed to be done.

Then Seamus found a small light of hope.

"What if, tomorrow night, I open a door into Gotham?'

To which a confused Easton asked, "I thought we were in Gotham."

The Nightmare understood. "We're in New York. Every country has a spirit, a land where its soul resides. For Ireland it's Erie; for England, Albion. The soul of our country lies in America. Some cities grow souls. Behind London is Londinium and Constantinople still lies beneath Istanbul. The soul of New York is Gotham, and it is there where we'll meet and confront this self-styled Bright One. Should we fail and the worse happens, the city and its people *might* be saved, but with its soul destroyed, well, it will no longer be the great metropolis it is now and could become another Harbor City."

As the apparent voice and representative of authority it seemed to Easton that everyone was looking at him, if not for approval then at least for his blessing. Taking a deep breath and counting to ten he finally said, "What the hell. What do we have to lose?"

The unspoken answer which all thought but none said was, "Everything."

They parted – the Nightmare and the Phoenix to spend what might be their last night together, Easton to convince his bosses to begin an evacuation of the as yet unaffected areas of Manhattan, and Seamus to devise the means and methods of doing so.

Again Shaw woke in the mid-afternoon. He spent it in his study, finalizing his affairs, making sure that his servants were cared for, that his friends were remembered and that his crusade would go on. He decided to leave Jerome Easton a set of his spare work clothes along with more than enough money to make him the richest honest cop in what was left of New York. He was imagining the look on the lieutenant's face when Taft, his house manager, knocked for entry.

"May I come in, Mr. Shaw?"

"Certainly, Taft." The servant entered. Behind him was most of the household staff – the maids Dolly and Eleanor, Jackson the groundskeeper, Wilson the chauffer, Mrs. Grant the cook, and Mrs. Kennedy the housekeeper. Harding came in last and closed the door behind them.

Shaw looked up; saw determination in his servants' eyes.

"This is a fine time for a mutiny. Or have you joined the socialists and I'm first on the list?"

Taft, who never did have much of a sense of humor, managed to both maintain his respect and show his disapproval of his employer's jest.

"You are going out tonight, are you not, Mr. Shaw."

"Yes, Taft, I had planned to. Why?"

"We know why, Sir," Jackson said, deliberately misunderstanding the question. "It's for the same reason you go out most nights. But tonight you're going out to confront the evil that threatens the city, and tonight is the night you may not come back."

Shaw thought to deny it, to dismiss their suspicions and once again act the idle playboy. But he had never directly lied to them and would not start now. Besides, he could tell by the looks on their faces that they would not believe him.

"How long have you known."

"Since the beginning, Sir," Mrs. Grant said, "when poor Tyler's daughter was killed. The police weren't doing nothing. Then we read how this Nightmare fought and killed most of the gang that done it. You were out that night, and when you came home we knew it was you."

Harding answered Shaw's unspoken question.

"Like you, Sir, I was in the War. The smell of gunpowder is quite distinctive. Your clothes reeked of it."

"Why didn't you, any of you, say something?"

"It's not a servant's place to say anything, Mr. Shaw," Taft replied. "To help him, yes. To support him, to keep his secret, to lie and fool the police and reporters when necessary – again, yes."

"So why speak up now?"

"Because, Mr. Shaw, from all we've read and heard, you might not come back. That will on your desk confirms that possibility. There are sufficient weapons in the house. We would like to accompany you and fight by your side – myself, Jackson, Wilson, and Harding, that is. It was with some difficulty that we convinced the women to stay behind."

Shaw sat and stared at his servants in sheer amazement. That they would, knowing the chances of survival to be low, make this offer filled his heart with pride and made him humble in the face of their loyalty and bravery.

How does one tell brave men that their service was not needed?

Sadly, slowly, Michael Shaw shook his head.

"If it were any other night. If we were to face any other enemy. But not this one. You remember the woman in black?"

They did. The women smiled, the men shuddered.

"This enemy would give *her* pause. I cannot face him in this world. I must travel to another to fight him."

"With the bird lady, right?"

"With the bird lady, yes, Mrs. Grant." ." *Nothing gets by these servants.* "It is not a world you could survive. Any of you."

Then, "I need you here. I have provided for you all in case … well, in case. But I need you here to continue my fight, our fight. There is a certain police detective who will need your help in adjusting to his new position in life."

"The one who wears the cheap, off the rack suits?"

"Yes, Harding, that one. If the time comes, please dress him better."

"You can be sure of it, Sir. And speaking of dressing, Sir, I think it is about that time."

"So it is, Harding, so it is. Would you like to assist me?'

"Sir, it would be an honor."

Shaw stood. Before his left his study he turned to his still gathered staff. "Thank you all very much. And should this be the last time … well," he paused, he had not the words. "Just, thank you." He left the study quickly. Feared vigilantes should not be seen with tears in their eyes.

The black Airflow pulled up to Moran's then drove past it, Shaw parking around back.

"What it the problem, Shaw Who Is Nightmare?'

"A crowd of men outside Moran's. Police, men I've helped in the past. I recognized some of them. Easton's with them."

"A trap?"

"On another night, maybe. But not tonight. Tonight they are brave men who want to do something foolish."

"Then they are no different from you and me."

Shaw smiled, told She Who Is how to enter Moran's from the rear, then got out of his car. Putting on his mask, becoming the Nightmare, he walked the darkness to the front.

Just at Easton thought, *He should have been here by now,* he heard a familiar whisper behind him.

"Inside, Lieutenant."

Once in Moran's, Easton said, "You know why those men are out there, don't you?" The Nightmare nodded as Easton continued, "They want to help. They need to help. It's their city as much as yours."

"I know, but they cannot walk my path." Then, "they are the bravest, the ones you trust the most?"

"Yes."

"Then whatever happens tonight, they will be needed tomorrow. Have them assist in the evacuation, but make sure they leave the island before morning. By sunrise, it may not be here."

"What about ..." the detective looked toward Moran.

"Thank you for your concern, Lieutenant, but I'll be fine." the bartender replied. "In fact, I'll be elsewhere. Moran's is just a building, it can be rebuilt. I was thinking of taking a vacation anyway." Looking at the Nightmare, he said, "Your lot may have to find someplace else to haunt. Now, lad, are ye ready?"

The Nightmare nodded. A door without a room opened near the front. With the Phoenix at his side, the Nightmare stepped through.

At first the Nightmare thought he was still in New York. Then he looked around. The colors were more vibrant. None of the buildings were in need of repair. The streets were clean. This was how the people of the city imagined it, preferring the fantasy to the harsh reality of their lives.

"Shaw Who Is Nightmare."

He turned to see the Phoenix as she really was – ablaze with light, both human and avian, nude but for the feathers that covered her, the wings on her back all the colors of flame.

How must I look to her?

"As you always do." Aware of his thoughts, she answered his unspoken question. "You are Nightmare, you are Shaw, and you are Michael – and none could exist without the other. Shall we hunt?'

"Not yet."

The Nightmare paused and thought back to Eire. There he was more than a man, one whose mask was his face and whose pistols never emptied. He was Tromlui, Nightmare Incarnate, a terrible creature who lived in the night and could drive men mad with just a thought. Afraid of what he might become, he had rejected this part of himself and saw it destroyed.

Now he wondered – could he, should he summon it back. There was no telling what minions Apollonius might have conjured in this land. He might need Tromlui's strength and terror to do what must be done. If he survived, he would then deal with the consequences.

He reached out but did not feel Tromlui anywhere. He had left that part of himself back in Eire. Instead he sensed something else. Something that called to him, something of which he was a part. He called back, allowing it to come to him.

It was Gotham. She came to him and named him "champion." He felt the pain that this Bright One had inflicted on her. He felt her joy at the willingness of so many to defend her. Then, as her spirit filled him, he knew her as a man knows his mother, his sister, his lover, himself. He knew every street and alley, every home and store, every guy and doll, every heartbreak, and every joy.

And he knew where to find Apollonius. He was in the Great Park. Waiting.

"Yes," said a voice in his head that he had heard once upon a time in another land. "I am waiting. Waiting for you. All this, for you. It was I who arranged for the others to be called away. I shall take your city from you, then I will take your land. Then in the war that is coming I will take it all and the Glory that I rightly deserve will be mine."

The Phoenix heard none of this. Again she asked, "Time to hunt?"

The Nightmare nodded. Then he laughed. It was a laugh that was heard throughout Gotham and which was echoed in New York. It was a laugh that caused evil men to shudder and gave brave men hope. It was laugh of defiance, a laugh of mockery, a laugh of confidence. It was the laugh of the Nightmare and, on that night, it was the laugh of the City.

"Time to play," he said and set out to meet his foe.

As the Nightmare and Phoenix moved towards its center, Gotham changed. The lights were not as bright, the streets not as clean, the buildings ramshackle and nearly tumbling. There was an odor of corruption in the air. It was as if all hope had gone or was at least fleeing.

When they arrived at where the war zone was in New York, the man in black and the creature of flame saw the source of the illness that was plaguing their city. A miasma of blight and disease hung in the air, its tendrils extending outward, ready to infect those that dared breathe it in. The Nightmare reached out to the City and she responded. There was a rumbling as purifying steam rose from street vents to dispel the noxious clouds.

The way clear, the pair proceeded, only to be challenged by the thralls of the Bright One. Men and women, those drawn from other times and those taken from the city, attacked them. Never all at once – five here, six there, a dozen later on. His guns roared and cut them down. Her fire burned and only ash was left. Never were their foes too many, always they were just enough for the Nightmare and Phoenix to handle. It was as if Apollonius did not want them stopped, merely slowed and tired, so they would be weaker for the final confrontation.

Street by street they fought their way; his guns never emptying, her flame always bright as the Nightmare drew strength from Gotham. Soon they neared the park. As they approached the place where the bones of the great ape still lay, the fighting became heavier, their opponents more fierce. Twice the Nightmare had to holster his guns and cut his way through using the long knife he had brought from Eire. And twice did the Phoenix burn their way through, incinerating some whose only crime was serving a false messiah.

It was on the Great Lawn that they encountered Apollonius. As in that other land, he was ensconced on a throne of his own making, the Park itself his royal chamber. By then the Nightmare and Phoenix were battle weary and exhausted, the City saving her strength for their final effort.

Finally, after much struggle, the crowd was forcibly parted and Nightmare and Phoenix approached the Bright One's throne.

"Burn him," the Nightmare asked of the Phoenix. She rose in the air. Her fire lashed out, but from his throne Apollonius waved it away.

"Do you think, Dark One, that I have not faced her kind before this? As it was then, so it shall be now."

Another wave of the Bright One's hand and the Phoenix was swatted down as if she were an insect. She fell and lay still, bleeding and broken but not dead. Dead, she would have burst into flame and been born anew. The false god would not risk what she might then become.

"And now it is just you and me. What is it you are called? Nightmare? A brave name for a mortal as yourself. It is too bad you left the better part of yourself in Eire. Too bad that this time you face me alone, without a companion or the weapons of a god. It is too bad that you are going to die without seeing the destruction I plan to bring to your city."

Even as the Bright One spoke, the Nightmare raised his pistols and fired once, twice, four times into Apollonius's body. As he feared, his bullets had no effect. This killing would have to be close and personal.

"Prepare to die, Nightmare. Then I will see your pet killed over and over again, each painful death coming just seconds after rebirth. And then … but why go on, you will be past knowing or caring."

"Never past caring," the Nightmare said to himself. To Apollonius he said, "If I must die at your hands, do it right" and tossed the Bright One a pistol.

The god laughed. "Why not. Every man should be able to choose his own damnation." Raising the automatic, he fired at the Nightmare.

The man in black felt the pain of the bullet's entry and exit. But drawing on the last reserves of the City's strength he stayed upright and took a step towards Apollonius on his throne. Another shot, another step. Over and over the Bright One pulled the trigger but still the Nightmare came on. Eight shots, nine shots, ten – each bullet taking its toll on the man in black. But on that night he was more than a man. He was more than the city. He was Gotham, the Dream of the City. And while men might die and cities crumble the dreams, the myths, the legends of cities do not.

Ancient Babylon fell but lives still. Troy was destroyed but never forgotten. Atlantis will one day rise and Eldorado waits to be discovered.

New York would not fall easily.

And so the Nightmare fought through his pain and toward the man whose death would make his own worthwhile. And with each step the would-be messiah's faith in himself lessened.

Five steps away, four steps, three. The Nightmare paused, his body dying, his strength nearly spent. He had but one last job in this lifetime to do, and he would do it then gladly lay down his burden.

Two steps away. Close enough. The Nightmare laughed, laughed in the face of death and the Bright One. And there was fear and doubt in the mad god's face.

Now.

The Nightmare drew his long knife, the one he had brought from the plans of Erie, the one he prayed still had the magic of that land within it. And before Apollonius could react, he plunged it deep into the Bright One's heart.

There came a scream that was heard throughout Gotham and was echoed in New York. On hearing it, evil men wept and brave men dared to smile.

The Nightmare remained upright just long enough to see the light fade from Apollonius's eyes. Then he collapsed.

No one to save me this time, he thought. He tried for one final laugh, but only spit up blood. His eyes began to close on the final darkness then,

"Michael!"

He found himself in the embrace of the Phoenix.

"You are dying," she said.

"Yes, and for me there is no return."

"There can be. There might be. I am injured, this body is broken and will not heal. It is my time. Let us burn together."

The slightest nod of the masked man's head. Then, as his eyes closed and his breathing grew ever more shallow, the Phoenix found the eternal spark inside her and ignited it.

The great flame was seen throughout Gotham and its heat felt in New York. It burned for hours, from the night into the day, its fires purifying the city and banishing the last remaining traces of the evil wrought upon it.

The Nightmare opened his eyes then closed them against the bright sun. Slowly he again opened his eyes. The sun was still there. Turning away from it, he painfully rose, his every muscle aching. Looking around he saw that he was still in Gotham, a much cleaner, brighter Gotham.

Then he saw a body that had been stabbed through the heart, the knife still in place.

At least he didn't fade away this time, he thought.

Again he looked around but did not see what he wished to see.

With a sigh of great loss he reached out to Gotham. "Take me home."

In his mind he heard, "You are home. This is, I am, your city."

"In that case, I could use a drink. And please make sure the police find … that," he added, pointing to the corpse.

There appeared a door without a room. The Nightmare passed through it and into Moran's.

"And where is … She?" Seamus asked.

The Nightmare returned a look and a shrug, each a mix of hope and loss.

He was sipping coffee laced with more than a bit of the drop when Easton came in. "Should you be out in the daytime?" he asked the man in black. "Isn't against union rules or something?"

"Special circumstances," came the Nightmare's whispered reply.

"Well, I'm glad you're here. I just wanted to say thanks, for everything. And to tell you that the body of an unknown man was found stabbed to death in Central Park this morning. I doubt if we'll ever find the weapon." He handed the Nightmare a cloth-wrapped package. "You might need this again."

"Thank you, Lieutenant."

"It's the least I could do, and never let it be said I did not do the least I could do."

For a moment Easton thought he could see the eyes of Michael Shaw looking through the mask of the Nightmare and that possibly that mask had been moved by a smile.

Sensing that the man behind that mask must be tired, the detective said, "Go out the back, the way is clear. That car is yours, isn't it?"

"Borrowed from a friend."

"Of course it is."

The Nightmare, or rather Michael Shaw, returned to his manor where Mrs. Grant and Kennedy fussed over him until Harding insisted that their master needed his sleep. Shaw slept most of the day, woke up then slept some more.

He woke again just before dawn, his rest disturbed by a song he knew well. Looking toward his balcony, he saw a fabulous bird whose plumage was all the colors of flame. He opened his doors, but she did not come in. Nor did she shift to a human form.

As Shaw waited, the Phoenix sang, her song one of love and loss. Shaw understood. He could not fly with her and share her song. So she gave that which had been her humanity to him, restoring his life.

"Thank you," he said as the Phoenix turned and launched herself into the sky, her cry the closing chorus of the song they had sung together.

JOHN L. FRENCH has worked for over thirty years as a crime scene investigator and has seen more than his share of murders, shootings and serious assaults. As a break from the realities of his job, he writes science fiction, pulp, horror, fantasy, and, of course, crime fiction.

In 1992 John began writing stories based on his training and experiences on the streets of Baltimore. His first story "Past Sins" was published in Hardboiled Magazine and was cited as one of the best Hardboiled stories of 1993. More crime fiction followed, appearing in Alfred Hitchcock's Mystery Magazine, the Fading Shadows magazines and in collections by Barnes and Noble. Association with writers like James Chambers and the late, great C.J. Henderson led him to try horror fiction and to a still growing fascination with zombies and other undead things. His first horror story "The Right Solution" appeared in Marietta Publishing's Lin Carter's Anton Zarnak. Other horror stories followed in anthologies such as The Dead Walk and Dark Furies, both published by Die Monster Die books. It was in DARK FURIES that his character Bianca Jones made her literary debut in "21 Doors," a story based on an old Baltimore legend and a creepy game his daughter used to play with her friends.

John's first book was THE DEVIL OF HARBOR CITY, a novel done in the old pulp style. Past Sins and Here There Be Monsters. John was also consulting editor for Chelsea House's Criminal Investigation series. His other books include THE ASSASSINS' BALL (Written with Patrick Thomas), Paradise Denied, Blood Is the Life and The Grey Monk: Souls on Fire. John is the editor of TO HELL IN A FAST CAR, MERMAIDS 13, C. J. Henderson's Challenge of the Unknown, and (with Greg Schauer) With Great Power …

One of these days John may get a website and a Facebook page. Until then you can email him at jfrenchfam@aol.com.

For more pulp action please see:
The Devil of Harbor City, John L. French, Dark Quest Books, 2012 – featuring Frank Devlin, aka "The Devil" and revealing the final fate of Wolf Hopkins

From the Shadows, Patrick Thomas and John L. French, Dark Quest Books, 2012 – featuring the Nightmare, Nemesis and the Pink Repaper

Souls on Fire: The Chronicles of the Grey Monk, John L. French, Padwolf Publishers 2014

Tales from the Pulp Side, John L. French, Patrick Thomas, Michael A. Black and Ray Lovato, Dark Quest Books 2013 – featuring the Nightmare, the Pink Reaper and Doc Atlas.

EDWARD J. McFADDEN II

<u>OUR DYING LAND</u> There is a dead zone in Arizona the size of Rhode Island, and no one can figure out what caused it.

<u>ANYWHERE BUT HERE</u> What would you do if your son and his dog disappeared into a rip in space- time? You would follow.

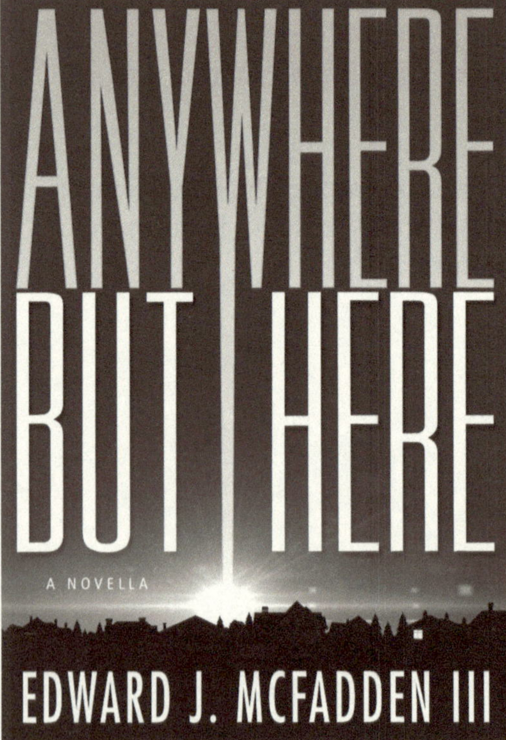

<u>DECONSTRUCTING TOLKIEN</u> In this collection of essays, stories, discourses, and tributes, Ed McFadden has gathered together a wide range of topics, perspectives, and outlooks on some of the most intriguing factors concerning THE LORD OF THE RINGS

Patrick Thomas

The First Drink Is *Always* On The House.

Find out more about other books by Patrick Thomas and enter the world of The Murphy's Lore series at:

Patthomas.net & Padwolf.com

THE ASSASSINS' BALL

When there's a murder at a convention of killers... everyone's a suspect.

Coming soon from
PATRICK THOMAS & JOHN L. FRENCH

IT'S A CRIME TO MISS OUT ON THESE OTHER GREAT BOOKS FROM

JOHN L. FRENCH

John L. French is a crime scene supervisor with the Baltimore Police Department Crime Laboratory. In 1992 he began writing crime fiction, basing his stories on his experiences on the streets of what some have called one of the most dangerous cities in the country. His books include THE DEVIL OF HARBOR CITY, SOULS ON FIRE, PAST SINS, BULLETS AND BRIMSTONE and HERE THERE BE MONSTERS. He is the editor of BAD COP, NO DONUT which features tales of police behaving badly.

PADWOLF
P U B L I S H I N G

More GREAT Science Fiction!

THE STARSCAPE PROJECT

As his quest begins, an artificial intelligence life form enters the galaxy and launches a series of covert attacks against the Empire. The Teconeans assume that the Federation is responsible, and galactic peace is about to unravel. As Stryker chases his nemesis into Teconean space, he finds himself thrown into the middle of the battle. Knowing that Earth will be the aliens' next target, Stryker must decide whether to let them destroy the Empire, or to join forces with his Teconean enemies against the invaders. The key to the mysterious aliens lies buried on the moon of Kennedy Prime, and it's up to Stryker to solve the puzzle before war begins. The fate of the galaxy is at stake.

ZONE OF THE TENTH DGREE

In 1912, an alien ship crash lands in the Atlantic ocean, setting up a secret colony that remains undetected for centuries, allowing them to manipulate some of the most important events in human history -- from the sinking of the Titanic to the Bermuda triangle to global warming. Now, the technology of the 26th century has discovered the aliens' distress beacon, and it's a race against time as the Navy tries to stop a terrorist armed with a nuclear weapon from destroying the colony and triggering an all-out war as the mother-ship approaches

Now available from

PADWOLF PUBLISHING

v i s i t p a d w o l f . c o m